Praise for CHINESE GUCCI

"Hosho McCreesh's *Chinese Gucci* is a raw portrait of modern American desolation and loneliness. Mesmerizing and unsettling, it takes us from the desert to the dark alleys of the internet. At its center is a lost kid, Akira, caught up in the gears of a wild world. A killer debut novel by one of my favorite contemporary poets."
— William Boyle, author of Gravesend & The Lonely Witness

"*Chinese Gucci*, in the embodiment of Akira Nakimura, is a fantastically written desolate portrait of today's rootless youth navigating this inverted totalitarian, tech-junkied, consumerist piece of steaming shit called America that has smugly sat its fat, racist, rotting lilly white ass on stolen land for over two hundred and forty years."
— John Grochalski, author of The Librarian & Wine Clerk

"I knew the sentences and images in McCreesh's debut novel would be topnotch, given his background as poet. But what makes *Chinese Gucci* so memorable is its main character, a kind of 21st century Holden Caulfield. Akira is compelling and terrifying, allowing us to occupy and understand a troubled psyche."
— Joshua Mohr, author of Sirens & All This Life

"Somewhere between a Harmony Korine film and a Tao Lin novel, *Chinese Gucci* is a book about desire and greed and being too spoiled to figure out your dreams. It's a book about being alive in the 21st century and maybe what all our futures will look like —buying and selling and gaming and drinking and drugging. Nights in Mexico. Days on the computer. Forgetting the difference between what's real and fake. The edges on this novel are sharp enough to cut the reader's throat. Filled with text messages and prose as clean as the best dirty realists, *Chinese Gucci* is a novel filled with characters no one wants, characters who do despicable things, characters who most of us are, and we all need to read it."
— Dave Newman, author of The Poem Factory & Two Small Birds

"*Chinese Gucci* is raunchy, scabrously funny, and downright brilliant. Hosho McCreesh has somehow written the funniest book about existential horror that I have ever read and I cannot wait to see what he does next."
— Tony O'Neill, author of Sick City

"With *Chinese Gucci*, Hosho McCreesh explores 21st century connection, disconnection, consumerism, and capitalism through the eyes of a lost Asian-American millennial on the New Mexico/Mexico border. And he leaves us wondering, once again, if the kids are alright."

"A *Catcher in the Rye* for the 21st century. *Chinese Gucci* is honest—at times experimental, at times skinned down to Hosho McCreesh's roots as a poet—and always trying to drill to the core of its drifting, unforgettable protagonist, Akira."

"I'm not sure how much a blurb from an obscure writer will help, I'm shit at blurbs. *Chinese Gucci* is uniquely American and reads very clean and lucid, a vivid representation of real American lives, as opposed to all that Hollywood crap. It's a great novel, amigos."

"In his first novel, Hosho McCreesh brazenly pulls no punches, just like he has always done with both his poetry and art. His ability to take risks, not only pays off, but sets him apart from other writers, who often follow conventions rather than their hearts, His uncanny ability to translate the human condition into words truly resonates and lingered long after I finished the book."

"*Chinese Gucci*'s main character, Akira, is maddening, endearing, troublesome, wounded, lonely, lazy, and a tremendously enthralling ne'er-do-well. A modern Ignatius J. Reilly selling knock-off Chinese Gucci on eBay. You'll love him and hate him, you'll want to save him and throw him off a building. Hosho McCreesh is a serious talent and *Chinese Gucci* is a tremendous debut."

CHINESE GUCCI

HOSHO McCREESH

DrunkSkull Books
Albuquerque, New Mexico
2018

For permission requests, or ordering information contact the author via his website:

www.hoshomccreesh.com

Or contact the publisher in writing at the following address:

DrunkSkull Books
4601 Paradise Blvd NW
Suite 113
Albuquerque, NM 87114

Cover Design by Ryan Bradley
Author photo by Freddie De La Cruz

Printed in and about the United States of America

ISBN: 978-1-937073-98-5

First Edition
10 9 8 7 6 5 4 3 2 1

CHINESE GUCCI

For Dr. Francisco Amprero—
who saved my mom,
and incalculable additional lives
as a result.

1

Akira sat in his new bamboo robe deciding over buying a "Manko" — Japan's "industry-leading" artificial vagina. It was not some cold, lifeless piece of Beijing plastic being strangled by truck drivers outside of Van Nuys. It was soft, shaped like a small woman, and had an underlying bone structure with a removable coin for increased suction. And unlike the rest, it came with an internal heating element, and a bottle of its own "viscous fluid," plus pulsing robotics that were supposedly unrivaled. Akira imagined them as the rhythmic, whirling arms of a car wash, only in miniature. A cockwash. It was self-cleaning to one hundred uses — no mess, no fuss — at which point the manufacturer recommended discarding it and buying a new one. During the special sale only, it retailed at just over $100 US — free shipping. A buck a throw, Akira thought. It was odd and lonesome and fascinating — and he was alternately delighted and disgusted with himself.

He clicked through every page of the website, watched the promotional video — considering. Details as to the unit's size and proper storage were vague, and PayPal wouldn't automatically calculate postage to Albuquerque without clicking a button asking, "continue with this purchase?" Akira wasn't sure if clicking would just move him to the next step in the process, or actually purchase the fucking thing. The thought of clicking both insulted and terrified him. He decided against it — something about using his mom's money for it just didn't seem right. He x-ed out the window, and ended up just looking at porn instead — masturbating twice before his father returned home.

2

Akira's father started in as soon as he was through the front door, on and on again about Akira being fired from Ginger's Burgerhaus. His father figured he'd been fired for stealing, and warned of the hidden dangers of "gateway drugs," and of the "crippling shame" Akira should feel about not having any prospects. Akira decided against another tension-filled meal across from his father — the entire time spent thinking up smart-ass things he wouldn't say, then regret, while his father nattered on. He waited for his father to finish, agreed to whatever, and escaped to his room.

Akira slumped on his bed, and stared up at the polished hardwood ceiling. His whole room looked like something out of a goddamned Crate and Barrel catalog. In fact, nothing about his house felt alive — just angular stone and steel, all sterile and cold as a slab. His mother always insisted he keep his room pristine, even though his friends said it made him look like a psycho. He thought about letting his room go now, but it was probably too late. "Girls love a tidy man," his mother used to say, laughing about how she wished she'd found one herself. "I'll raise a clean boy if it's the last thing I do," she'd said many times.

Akira decided he was hungry, and started scrolling through his phone, looking for someone to ask about dinner. He flicked past each contact, considering a call before reminding himself of whatever lousy thing each had done to him. Akira knew he should probably be over all that shit, that it was a long time ago — but he wasn't. Name after name, some Akira hardly remembered and wondered why he even bothered to keep them. Most were off at college anyhow, or had new numbers, new lives, and probably deleted his number a long time ago. He landed on Kurt. Boring ol' Kurt. He was nice enough, sorta funny, but always too worried about disappointing his parents. *At least he has a fake I.D.*, Akira thought, and dialed.

"What's up, *joto*?" Akira said.
"Oh, hey man. Nothing. You?"
"Almost bought this sweet pocket-pussy from Japan."
"Seriously?" Kurt said, "what's with you Nips?"
"Don't hate, yo. We likes what we likes."
"How much?"
"Hundred bucks."
"What?! Might as well just get a girl. Applebee's and a movie's gotta be cheaper."
"Shiiiit," Akira said. "You been to the movies lately?

Besides you'd have to, like, sit there and pretend to care and everything."

"True that," Kurt said.

"And eat at Applebee's."

"You're right: a hundred bucks is a steal."

There was a pause, and Akira thought maybe the call had been dropped. But no, that was just Kurt. Akira remembered that whenever Kurt didn't know what to say, his brain just log-jammed. Akira laughed: Kurt was buffering.

"Hey, so, did your folks—" Kurt said, "or, I mean…your dad flip out about you getting fired?"

"More like *IS* flipping out. Present tense. He won't let it go."

"Yeah, my folks are 'very disappointed.' What does that even mean?"

"As if my dad can even talk. He hasn't had a job for, like, months." Even thinking about his dad's fucking hypocrisy made Akira want to smash something. "Besides, my mom told me he used to smoke pot. Like at Woodstock or whatever. 'Back when he was fun,' my mom alway said! He can't even say shit to me."

[buffering]

"So what are you gonna do for work?" Akira said.

"I don't know," said Kurt. "You?"

"Be a writer or something."

"How do you do that?"

"Just write some shit. Make a book, *dawg*."

"Yeah, then sell it on Amazon."

"Sell it everywhere, like crack. Fat stacks, man. Chicks all over my shit," Akira said.

"No doubt."

"Sippin' Cris. Rollin' my murdered-out Bentley. Making it fucking rain."

"Spinnin' around like a pimp in a white Armani."

"On a yacht, *dawg*. In, like, Paris."

"Paris ain't got a harbor, dude," Kurt said. "Just a river."

"Why you gotta shit all over my dream?"

"It's not me, man. It's France."

"Everything is France's fault."

"Getting fired from the Burgerhaus: France's fault."

"Stupid France," Akira said.

[buffering]

"Hey, so, you hungry?" Akira asked.

"Yeah."

"Double Gay-bow?"

"Sure. Which one?"

"Paseo, man — for sure. Juan Tabo has no talent and Central's full of hipsters and hobos."

"Maybe what's-her-name will be there. What's her name?"

"I dunno," Akira lied. Her name was Zoë and Kurt better not get any bright ideas.

"She's hot."

"I guess," Akira said. "You leaving now?"

"Yeah. You?"

"Already rollin,' *puto.*"

3

Zoë wasn't working.

Akira had searched the tables, searched the bright, earthy pastel walls, the giant windows and exposed industrial elements, and the stacked stone columns lining the airy room, past all the beautiful faces of the untroubled, upper-middle-class pricks, hoping — but knowing he wasn't lucky enough to catch her working. He waited the hour or so for shift change, eating slowly, and texting people, and sharing idiotic videos of dudes putting Mentos in a two-liter of Pepsi, or of some kid fighting invisible Stormtroopers with a Photoshopped lightsaber with Kurt, even though Tuesday wasn't a work day for her. She sometimes hung out even when she wasn't working, but no such luck today. Without her, Akira hated the place — even though the overpriced food was pretty good. Everything from the dull and obvious lifestyles, to the idiotic conversations he spied on — these people and their adorable, so-called problems — was fake and infuriating.

"Everything's some cheap-ass imitation of the way shit is supposed to be, you know?" said Akira, picking at the last of his turkey jack and fries.

"True true," Kurt said. "It's like I don't even know what my life is supposed to be."

"I'll tell you what life *ain't*," Akira said. "Working at Ginger's Burgerhaus."

"That's no bullshit right there."

"Fuck that place," Akira said. "I'm glad we got fired."

"You think Mrs. Beckley knew about the weed?"

"Who cares?" Akira said, checking his Facebook. It was full of stupid, self-important shit — as usual.

"It seems like she knew." Kurt said, still worrying about it.

"I mean, yeah, we weren't good employees—"

"Damn right we weren't!"

"But they usually don't fire you just for that."

"Look at that dumbass, Sam," Akira said

"Dude couldn't do anything right."

"He keeps his job but *we're* out?" Akira asked.

"They had to know," Kurt said. "I hope they don't tell my parents."

"Whatever," Akira said.

Kurt was such a bitch. He'd be a whole lot better off if he stood up to his parents for once in his miserable life.

"Fuck Ginger...right in her *Burgerhaus*," Akira said.

[buffering]

"Check this," Akira said, turning his new MacBook around to show Kurt another video. It was titled *'What's in my bag?'* and in it a pretty girl talked about everything as she pulled it from her purse. "She talks for fourteen minutes about what's in her purse."
"Sounds riveting."

The video played. The girl was beautiful: perfect teeth, perfect complexion. She had the newest iPhone — she'd just upgraded.

"Fourteen minutes," said Akira. "I could *maybe* talk for, like, eleven minutes about wanting to kill myself."
"She's hot," Kurt said.

They watched as the girl explained why she had all the crap in her purse. She dragged out a hand-held Scrabble game — one built into a travel dictionary. She said she used it to look up any new words she heard. Then, when she knew what they meant, she used them in sentences all day, to really burn them into her brain.

"Precious," Akira said, "working on her vocabulary."
"She could work on MY vocabulary..."

Akira rolled his eyes. "What does that even mean?" It annoyed Akira to watch Kurt act like he even had a chance with her.

Of course the girl was selling something. It was some kind of purse organizer that her and her sister made. They'd started a company called B&R Fashions, B for Blaine, R for Rachel. She was Blaine, apparently.

"What the hell is a purse organizer?"
"Hell if I know," Akira said. "How many do I have to buy for her to fall in love with me?"
"With you? Shiiiiiiit," said Kurt. "More than she's got."
"Better get my Burgerhaus job back."

They watched in silence for a while. It was all so stupid. Did people really do shit like this — just make up a company, and sell stuff? It didn't seem possible. All the shit, all over the Internet, everywhere…how did anyone ever sell anything?

"My god," Akira said, "I'm in love with this chick."
"You and 347,819 other psychos," Kurt said, joking about how many likes her video had.
"Holy shit…is that a tampon?" Akira said.
"Jezus…she didn't!"

They both watched in fascination and fake horror as the unbelievably sexy girl talked openly about tampons.

"She's like a smoking-hot, girl MacGyver," said Kurt.
"She's like Woman vs. Wild…if wild is the hip bar scene," Akira said.
"How old do you think she is?"
"Who cares? I'm gonna send her an email." Akira pretended to type a fake email in the air. *"Dear Blaine, it's your boy Akira. How does spring sound for our glorious nuptials? We'll honeymoon in Bora Bora, summer at Martha's Vineyard…"*

[buffering]

"Oh my god," Akira said. "Did she really just say she uses a notebook to 'keep track of everything she puts in her mouth?!'"
"That's what she said."
"Better get out your notebook, honey…" Akira said, *"Zzzzzzziiip!"*

Akira paused the video so they could both laugh. Next Blaine pulled some hunter-safety-orange earplugs from her bag.

"What the fuck?"

"If she pulls out a Glock, I swear to god, she's not real!" Akira said. "She's a robot, created by my future self, who somehow sent her back through time to get to me!"

The video ended, and Akira was disgusted to realize he just wasted fourteen minutes of his life on Blaine and everything in her stupid fucking purse.

"Why are you even Googling purse videos?" Kurt said "It was a typo, yo. I was looking for something else…"

When they finally finished eating, a man came by gathering empty plates and bussing tables. Akira looked at him. He figured the man was as old as his father, probably older. The man dumped uneaten food into a trash bag mounted to his push-cart, then put the dishes in a soapy water bin. It didn't look like it bothered the man — bussing tables, picking up other people's goddamned slop.

"Look at that dude," Akira said. "He's older than my dad." "Yeah?"

Akira didn't know how that could be. He watched the man work, a quiet smile on the man's weathered face, mind clearly elsewhere, unaffected. Akira thought maybe the man was slow or afflicted somehow. He'd have to be…no one could smile doing that shit job. The man approached their table.

"Evening gentleman," the man said. "Can I take these out of your way?"
"Sure," said Kurt. "Thanks."

The man cleared the table. In his back pocket, Akira spotted the worn edges of some old book. It didn't make any sense. What the fuck did he need a book for? The man ran a damp rag over the tabletop, and pushed on to the next. Akira watched him go, still not sure what to make of him.

"If I was that guy," Akira said, "I'd kill myself."

They hung out, showing each other posts, Tweets, memes, or videos on their laptops or phones until the Double Rainbow staff began putting up chairs and vacuuming around their feet.

"Subtle," Akira said, and Kurt laughed. "You wanna go catch a drink?"
"I can't," Kurt said. "I lost my fake."

"Seriously?"

"Left it in my jeans. My mom washed it."

"That was a dumb move."

"Like I said, they're 'very disappointed' in me."

"Well so am I," Akira said. "Now I have to be the scary, drinking-by-myself loner."

The staff got closer with the vacuums. Miffed, both Akira and Kurt gathered up their stuff and left without tipping.

4

Akira found his father sitting up, waiting — straight-backed and unmoving like usual. He was listening to Chet Baker and drinking a few fingers of Lagavulin — the weeping trumpet tumbling around the crypt of a living room — Akira's mom's potted calla lily the only life. Clearly there would be a serious discussion. Akira had his headphones in, even though no music was playing. He hoped his father would not see or hear him, that maybe he could sneak by.

"Akira."

Akira froze and rolled his eyes.

"Sit down, son."

Akira stared at the back of his father's head.

"Please," his father said, waving a hand towards the couch.

Akira sat.

"Where have you been?"

"Eating."

"We have plenty of food."

"I didn't want any of that."

"What's wrong with it? It's perfectly good food."

"I had yaki soba, like, twice today. I wanted a sandwich."

"Yes, I found your mess in the kitchen."

"Señorita Vasquez comes tomorrow. She'll clean it. That's what we pay her for, isn't it?"

"Did you look for a job today?"

"Did you?"

His father's eyes glinted for an instant, followed by a deep, deliberate breath.

"I'm retired," his father said.

"Retired?"

"Semi-retired," his father said. It was bullshit. Akira knew he'd been laid off from his job on base because he was depressed.

"Well, how can you quit working when we don't have enough?" Akira said.

"You're the only one who never has enough."

Neither said anything for a bit. Akira wanted to destroy

him, but couldn't think of what to say.

"I'm sorry. We're talking about you," Akira's father said, "your situation."

"And where should I look for a job?"

"Your computer. It's good for things besides wasting your life away, you know."

"Fine, I'll look tomorrow."

His father took a long, slow drink of his Scotch, then gently set it back on the slate stone coaster. This was how their conversations went: Akira's father talked between long, slow drinks, and Akira waited for it to be over.

"Akira, you need to be serious about things. Tell me why were you fired?"

"I already told you a million times: my manager hated me."

"What reason did she give you?"

"She didn't give me a reason."

"What about this marijuana business?"

"It was a customer's," Akira said. "Mrs. Beckley tried to say it was mine, but it wasn't. She just blamed me so she could fire me."

"Then stand up for yourself," Akira's father said. "Demand your job back."

"I don't even care. That job sucked."

"All jobs are hard…that's why they give you money to be there."

"I was gonna quit anyway."

"Oh you were? And how will you get money?"

"I don't need money."

"Since when?"

"Look," Akira said, "I hated that stupid job. I'll find something else. Something better."

"How?"

"I don't know."

Akira's father took another drink. Akira wanted to bolt, wanted his dad to fuck off with all his bullshit insinuations and accusations.

"Akira, " his father said. "You have to work. I have to work. We must earn a living, must be proud, and work, and prove to people you are reliable."

"Okay, already…"

"What about college?" his father said.

"I said I'd find a job," Akira said.

"Your mother and I made many sacrifices. You must honor her…"

His father kept talking, but Akira heard none of it. All he could think of was how his mother was getting ready to divorce his father. She'd built up her eBay store, and was saving up. Akira was furious to hear his father act like everything was fine between them, like his father had ever done anything right. His father blathered on, and Akira simply agreed to do whatever he said without paying any attention. *Just let the stupid, old fool talk*, Akira thought, *he never knew a thing about her...* His father finally shut the hell up.

In his room, Akira threw on B.E.T. and calmed down some. 106 and Park was counting down the day's top jams and as he watched the video chicks bounce their asses, he tried texting a few friends, but no one hit him back. He knew people probably had their phones with them — like they always did — but still no one replied. Buncha fucking assholes, that's what all his so-called friends were. They didn't care about him. No one did. They all just used him like some kind of fucking prop in their lives. He thought about trying another round of texts, or maybe some Facebook messages, but decided he was only gonna respond now...he was done trying to initiate. After ten minutes, someone finally got back to him.

> where u at?
> home, bored. dad's totally buggin'
> u going out?

> nah. u?

> u know it! gonna get my party on!

> sux I'm stuck here. whaddya gonna do, eh?

> ??? wtf?

> I meant like a mafia guy: "whaddya gonna do, eh?"

> O. sry. ya, sucks man. L8

> L8r

Akira's phone beeped — low battery. He took the phone to his dresser and plugged it in. Even though it was late, he tore the plastic off *Operation Overlord* for XBox, put it in, and started playing. It was a brand new game about invading Normandy, like in World War II. He stuck his Bose earbuds in, his iPod cranking Snoop Dogg, as he slaughtered wave after wave of faceless soldiers. He'd tried, at first, playing the game as one of the Allies — fighting his way from an amphibious vehicle, up the beach, trying to break through the German line — but he could never make it. So then he tried playing as the Germans, and murdering his earlier self over and over again from a pillbox. His XBox controller bucked as he blasted and sang along with Snoop, *"Guess who's back in the muthafuckin' house…,"* trying to decide which of the little men storming the beach was J.D. Salinger. No matter which side he played on, Akira couldn't beat the level — he could never kill everyone, never kill enough. Akira decided the game sucked, the slaughter was too cartoony, another stupid waste of money, and he shut it off.

He sat for a while, hoping to figure out what to do. He didn't feel like going anywhere or seeing anyone or anything, and it was too late anyway. He didn't feel like staying at home, didn't know what he wanted, so he sat — waiting, staring — until he eventually fell asleep.

5

In the morning, Akira opened his MacBook Air and fired up YouTube — hoping to find some new, epic fails. Idiots on skateboards, or bikes, or motorcycles, or some other thing — all of them crushing themselves into the earth. Or the backs of cars. Or buildings. Or cement embankments. He loved that stuff. But it wasn't working this morning.

Akira thought maybe he'd try to find some cheat codes to beat *Operation Overlord*, but instead typed "people hit by trains." He wasn't even sure why. The screen filled with video thumbnails. They seemed to be either hand-held, taken by people standing around just before something happened, or these eerily still, silent surveillance-type videos. The hand-held videos had grainy audio, and hysteria, and the camera work was awful. He much preferred the latter. In them, the footage was unblinking, which made it all the more compelling. Hearing none of the sounds and just watching from high above it all made it almost feel like he was making it happen. In video after video, some poor sap would try to hurry across the tracks, or maybe step out from behind a train that was stopped, and POW! Akira just didn't get it. How could anyone be so stupid? How could they all be surprised by such a huge, loud, thing…so blatantly unaware of a giant, screaming, shrieking machine hurtling towards them down the tracks? It dumbfounded him. He laughed, deciding his dad was just like one of these idiots. The divorce freight-train was heading right for him, and the poor sap didn't even have a clue — then fate bailed him out. It was funny, in a way. The not knowing made it funny. Akira watched the surveillance-type videos until he was bored.

Next he found some war videos, recorded in Iraq or Afghanistan or wherever. Like with the train videos, the static shots, recorded by a sniper camera, or maybe some kind of reconnaissance footage were the best. In them, some fucking enemy would be walking around between crosshairs, totally oblivious, just before their heads popped, and their bodies dropped like wet cement. In others, there were people standing by a truck or a car one second, and in the next — the screen was instantly filled with black smoke and dust. When the smoke cleared, there was nothing left anywhere.

Akira's favorite was this eerie, green, night-vision footage, shot from a high angle, of four men trying to hide an IED in a shallow hole in the road — the fucking cowards. It pissed Akira off, how it could indiscriminately blow up a bunch of kids wandering by and these cowards didn't even care. Anyhow, one dude was trying to set the bomb in the little hole, all careful and sneaky-like, while his buddies stood watching out for troops or whatever. The guy started tapping on something really soft-like, and everyone's probably saying, "C'mon, what's taking so long?" and then — BOOM! — they're gone. Akira laughed, thinking *Ha...Ha! You stupid...mother...fuckers!* He watched it over and over, cackled like he was watching Looney Tunes. The bastards were like real-life Wiley Coyotes — it was hysterical. After laughing, he felt better.

Akira logged on to Facebook to post the link, and tell everyone about the hilarious video he'd found. Nothing was happening anywhere, and everyone was fucking boring. He sent a Tweet asking people to forward him more videos of people getting fucked up or whatever. He stayed logged in for a few minutes, but no one Tweeted back. He started looking at porn. He'd taken to Latina women recently. They seemed fiery and passionate, with crazy-curvy asses and big boobs. He wanted to be fiery and passionate. He was masturbating when a chat window from Rodney, one of his old friends popped up. Fucking Rodney, Mr. Ladies' Man. That bastard had cock-blocked him over Chrissy all senior year. Apparently a few of the people he knew from school were going on a road trip, "gonna get fucked up in Juárez," they said. Akira wrote:

akinaki93> whos going, yo?
long_derp_dong> d, maybe brodysattva. not sure who
else.

Darius. That jerk cheated him out of keg money
Homecoming weekend, then didn't even tell him where
the party was at. Then there was that whole Amy situation.
It was Rodney and Darius who told Akira she was hot for
him. He spent a good month junior year fawning all over
her like a jerkoff, trying to make it happen. High on
mushrooms one night, Darius let it slip that it was all
bullshit, otherwise Akira might still think she liked him.
Yeah, those pricks had a good laugh about that shit.
Broden was cool, though. He was a fucking brainiac, for
sure — but he was always busting Rodney and D's chops,
which was *high*-larious.

akinaki93> when R U going?
long_derp_dong> 2nite after b is done w work
akinaki93> whos driving?
long_derp_dong> no clue

Akira hadn't seen any of them in months and he'd never
been to Juárez. He'd heard bad things about it — drug

cartels, crooked cops, murders, and all. It was obviously a terrible idea.

akinaki93> I'll drive.
long_derp_dong> dude! kickass!
akinaki93> every1 pays 4 gas. especially D!

They settled the details, deciding to leave at 10:30pm. Akira tried to finish jerking off — but couldn't concentrate. He gave up, set an alarm, and laid down for his daily nap.

At 9pm Akira woke, jumped in the shower, got dressed, and threw some clothes in a duffle bag. He tip-toed out of his room, leaving a note for his father on the concrete kitchen island. In it, he said he was taking a road trip with friends, that he'd be back in a few days, and snuck out as quietly as he could.

6

Akira spent the next hour gathering his friends for the trip. Broden was up, ready and waiting with his backpack and a water bottle — the fucking Boy Scout. Rodney and Darius were drunk and hard to keep on task — both of them choking down a half-baked frozen pizza instead of getting their goddamned gear ready. It was 11:37 pm before they were finally able to hit the road.

At the southern edge of town, Akira found a gas station with an ATM nearby. He set the nozzle to pumping full blast, then ran to the cash machine. He stuck his mom's card in the slot and punched in her pin. He took $400 from her savings, the max allowed per day. The gears whirred and the machine spit out a stack of bills. He stuffed them in his pocket. When asked about a receipt, Akira decided he should probably know just how bad it had gotten, and clicked "yes." The receipt slid out: $4,805.04. *Jezus*, Akira thought, *I have to do something*, shaking his head. *This is no way to live*. Then he crumpled up the receipt, stuck it in his mouth, and chewed it to pulp.

Inside Akira's Nissan Skyline, everyone was texting, or

posting pics, or bragging about the trip to people who couldn't go. They tried to make everyone jealous by talking about all the things they were gonna do, all the chicks they were gonna bang, how fucked up they were all gonna get. Akira plugged his iPod into the dash.

"Driver picks the jams, bitches," Akira said.
"Try not to pick any shit," said Rodney the cockblocker.
"Ain't none in my library, son. My shit's solid-fucking-gold."

Akira punched up *Leeches of Lorechestra* and pushed the Nissan south in the black, empty night. Everyone bobbed their heads, especially the drunks, wilding out every time the Nissan passed another car. They passed the airport just as a plane was landing over the highway, and Los Lunas, then Belen in no time. The road hummed up through the tires, the steady vibration and motion charging them up as the miles ticked by. The cool, cloudless desert night clung just beyond the windows, as they all talked over each other.

"Check it," Broden said, "we can probably find some Cuban cigars."
"Oh, no shit?" Akira said.
"Mexico doesn't have the same embargoes."

"Boss!" said Rodney.

"And booze!" Darius said. "We can get a shitload of booze."

"For sure!" said Rodney.

"Well, you can get it," Broden said, "but good luck bringing it back across."

"Ah man, that's dogshit."

"Guess we'll just have to drink it all in the hotel," Akira said.

Darius said he wanted to get a bunch of pills, that they sold ecstasy right in *la farmacia*.

"There's no way that's true," said Brodysattva.

"I swear to god!" said Darius.

"Yeah, it's, like, this experimental treatment for PTS," Rodney said.

"You mean PTSD?"

"Whatever. I saw it online or wherever."

"We'll see, I guess," said Broden.

"I'm getting some Mexican viagra," said Rodney.

"Spanish Fly!" said dumbass Darius.

Broden just rolled his eyes, saying, "You know you're not supposed to use it on yourself, right?"

"Says who?" Darius said.

As the early energy faded, there came long, silent stretches as each yawned, or napped a bit. The shrouded New Mexico landscape trundled by. Darius told everyone if they got jammed up by the cops, to just bribe them, and Broden said that sounded like terrible advice. Akira laughed every time Broden, who almost never said anything he didn't know to be true, corrected Rodney and Darius mercilessly.

"My brother told me. Watch, you'll see," said Darius. "Well," said Brodysattva, "I certainly hope not." "Yeah, no shit, right?" said Rodney, elbowing Darius, "dumbass."

They gassed up the Nissan in Las Cruces, Akira careful to get money from everyone, especially Darius — needling him again over the keg Homecoming weekend. The sun threatened at the Eastern horizon, despite it still being an hour or so off. Everyone was tired, bored, and hungry.

They wanted fast food, but Akira would have none of it. They had breakfast outside of Las Cruces at an all-night truck stop, the only place they could find that was both open and close enough to the highway. Akira hated the idea, but couldn't stomach waiting until El Paso. The food wasn't good and the waiter took forever.

The desert stretched out in long, lonely morning shadows

as they piled back in the Nissan. Darius said he wanted to buy a sombrero.

"Why?" said Akira, "so you'll have something to wear to the donkey show?"

Broden about hacked up a lung laughing, before saying, "Man, that shit ain't real."

"No, it is," said Darius.

"Yeah," said Rodney, "my uncle saw it once!"

"That's code for 'my uncle was in the show once,'" Broden said, and everyone laughed.

They talked about buying switchblades, or brass knuckles, all kinds of wacky shit, and every time Broden reminded them that buying something, and actually getting it home were two separate things, and every time Akira laughed.

"Fine, what about you, asshole—" said Darius, miffed, "what are you gonna buy then?"

"Check it," said Akira, "a black velvet painting of Elvis. Or 2Pac — whichever I find first."

"Who's Elvis?" Darius said.

Everyone laughed, and had to give Akira propers — agreeing that was pretty kickass. Akira thought sure, they could be assholes, but sometimes they were all right.

7

El Paso was a shithole, and Akira immediately started to
worry about Juárez. He'd always heard El Paso was
glamorous compared to Juárez. He felt the whole trip was
already a mistake — a huge waste of time. They all argued
about whose GPS was right as they pressed on, looking for
the highway exit to Juárez. According to the signs, a long
flyover lane on the left would take them across the
Cordova International Bridge and down in to Juárez.

"You guys sure about this?" said Rodney. No one said
anything either way.

The road dumped them into a barricaded lot, with long
entry lanes lined with speed bumps and signs featuring
handguns with red "no" circles around them. Akira felt
panicked, but the sharp metal humps had teeth that
promised "severe tire damage" if Akira turned back.
White vans reading "Field Operations" sat just outside the
concrete barriers that lined each makeshift lane, and a
short series of long wooden arms raised and lowered like
metronomes between each car that passed.

"We're gonna get fucking murdered," Akira said as they reached the armed men guarding the border.

Following a cursory conversation about what they planned to do while in Juárez, the guards waved them through the series of checkpoints, and eventually out on to a broad Mexican street lined with a few tall palms. Everything seemed dusty, maybe a bit rough, but still okay. A few gap-toothed smiles punctuated conversations the poor folks were having while loitering on the sidewalks, or park benches as Akira tooled toward what felt like the old center of town.

A few wind-blown characters, older, poor and possibly homeless, clung to the medians — hawking trinkets or begging change. Akira was sure everyone was looking at the Skyline, measuring it for scrap, and sure that every car behind them was full of gunmen, dirty cops, or drug lords that would force them all to mule heroin-filled condoms that would rupture in their stomachs. When they did crest the occasional hill, Akira looked out over the sprawling, desperate city. Everything was crumbling — the stucco and adobe ruins of a civilization gone to rot.

The roads became steadily smaller as they inched farther and farther into Mexico, and things began to look worse.

Shanty-town squalor. Bullet-pocked cinderblock walls. Stray dogs and chickens and military trucks. Hard-eyed people milled about ramshackle shops and dirty food carts and *helado* stands with broken umbrellas. A raw-boned old Mexican sat in a plastic lawn chair selling iced Juaritos from a 5-gallon bucket. Akira drove past sun-dulled buildings with towering barbed-wired fences and rooftops, past bars with hand-painted signs or splintering billboards of Mexican women in string bikinis. Junk shops of every stripe littered the long, dense blocks of the city as it began to wake. Flat-bed trucks and buses spewed diesel fumes and clogged the thin streets. Above it all, a few birds gathered on street poles and in the massive tangle of wires that seemed to lash each crumbling building to the dusty desert floor.

"What the fuck are we doing here?" Akira said. "I thought it was gonna be like a resort."
"Relax," said Rodney from the back seat, "once the bars open, the *chicas* come out, you'll forget all about it."
"I'm not parking my fucking car here," Akira said.
"What, are you gonna drive it back to Texas?" Darius joked.
"Just wait, man," Rodney said. "It'll be fun. You'll see."
"Jezus," Akira said, "this place looks like Baghdad."
"As if you even know," said Darius.

In the center of the old city was a church — one clearly only held together by the faith and earthly toil of her believers. Crawling the streets, Akira saw fat women fanning themselves with mangled newspapers, the stray *pachuco,* and *padrotes,* and *narcotraficantes* with gold teeth, taco hats, and pointy boots made of nippled leather or naugahyde. He knew they had switchblades, all of them. They passed a man wrapping single roses with cellophane, and people carrying sacks of aluminum cans, or bottles of water, or empty fruit boxes, or crying babies. Shopkeepers barked about *piñatas,* baseball caps and sports shoes. Headless mannequins with erect nipples wore skin-tight, hot pink or electric blue spandex dresses. Trucks and SUVs lurched and belched. Signs everywhere hustled *internet compu-rent, dentista, farmacia, dulceria,* and *dólares - compra - venta.* There was a sad, leathery man wearing a sandwich board for a company selling bus tickets: Las Cruces, Albuquerque, and Denver, and children hustled flats of "chicle, chicle, chicle," or sacks of tiny oranges — knocking on Akira's windows with their filthy knuckles.

"Mongrels!" Akira said.

Everyone's cell phones got patchy reception, and Akira was relieved to get just enough from the GPS to get them to the Hotel Tulum. When the white stone building shone in the cool, late morning light, it was a comforting bastion of culture in a fucking wasteland.

"We're taking fucking taxis," Akira snarled as he valeted the Nissan.

The expansive lobby was filled with a cool, damp air, and open clear to the skylights on the roof, a bank of three glass elevators in the center. Behind them, a waterfall tumbled to aqueducts that lined the second story interior, with smaller waterfalls feeding a smattering of fountains, indoor palms, and even patches of real grass. Behind it all, a bank of windows divided the indoor pool from the outdoor one. The pyramid-shaped structure meant the open hall outside each room had a balcony that looked out over the fake paradise below. Everyone pulled faces, and raised eyebrows at how fucking pimp the whole set-up was.

"See *that's* what I'm fucking talking about!" said Rodney. "How you like me now?!" said Broden. "Told you this shit would be dope."

Akira paid for a two-queen-bed room with his mother's debit card. He was an approved account member, and all charges were automatically deducted from what his mother secretly called her "divorce account." His mother kept whatever money she made from her eBay store in it, and used it for gambling, or for fun money. Akira set it all up so her sales were deposited directly, and made sure it was an account his father knew nothing about. His mother had a friend back in Japan who sent her boxes full of anything she could buy in bulk at the 100-Yen stores: cheap sake sets, sushi-rolling mats, dishes, clay samurai figurines, mass-produced woodcut prints, winter hats, gloves — anything she could sell at a profit. Akira's father had no idea that her eBay store had done so well, earning a "Powerseller Ranking," and banking thousands in the process. She paid Akira an extra allowance for working and conspiring in her eBay store and secret finances. As far as his mother's bank was concerned, she was still alive and well — consuming quality services and sundries, and being charged moderate fees on her active accounts. Akira had been burning through the account for the last three months — buying his MacBook Air, a new phone, all kinds of stuff.

Just off the elevator they all leaned over the balcony railing. Across the expansive atrium, it was easy to see the front door balconies of all the other rooms, and the waterfall tumbling down from somewhere near the ceiling, filling a small reservoir that fed a lazy-river for guests to float in with tubes. It wound its way to a pool, and the mouth of a small water slide that splashed into the pool outside. The *El Acueducto* bar, and the hotel's restaurant were carved out of the lush jungle-scape four stories below. The air was hot and moist despite the nippy October air outside.

The room itself was clean, two beds, a bathroom with separate tub and shower. There was a dull watercolor of a beach palm tree, bent to an impossible angle by the wind — her fronds splayed by some unseen, approaching storm. Akira threw open the curtain on a window that overlooked the roof of some lower stories, a gas station, and a busy street trailing off to the left. He tried to open the window but it caught at six inches and a cool, dusty breeze blew in. *No jumping from this room without going through the glass*, he thought. It insulted him that the hotel had the nerve to think that a suicide wouldn't just go through the window. He figured if he ever ran a hotel he'd insist the windows not have suicide catches. If someone did jump you'd have a corpse to scrape up *and* a window to fix. Better just the corpse.

The city seemed to be built on a tilt — as if no level ground existed anywhere and the rocky peaks of mountains poured off at a slant. The sun-baked colors of signs and walls were almost beautiful. The skyline was torn by jagged metal spires, the border wall, and cell phone towers — not that any of it worked worth a damn. Occasionally they could catch an El Paso cell tower and get some patchy service, but otherwise their phones were pretty useless. Everywhere on the street below it seemed something was being sold. Akira scanned the little slice of the city the window allowed, back and forth to the distant crags on the horizon. Everything about the life he imagined here seemed hard, dry, dirty, and unforgiving — everyone dying under the merciless winter sun.

Even though it felt too early, everyone was frantic to get out into the filthy streets. Akira didn't want to go. He wanted to rest a minute, relax, gather himself up — maybe re-think this whole thing. He lied and told everyone that he wanted to take a bath.

"A bath?!" Rodney said, mortified. "You bring some bath pearls and scented candles too?"
"Yeah, seriously," said Darius, giggling, "Did you bring some tampons?"
"Man, fuck you guys," Akira said. "I'm Japanese. A nice, hot bath is, like, cultural."
"C'mon," said Rodney, "we're wasting drunk time!"
"Go on then, you savages," Akira said. "Get your finger

cut off for your class ring…wake up in a dirty bathtub with a kidney cut out!"

"What is your problem, man?" said Rodney.

"He's joking, right?" said Darius, looking at Broden — who just shrugged and smiled.

"Just go," Akira said. "I'll text you when I'm ready and we'll just meet up."

Akira didn't feel like paying for their fucking taxi ride anyway.

"Our phones barely work, man," Broden said.

"C'mon, let's go to the dog races!" Darius said.

"Fuck that. Let's get some drinks, y'all!" said Rodney, heading for the door.

"Just send me the name of wherever you are, and I'll meet you in, like, an hour."

"I'll try," said Broden.

The hotel door slammed, and Akira listened to the pack of them as they clamored down the hall.

Akira caught himself hoping maybe someone would come back to try and convince him to go along. *If they do come back*, Akira thought, *I'll just go.*

When no one did, he plugged the drain, and turned on the water as hot as it would go.

8

Akira sat listening to the faucet drip, wondering why he didn't just go.

He replayed images of the filthy town in his mind. Switchblades, and gold teeth. Dirty children. Plumes of diesel exhaust from dusty buses. Trash in the gutters. The squalor sprawling out into the naked hills. Now he'd have to brave it all alone. He scrubbed with a grainy bar of hotel soap until his flesh was pink.

He spotted a radio on the vanity. He climbed out of the tub, dripping everywhere, and dried his hands. He fidgeted with it until *ranchero* music leapt from the speakers. Trumpets bleated as a fat acoustic guitar thumped out the rhythm — the singer caught halfway between a laugh and a cry. *"Nada me han enseñado los años,"* sang the man, and violins called to trumpets, swirled in long, drunken notes. The sad, weary feel was somehow similar to the lonely *koto* and *shamisen* music his mother loved, though he couldn't say how. The words were strange and melodious, sung by what Akira imagined was a fat and lonely man with a big white handlebar mustache and dark, sun-tanned skin — a man crushed under life and love's heel. Akira was oddly stirred.

He slid back into the water. The singing stopped and a guitar plucked out a solo. Maybe there was even an accordion squeezing the breath from him. When it seemed he could stand no more, some lonesome trumpets cried out, crushing him.

Akira smiled at how sad the world was as the haggard hours of driving began to sink from his bones.

9

Out of the tub and dripping wet, Akira tried calling Broden, then Rodney but either his phone didn't work or theirs didn't. He typed out a text to Rodney:

> where u at, *joto*?

Finally, a response:
> bar w/hot chicks from nmsu. phone is 4 shit

He responded:
> dibs hottest 1 - no duffs!
> 2 bad 4 U shes mine
> Send pics of chicks & bar!

Akira's phone kept getting error messages, and pics that wouldn't load. He'd have to x-out of them, and try to reload. Eventually a picture came through. It wasn't especially clear, but Akira could make out the bar's name, and hoped it wouldn't be a problem getting there.

Akira texted back:
> B there soon 2 steal all the bitches!

Akira finished getting ready, and went down to grab a taxi. He told the cabbie the name of the bar, showed him the lousy picture. The cabbie seemed to know the place. *Probably it's where every dumbass, snot-nosed American punk from the hotel gets dropped off*, Akira thought.

On the road, it was the sounds that hit him, an indistinct kind of electric hum under the ebb and flow of traffic. He heard a train far off. He heard music spilling out of old car radios and percussive, electronic notes and accordion music throbbing out of club doorways and open shop doors as they inched by. A wail of sirens drove everyone else to a standstill. The battered Ford truck in front of them was pulling a trailer filled with sheep. There was a plastic kiddie pool spilling water, and hay lining the flatbed. Akira thought sure they were being driven to slaughter. But maybe not. After all, you probably didn't feed things right before killing them. No, they were headed to a farm, to make milk and keep some sweet grass chewed down. It had to be.

Two official-looking white vans passed the taxi and the traffic reshuffled back to gridlock crawling the streets.

"Every goddamn building looks like a safe house," Akira

said to the cabbie. The cabbie said nothing. In the shade of a palm at another red light, Akira craned his neck out to see the sun flickering through the swaying fronds. People milled about, bundled up against the wind, carrying plastic sacks and dragging tired children by the arm. *This was real life,* Akira thought, *these people were really living it.*

Akira rode the rest of the way — somehow sad he didn't live in Juárez.

10

"*Señor*," Akira said to the bartender, "another round plus tequila shots for all those drunks!" He pointed to the table where his friends were sitting. While waiting on the order, he tried to decide which girl he liked best. He settled on blue glitter top. He liked her hair.

The bartender stacked a tray with a bunch of tiny plastic shots around a galvanized bucket of Coronitas, and a couple of umbrella drinks. Akira followed the waitress over.

"Hey," Broden said, "there he is!" Akira paid, flashing his wad of bills.
"Enjoy your bath, homo?" asked Darius with a smirk.
"I did," Akira said. "Try as I might, I just couldn't get your mom to take any money. She always does such good work..."
"OOOOHHHH no he didn't!" laughed Rodney.
"To mothers!" Akira said, raising a little plastic thimble of tequila. Everyone raised their shots, drank them down.

Introductions were made, and Akira immediately forgot all

the girls names. Everyone sat talking, and drinking — each trying to impress the girls, each girl scoffing. They were all students at New Mexico State, ditching to blow off some steam before mid-terms. One graduated from Manzano, and her parents still lived in the foothills. The other two weren't from Albuquerque. Blue Glitter Top, whose name Akira had forgotten, was from Ruidoso. Akira didn't know where that was. No one did. She tried to explain it, but no one knew any of the other places she said it was near either. Everyone laughed a little. Akira told Blue Glitter Top that he loved wandering the streets of Juárez, that folks here were living real life, salt-of-the-earth people. She smiled.

After a few more drinks they all hit the streets. The autumn day felt unseasonably warm. Shopkeepers barked at them as they walked along, promising the best prices on all kinds of wacky junk.

"Oh my god," said one of the girls, "that's totally my sister's birthday." It was a picture of a young girl, missing, taped to a street pole. "That's, like, fucking creepy, right?" she said. Everyone agreed it was.

Everyone shopped for some junky trinket, some souvenir of the day. They asked shopkeepers about sombreros and velvet Elvis paintings, but they didn't have much luck finding anything worth buying. The girls from NMSU kept looking at all the fake sunglasses, shoes, and purses — talking about which looked most like the real thing. The shopkeepers swooped in like flies, buzzing with broken phrases about "maximum quality," "*sí, sí...mira aquí...*," "best deal," and "number one good priiiiice."

"This is, like, a really good fake," said one of the girls, looking closely at a purse. Her friends quickly caught wind of it and wandered over.
"Let me see," said Blue Glitter Top. They talked about what made the fake purse look real—good stitching, with patterns lining up right, a leathery smell instead of plastic one. They were all super impressed.

"You want it?" Akira asked.
"Really?" said Blue Glitter Top.
"What about us?" said one of the other girls, smiling as she horned in.
"*Si, si*...you buy all the girls!" the shopkeep said.
"Sure—" Akira said, "whichever you like."

The girls squealed and tittered with excitement as they plowed over the purses on a spinning rack. *Jezus*, Akira thought, *what the fuck am I doing?*

"I give you extra special price, *Señor*," said the shopkeep. "You buy five, maximum deal."

"Man, what I'm gonna do with five fake-ass purses?" Akira said in his best gangster rap drawl. The girls were lost in the bags: Louis Vuitton, Prada, Dolce & Gabbana. They bubbled, and posed, and laughed.

"Thirty dollar each," said the man, "greatest deal."

"Which one," said Blue Glitter Top. "This one, or this one?" A bag dangled from the back of each wrist — one Coach, one Gucci.

"Hold them by your sides," Akira said. She did. "Now show me both together." She twisted the bags in front of her. Akira watched her breasts come together, and cleavage peek out from her neckline. "Perfect...they're both perfect," he said. "Get both."

"Thirty each," repeated the man. "Best price in all Juárez." Blue Top was off trying on sunglasses now.

"You girls pick another one," Akira said to the others. The girls shrieked, jumping up and down together.

"Six bags, twenty-five each, American..." he said to the man. "And free sunglasses...for my girl."

"Aw...now you steal from me! Thirty dollars!"

"Twenty-five. Or I go ask that guy right there," said Akira, pointing at the *Mercado Reforma* across the street, "for the same deal."

The man pretended to think about it. "My purses are better. Number one quality," he tried.

"One-fifty," Akira said as he began to peel off bills. "American."

The man agreed and Akira paid. The girls were already snapping selfies — pouty, duck-lipped, and angled down their shirts all sexy-like as they posed with their purses.

"Thanks a lot, man," said Rodney, stomping off. Akira was tempted to say something about Chrissy, about how it ain't so fun being the cockblock-ee — but he couldn't think of anything clever so he let it drop.

"This is so awesome!" Blue Glitter Top said, lifting her huge sunglasses and kissing Akira on the cheek.

"Yo," Akira said, "text me those pics…" but the girls said their phones weren't really working.

11

Akira wanted to go to the dog track. Everyone was drunk and happy, so no one complained. A few races in, Blue Glitter Top said she needed to go to the bathroom, and look around a bit. Akira felt like she was bored.

"I'll go with you," Akira said.

"No...I won't be long," she said.

"Just let me bet and we'll get another drink." She shrugged, trying to send a text.

Akira went to the betting window. He didn't know how to bet, so he just copied what the man in front of him said. He grabbed his ticket and turned around, but Blue Glitter Top had disappeared. He tried the nearest bar. Nothing. He tried a snack bar, tried waiting outside the closest bathroom.

He checked back in with his friends. The dogs were running, but no one was even watching — too busy snapping pics and trying to get their phones to work. Blue Glitter Top was gone. Akira told everyone she was missing, but they didn't care — they wanted to get *churros*, and Mexican Cokes, and a trucker cap with the dog track's logo on it.

"She's just like that," one of the other girls said. "It's no big deal."
"Not a big deal?" Akira said. "In Juárez?"

Twenty minutes later Akira was still looking — stomping around and pissed. He was sure she was being raped at that very moment. When he finally found her in an upstairs bar, she'd just knocked back a tequila shooter and raised her arms in victory.

"Whooo," she yelled, and wiped her mouth with the back of her wrist. Some Mexican guy was buying — the kind of guy that probably spent too much on an old, broken down Corvette just to say he drove a Corvette. *That* kind of prick, always wearing too much dollar-store knock-off cologne. "Oh, how sweet," she said to the Mexican. "He came looking for me!"

She ran up and tried to hug Akira. Akira felt sure she was just trying to start something between him and the other guy. Akira figured she wanted him to threaten the guy, say he was going to smash his face in or something. He felt sure it was all some kind of test, or punishment for boring her with dog races.

"Hey…how much?" Akira said to the Mexican, "How much if I let you fuck my girl?"

"What?!" Blue Glitter Top said.

The Mexican started laughing.

"No shit, amigo. Two hundred, American." Akira went on like a shopkeeper, "*mira, mira*…number one best priiiice."

"'Your girl?'" she said. "Fuck you, pal!" She took three steps, stopped, and turned — yanking everything from her fake Gucci. "You can keep your shitty bags," throwing both at Akira's feet. She walked a few more steps then stopped. "And you're fat too!" She stomped away. Over her shoulder she yelled, "And you have awful skin!"

Akira stooped, picked up the purses, tempted to say something about the sunglasses. He couldn't think of anything. He pretended to laugh. He ordered a beer, and drained off half with his first few gulps.

"*Putas*," the Mexican at the bar said, raising his Bud.

"Yeah," said Akira, "*putas*," raising his can before draining off the rest.

12

"What'd you do, man?" Rodney said, grabbing Akira's shoulder. They'd found Akira still sitting at the upstairs bar with his purses, knocking back a tequila shot.

"Man, fuck those chicks," said Akira.

"Dude," Rodney said. "Everything was totally chill. Then their friend comes back saying you're a psycho, and they're gone. What the shit?" Rodney handed Akira two more purses. "They said they didn't want these."

"They were just juicing us for drinks, man" Akira said, "playing us for chumps."

"Playing you, maybe," Broden said.

"Whatever," Akira said.

"Dude, they were cool," said Darius.

"Then go run after them, why don't you — Dairy-Ass?" Akira said, jumping up from his bar stool. No one moved.

"Go on!" Akira repeated. "Go chase them down…kiss their fat asses!"

Again, nothing.

"Yeah," Akira said, "that's what I thought." Akira grabbed

his purses off the bar and started walking out. His friends followed. They wound down the staircase saying nothing, headed for the front door on the ground floor.

"They were cool, is all," Rodney said.
"You buy all their fucking drinks then!" Akira said, shoving the glass door open.

Out front, they hailed a cab. They packed in and were soon bouncing down the dusty streets on the way to whatever was next. It was blocks before Akira realized he'd forgotten to check his ticket to see if his dog had won.

13

Akira leaned way back in his chair and stared at the ceiling, the table littered with empty plastic cups. After wandering around, trying to find some shit to buy, they'd spent the last two hours in this idiotic strip club. It was the first time, since sitting down, that he noticed the ceiling. It was acoustic tile, all painted black, with a string of Christmas lights dangling from bent paperclips strung around the edges. A dusty vent above him belched stale air. In the far corners, fans spun against the smoky air. A stage sat in the middle of the room, a single pole reaching up through the black. A small-breasted girl writhed against the pole, her bikini strings dangling, swaying to some lousy *tejano* pop.

"This is horseshit," Akira said.
"Dude, just shut up," Darius said.
"This is about as sexy as an autopsy..." Akira said, trying to get out of his chair. "I gotta take a leak."

He tried again. Finally, he found his feet. Akira pin-balled between tables, knocking over a few empties. He noticed the black paint worn from the metal chairs by years and years of hands and strippers and sweat and spilt beer. *This place is a dungeon,* he thought, *full of coked-up ghosts.* He imagined his mother, imagined her accusing eyes. She'd be disgusted with him, here he was in Mexico, pissing away her hard-earned money. And in a terrible Juárez strip club no less…not the clean boy she'd raised after all.

In the empty hall outside the restrooms, Akira felt his eyes start to water — so he punched himself in the side of the head to stop. In the bathroom, Akira leaned sideways against a cold wall as he pissed. He finished, washed his hands, splashed some water on his face. He checked his eyes to make sure no one could tell. There were no paper towels, so he dried his face on his shirt. As he finished he found a man staring at him, blocking the door.

"Sup," said Akira, trying to pass him.
"*Órale,*" said the man, who didn't move. "Why don't you take off, *ese?*"

The man was big, with a tough, weathered face, scruff, and wore a leather vest with patches.

"What?" It didn't make any sense. Akira was trying to leave and this dipshit was blocking the way.
"I said, 'why don't you and your *güeros* take off.'"

"*Güeros?*"

"You, and your faggot friends get the fuck out of here."

There was a chain at the man's belt, and what was surely a knife in his front pocket. The man's ringed fingers lurked near it as he crowded Akira even more.

"Hey man," Akira said, "there's no problem..."

"I know...that's what I'm telling you, *pinche chinito*. Right now, there's no problem..." the man said.

Then another man, even larger, appeared just behind the first man's shoulder. Both stared at Akira, smirking.

"But in five minutes," the first man said, "*no sé*...maybe there *is* a problem. *¿Comprendes, Mendez — o te explico, Federico?*"

"Okay, okay," Akira said.

Akira walked back to the table. He told his friends that they had to go, that he'd talked shit to some guy in the bathroom, and they better leave. Everyone gathered up their idiotic purchases, sombreros and burlap Corona pull-overs, and quickly climbed the stairs. Painted on the stairway walls were vultures and cactus and cow skulls and a blistering desert scene. They found a taxi and just as they climbed in, the men from the bathroom came outside, a few more burly friends in tow.

Akira laughed and flipped them all off as the taxi pulled away.

14

Everyone argued in the cab.

Akira said he was just sticking up for everyone, that at least he had some balls, that the fucking Mexican had threatened him first.

Rodney said that Akira had been causing problems all fucking day. Broden tried to calm everyone down. Darius said they should leave, tonight, as soon as they could pack up all their stuff.

Akira said he was fucking staying.

They said fine, whatever, to stay by himself — if that's how he wanted it.

In front of the Hotel Tulum there was a scuffle. Akira said someone pushed him getting out of the cab, and that was the only reason he fell. Rodney said no one fucking touched him, that he was just drunk.

Akira threw a haymaker, catching Rodney just above the

ear and knocking his stupid sombrero off. Darius grabbed
Akira while Broden tried to break it up. The three tumbled
around for a dusty minute, swearing at each other.
Someone from the hotel came out front, yelling as they all
found their feet and stood there panting.

They heard a police siren, so they gathered everything that
had spilled from their bags — liquor bottles, pills, cigars
and trinkets, Rodney's bent-up sombrero — and scrambled
up the stairwell inside.

Back in the room they sat in the dark, quiet as church mice,
hoping management or the cops wouldn't come knocking.

When it was clear no one was, everyone decided that they
shouldn't risk going back downstairs, that no one was
leaving Juárez, not tonight — it was too dangerous. The
only thing they risked was trips to the ice machine.
Everyone cracked open their bottles of booze, and showed
off all the dumb shit they'd bought. No one said anything
about the girls, or the scary dudes at the strip club, or
anything like that. Eventually they fell asleep — Akira and
Broden in the two beds, Cockblock on a chair, and Dairy-
Ass on the hotel room floor. Everyone was haggard, and
hungover, and already sick of Mexico.

15

The hotel room phone was blaring.

The clock radio said it was almost noon and the front desk wanted to know if they were checking out, or if they wanted the room for another day.

"Another day," Akira said, "maybe more." His friends all traded looks. "And send up more pillows — these ones suck." He hung up.

The room was littered with half-empty liquor bottles, empty bags, and all the stupid trinkets they'd bought the previous day. Akira picked up a scorpion, encased in a plastic dome, with 'Juárez' spelled out in tiny rocks on the sand in front of it's open claw.

"Dude, I have to, like, go home n' shit," Rodney said.
"Seriously. My folks aren't even gonna let me stay here all weekend," said Broden.
"Fine then," Akira said, "go."
"Go? How? We all rode with you..."
"Yeah, and I'm staying," Akira said. "I like it here."

The heater, which didn't work worth a damn, switched off, and the room went silent.

"I have to go home today," Rodney repeated. "Tonight, at the latest."

"Are you deaf?" Akira snapped. "I said I'm staying. You can stay and ride back with me...or you can leave."

"Dude — fuck..." Broden said, exasperated. He grabbed a room key, and left.

"What are we supposed to do," Rodney said, "take some Mexican cab all the way back to Albuquerque?"

"Just stay," Akira said. "Let's go find some girls..."

"I can't. My folks already said no way."

"My folks don't even know I'm here," Darius said. "I told them I was staying at Rodney's."

"I'm staying," said Akira, and that was that.

A half hour later, Akira's so-called friends had decided to catch the Juárez-to-Albuquerque bus Broden had found for them — forty bucks each, one way. The Hotel Tulum even offered a courtesy shuttle to the depot. And even though Akira told them it looked like a hurtling death trap, and that they were insane to even consider getting aboard, his so-called friends climbed on and left him in Juárez alone.

16

Akira slept until late afternoon. When he woke and looked around the room — at matchbooks from bars, half-drunk bottles, the fake purses, all the shit his friends left in the room — and got pissed all over again. He decided he'd have to switch rooms, there was no way around it.

Downstairs he struggled through a long and drawn-out conversation with both the girl at the front desk and eventually a manager. He ended up with a suite on the 8th floor with a king-sized bed and a small private outdoor patio.

"Perfect," he said to the manager, "this'll do nicely."

After moving everything to his new room, Akira thought he'd like a swim, maybe find some girls to talk to. The pool had a hot tub and a swim-up bar that connected to an aquarium in *El Acueducto* bar. He imagined meeting some really cool girls, hanging out all day, and, in the end, maybe one would go back to his room with him. He imagined telling everyone all about her, and how jealous they'd all be, and how they'd regret leaving. "Oh, if only we would've stayed," he imagined them thinking, "then we might've got a little ass too!" But after looking around, Akira realized he didn't have anything that would pass for swim shorts, and besides, he wasn't feeling too great anyhow.

He sat on the patio, his feet up on the railing. The city crawled up the crevices of the mountain in the distance and the long, slow, off-kilter grade of the city was obvious from the 8th floor. There was movement below, slow and deliberate, but it felt routine, like there was no one and nothing interesting going on. From the street, Akira could hear some announcements crackling over the static of a loudspeaker. He tried to see what it was all about but no one paid it much attention. Akira couldn't tell where it was coming from, but it must've been some kind of goddamned sales pitch. No one cared. The cool air blew. Akira dragged his chair back inside and closed the door.

He tried the TV, but found only religious channels and zany commercials. In one, a cartoon turtle was talking to some sad people about the pill they should take if they wanted to be happy — some kind of anti-depressant prescription . Now that he was taking the pill, he was a new turtle, and everyone wanted to be like him. He was the center of attention at the cartoon animal party, and all the other animals were delighted to see him in such good spirits. Especially the sexy turtlette — who batted her turtle eyelashes and blushed as the turtle peeked over his sunglasses. The commercials ended, and then it was a sports highlight show about Mexican soccer. He clicked it off.

Buncha bitches, he thought. *They should grow some balls… stand up to their stupid parents.* He tried checking his email on his phone, Facebook, checked for texts — but the windows would just sit there trying to load until he gave up and x-ed them out. Twitter seemed to work though, and Akira tried to think up a vague insult to Tweet — something that would really burn his friends' asses good. He couldn't think of anything and when he tried to refresh the feed, Twitter had stopped working too. The whole fucking country apparently had lousy wireless because he kept getting disconnected. It didn't matter. No one missed him or cared.

Akira dialed the front desk. "How do I make the wireless work?"
"So sorry," said the woman on the phone. "We have no power wireless service. You can use the computers in the business center for no extra charge."
"Well, how do I make my cell phone work?"

There was some long, drawn out explanation of services and roaming fees and different prices, and the end result was basically buying some Mexican burner phone or a calling card. They all sounded like scams, so Akira decided he'd figure it all out later. The things she said made sense in context, but she sounded like an idiot. *Why don't they hire someone from El Paso to speak fucking English?* Even as he thought it, he remembered, as a kid, a man at his school yelling at his mother to, "Speak English!" Akira instantly hated himself.

"Forget it." said Akira. "Just send up some more pillows."

Akira took a leak, and messed with the clock radio on the vanity. He couldn't find the station he'd listened to before. Nothing was working. He punched the plastic keys on the heater. Blue. White. Red. Still there was no difference in the stale air that came out.

Akira crawled back into bed. He stared up at the ceiling, at the odd patterns and textures created by the shadows and the light. He tried to imagine things. He decided it would work better if he had some music. He plugged earphones into his iPhone and found a Pink Floyd song someone had told him about in his iTunes playlists. He put the song on infinite repeat. Akira looked at the shadows, and mostly they looked like birds — either in flight, or maybe standing there with long necks — geese or maybe cormorants. The more he looked, the more intricate the pictures became. He used his iPhone to film a movie of the ceiling, and the birds he imagined there while singing along with Pink Floyd. He panned around slightly, and zoomed in a little on the best looking birds. The light fixture in the center of the ceiling seemed to get brighter and brighter. The more he stared, the more he figured it looked like a mushroom cloud from above, one destroying Hiroshima. All the birds cowered, or flew as hard as they could trying to outrun the blast. It was all for nothing. The blast enveloped everything — turning all the beautiful birds to ash.

It reminded him of a program he once saw on the National Geographic channel. It was about some Golden Record, and the life cycle of the sun, and how it was basically a huge bomb — one bigger than man had ever imagined. When it went, it would destroy everything near it. They described the planet earth as "a pale blue dot," and how the entire human race, if it still existed, would basically be vaporized by the angry, dying star. Every good and terrible thing would be gone. Whatever humans dreamed up, or did, or made, or ever loved would be scattered across the universe like dust, like atomic sand and grit and all evidence of humanity would be erased in a blink. It said only some Gold Record, and a few other wacky bits of space-junk we'd somehow shot beyond the sun's reach would survive. It was all but certain.

He suddenly felt like it didn't really matter that he was born. He felt sure that he was nothing but a disappointment, an inconvenience to his father. And his mother…well…that didn't much matter anymore. He teared up a bit and closed his eyes.

Some time later he felt something moving in his room, someone even. He started.

A bellhop stood just inside the door holding two flat pillows, and saying something Akira couldn't hear over the music in his headphones.

Akira said something cruel to the bellhop, but the man didn't understand — he just kept bowing and apologizing and backing up. Akira grabbed the pillows and the man scurried off. Akira wondered how much the man had seen and if he'd fucking tell everyone.

Akira looked around the room. It was messy but livable. His plastic sacks full of everything sat on the floor, and he remembered the snacks and bottled water. He dumped the bags out on the bed. Three bottles of water — one empty, two full — his scorpion, the purses, some tequila, vodka, some Dominican rum, a Cuban cigar. He drank down a bottle of water in greedy gulps. Akira sat in a chair thinking, listening to the recorded message from the gas station below, heard it echo while staring and trying not to think of Blue Glitter Top or anything else.

Then, an idea...

17

Akira got a few looks from people in the lobby while carrying one of the purses. He didn't give a shit. He bought a beer at *El Acueducto*, then sat in the business center drinking and searching online for pictures of a matching purse. He found a few that seemed similar enough and tried to download them. They were copyright-protected. He took a screenshot, then pasted it into MS Paint, then cropped out everything he didn't need.

"Nice try, jerkweeds," Akira said to the unseen, unnamed people who tried to copy-protect the Gucci purse photos. He saved each pic and emailed them to himself. They were a little grainy, but they'd do.

He sat for a bit, trying to remember the password to his mom's eBay account. He'd quit posting new items in her store, sending out the last of her orders months ago. He just got tired of thinking about it. The last time he'd logged in, he'd set her entire inventory of cheap Japanese shit to "sold out" and hadn't been back to the storefront or answered emails since. He tried a few different password combinations before finally remembering hers.

He uploaded the best photo, and posted the Gucci purse as a three-day auction. He looked around at what his competition was selling, and his purse looked no different. One even used the same photo he'd stolen. He checked their sales history, and found that purses usually sold for a few hundred dollars. He felt like it might work. He wrote up a quick description, stating that the photos weren't of the actual item itself, but rather an accurate representation of the style of purse for sale. He told potential buyers to bid with confidence for this beautiful product from an eBay *Powerseller* with thousands of sales and hundreds of happy customers. Satisfaction was guaranteed, and that items shipped USPS Priority upon receipt of payment, PayPal preferred.

He launched the auction.

Akira figured he'd get some of his goddamned money back, and that would show those dumb NMSU bitches that he was no chump. He tried to imagine some kind of scenario where he could find them, and prove how wrong they were about him…how sorry they'd be for doubting him. Then he'd say something cruel to Blue Glitter Top because she was no fucking prize herself.

Akira spent a few dull hours at the pool, drinking more beer and playing stupid games on his iPhone while looking at girls. One girl, his favorite, was sorta tomboy hot, swimming in a yellow T-shirt with an old-timey radio on it. They were all a bunch of touristy Americans hiding out in the safety of the Hotel Tulum. Her and her friends were pretty, but he was sure they were all stuck-up.

When his battery got low, he decided to go back to the business center and check on his auction. The purse was already up to $137 even though there were still days left on the auction. Seventeen people were watching it, and so far there had been five different bidders. Akira could hardly believe it.

So why stop?

Akira quickly set up auctions for the other purses he had. With each new auction he launched, he imagined his new life: living in the Hotel Tulum, buying more purses every couple days with whatever profits landed in his mom's account. He'd hang out at the hotel all day — meeting people from all over, having awesome conversations, and everyone would wonder how a kid like him got so goddamned rich while they all slaved their asses off like chumps. Of course, he'd meet lots of hot girls — all on vacation in Mexico and itching to hook up. He'd show them around, take in the sights only hip locals knew, and everywhere he went everyone would know him when he walked in. It was easy as shit. He would toss money around like a fucking rapper, get drunk, and score a different chick every night. And every new day there'd just be *more more more more more*.

18

Akira pulled two hundred dollars from the ATM in the lobby of the Hotel Tulum — the maximum daily out-of-country withdrawal allowed. There was a $3.50 ATM fee for the transaction, which Akira hated but accepted. The machine asked if you wanted dollars or pesos. He took dollars.

He tipped the valet two bucks and slid into his car. He drove out in the vague direction the cab had gone the day before. He recognized a few landmarks, and, after a while, found his way back downtown. The traffic was oppressive and overwhelming, all the streets and all the people and all the shops looked the same. After a half hour of looking, Akira found the old church surrounded by a few streets he recognized and somehow found the shop with the purses.

"*Señor!*" said the shopkeep, recognizing Akira. "Back for more bags?"
"Yeah, I'm looking for a deal."
"I have! Best in Juárez!"
"Do you have ten?"
"*Sí, sí* — I have many."

The man began digging behind the hanging racks of
clothes, pulling out boxes. He pulled a box of T-shirts from
under a table, then put it back. He tried another box. He
finally found his box of purses stuffed behind a broken
register in the back. He brought it out. The box was
covered in shipping labels and *hànzì*, along with the
occasional word or phrase in English. The man removed
purses, counting aloud, *"uno, dos, tres…"* and stopping
when he'd pulled ten from the box. They looked every bit
as good as the ones Akira bought before.

"How much?" Akira asked. "Remember, you promised me
a deal."
"You give to many pretty women, eh?" The man said,
scheming.
"Gotta keep my bitches happy, yo," Akira said, waiting.
The man laughed. Finally the man said, "Two hundred,
U.S. Best price. Number one."

Akira tried on some fake Ray Bans, pretending to think it
over. Next he tried some fake Oakleys, deciding only
buffoons wore Oakleys — real or fake. Akira put the Ray
Bans back on, running his finger through his hair as he
checked himself in the small mirror.

"Ah, *lente oscuro, marijuano seguro…*"

"Excuse me?"

"Oh, *nada, amigo,*" the man said. "You like the *gafas*?"

"They're okay," Akira said. "You get these here in
Mexico?"
The man shook his head. "Mexican is shit!" the man said.
"Too expensive!" he laughed. "I get from China…you from
China, yes?"
"Man, fuck China," Akira said. The man smiled and was
clearly confused. "That's like me calling you a Texan."
Again the man smiled like *yes yes*, but didn't understand.

Akira told the man two hundred was too much, but the
man wouldn't budge. Akira told the man that if these
worked out he would come back for more. Still he
wouldn't budge.

"Okay, throw in these then," Akira said, holding up his
fake Ray Bans. The man agreed. "Plus you remember me
next time," Akira said, "and give me a better price, right?"
"*Sí, sí,* I remember," the man said. "Good price…number
one price."
They shook on it and Akira paid the man.

97

19

Back at the hotel, Akira checked back on the auctions. Gucci had climbed another $30 and two more people were watching. The other three all seemed promising too. He imagined a last-second flurry of bids, everyone trying to snipe each other, driving up profits on each one. Akira decided he was a fucking genius.

He bought a beer at *El Acueducto*, and went up to his room. *It was all so fucking simple! Why hadn't anyone figured this shit out?* He felt like celebrating. On his phone he tried logging on to Twitter. It seemed to work, so he Tweeted about buying a really expensive HD movie camera when he got back to town, saying anyone who wanted to be in his movies should hit him back — that roles would be first come, first serve. He then jumped on to Gmail to send a few emails. He was going to tell friends he was going to be a producer/director, but of course he couldn't get Gmail to work on his phone.

He went back downstairs, thinking he'd maybe send the emails from the business center. He stopped at *El Acueducto* instead. He got drunk talking to a bunch of people about his latest film. He was well known in Tokyo, people there loved his shit. He was gonna shoot all over the southwest and Juárez in HD, just like *Breaking Bad,* because the quality was getting so damn good and because there were big tax breaks and shit. He bragged about there being over three hundred days of sunlight and New Mexico being a totally photogenic location.

Some fucking blond dude from Arizona said Akira seemed too young to be making movies, and someone else asked if they could find him on IMDB. Akira said it just went to show what they knew, the rubes…that filmmaking was a young man's business, and that real movers and shakers didn't have time to fuck about on the internet, posting shit about themselves, and bragging about projects — they were out fucking hustling.

His lies got more intricate with each drink. Soon he was taking fake calls with semi-famous people on his dead iPhone, giving the people in the bar the 'just a second' finger when they tried to ask him stupid questions. He slurred through a call from Freida Pinto's agent.

"Bobby. Bobby. Bobby…you're not hearing me," Akira said. "Are we gonna do this thing, or are you gonna keep tickling my balls?" The bartender rolled his eyes, interrupting to tell Akira the bar was closing.

"Great," said Akira. "I'll just chill over here for a few minutes and finish my drink."

The bartender said, "No," that Akira needed to cash out and go.

"Fine," Akira said, "then send a few bottles of *Negra Modelo* to my room then." When the bartender asked him how he wanted to pay, Akira said "Charge it to my room — Jezus, I'm busy."

Back in his room, Akira realized he was starving. He rang up room service to ask about his goddamned beers. They didn't know a thing about them. Akira placed a big order, then sat dizzy and spinning on the bed, waiting. It was all he could do to plug in his phone to charge. He looked for the birds in the plaster as the ceiling spun but couldn't find them. He went to the bathroom and fell half-asleep sitting on the commode.

He woke to knocking on his room door. The pillow man from before had a big tray covered with silver discs. Under the lids were a hamburger and fries, a plate of *taquitos* with salsa, a Cobb salad, and a piece of chocolate cake. There was a tall glass of milk with saran wrap on top, and a bottled Coke to drink. Akira told him that the bartender downstairs didn't send up his goddamned beers and should be fired, but the pillow man didn't seem to understand.

Akira tipped the man a dollar, then ate until passing out.

20

In the morning, Akira checked his auctions on the business center computer. The first was up to just over $200. He decided to stay in Juárez for another day.

"I have to be back in Albuquerque tomorrow," Akira said to the girl behind the front desk, "gotta handle some very important business..."
"Movie business?" the girl asked with a smile.
"What?" Akira said. Then he remembered all his drunken babble in the bar the night before. "Oh yeah, yeah. Gotta meeting — Albuquerque Studios..." A few employees seemed to be lingering within earshot, snickering even. "But I like it here. I'll stay another day."

Back in the business center he checked his email, tried Facebook, and then Twitter. No one had asked to be in his movie.

In his room, he ate the cold room service leftovers: taquitos, some stale fries, and a Coke without any fizz. He ate while watching more Mexican TV. There was a fat man in a white suit. He was on the phone with two women, threatening them somehow. Whatever he said really scared them. One was holding a baby. Then there was a guy standing in a field. A woman wearing a nurse's smock ran to him. It seemed like she was delivering a harvested organ in a small, styrofoam beer cooler. They kissed. Another woman drove up in an SUV, apparently too late to stop them.

During the commercial break, Akira understood nothing but the names of the companies. Chevy. Qwest. Domino's. Sears. Back on the show, the SUV woman also had a baby with her. Akira couldn't tell if it was the same baby from before. Everyone argued, and then the SUV woman fainted. Then there was a wise old priest with a white beard — maybe he was dying. Akira figured that, with all the babies, the organs, the nurse, and the dying priest, it was clearly a riveting drama about selling babies and harvested organs on the black market. It all pointed back to the menacing fat man in the white suit — that's how the show ended.

Akira decided that if he was running this show it would be called *Black Friday*, however you said that in Spanish — and it would be on Friday nights. He even thought up a good tag-line — "In a world where everything is for sale… everyone has a price!" It seemed like the next show was about a champion girl boxer, a race car driver, and a famous *Luchador*. Akira couldn't figure how it all connected, and he felt sure he was going insane. He had to shut it off.

He started to regret staying another day. He thought about going back to the desk, saying that he couldn't stay, urgent movie business, change of plans, whatever. But he was sure they'd laugh at him some more, so he didn't. Instead, he figured maybe he'd just get drunk again, and pretend to talk to famous people or their agents. But he didn't have the energy for it.

To save money — he thought about walking to a nearby gas station for beers. Out on his patio, he stared down at the streets below. They hummed with a slow, steady energy. Everyone seemed to be busy doing something, but no one seemed stressed or worried. Akira told himself that was why he fit in so well down here. He closed the patio door, but couldn't make himself leave. He promised himself he'd walk to the gas station later. He tried Tweeting bits about his new Mexican TV show and his new Mexican life with his iPhone. He couldn't tell if it was working, got bored, and fell asleep.

When he woke it was late afternoon. He opened the patio

door and the air was electric and cool — maybe there had been rain. He sat near the door, smelling the sweet air, playing Angry Birds on his phone. As far as he could tell, no one had called him, or left him any messages. He could easily be dead in Mexico, and no one would even know it. *All these so-called friends,* he thought. He told himself he'd remember this next time they were all hanging out, trying to use him for his money, remember it when he was a big-time movie director.

He walked to the gas station behind the hotel, the sun sinking low. The sky was deep orange, then red; and the high grey and purple storm clouds were pink with highlights on the underside. He walked along with dirty people, folks who had nothing yet seemed happier than him. He wanted to talk to them, ask them how and why. Maybe they just don't know life can be better than this? Akira wished he understood.

He bought bottles of water, some candy, and a big bag of chips — *El Sabroso Salsitas.* He added a pack of gum, a bottle of juice, then some cookies. He didn't know what he wanted. He grabbed a tall can of beer, some beef jerky. He asked the clerk for some vanilla-flavored cigarillos. The girl rang it up. Akira looked around for a dirty magazine, but couldn't find one. He was too embarrassed to ask where to get one and didn't think he could make her understand anyways.

Walking back to the hotel Akira heard sirens, and saw cops stretching out crime scene tape — blocking a side street. He couldn't stop himself, he had to see. By the time he got there, a small crowd had gathered. One man was crying, surrounded by a few people trying to comfort him. A Ford truck had been shot full of holes, and a dead pair of legs lay on the ground, sticking out from behind the back tire. Most people just shook their heads and walked away. A news van parked and the reporter tried to interview the cops, but no one said much of anything. It seemed routine. Akira looked around at all the faces and they looked back at him — uncaring and suspicious. He didn't belong here. His was probably the next corpse to be ignored in the streets.

He sat in his wretched room, thinking about the whole scenario: the people; the cops; the news people; the legs. No one cared. Akira didn't know how that could be. He remembered the people being hit by trains, how funny he thought it was when he watched it. But maybe it wasn't funny. Maybe nothing was. He thought again of his mom, and how the legs were just there.

He'd stayed as long as he could, eating gas station junk as the walls closed in on him. He tried to find the news station that had filmed everything, find out what happened, what the explanation for the shootout was — but couldn't. He wanted to go, right away — but he was too terrified to set foot outside.

Akira didn't really sleep, and checked out just after sun-up. He drove, a bit spooked, straight toward the border crossing, surprised he knew the way. When he made it to the border, traffic was three long lanes, bumper to bumper, leading to a blue-roofed tan structure. "*PC-51 Puente Internacional Paseo Del Norte*" it said, and the exhaust-ridden palm trees choked and died while everyone waited. Leaving Mexico was easy.

On the American side, it was *Alto Aquí* - xCLOSEDx xCERRADOx - Open - *Abierto* - Have Documents Ready - *Tengan Sus Documentos Listos* - all flashing lights, green, red, and yellow. The closer he got the faster they seemed to flash. It was nerve-wracking. There were cameras, barriers, thick concrete-filled posts, and a bunch of badged, pot-bellied, paramilitary types in boots and ball caps, dragging drug dogs from inspection booth to inspection booth and car to car. Akira tried to imagine what they'd say about the purses, wondered if there'd be any problems.

When he arrived at the check-point, the Border Patrol were really only interested in alcohol, tobacco, medicine, and fruit, none of which Akira had brought with him. He was oddly relieved about being surrounded by Americans again, even if they were cops and border patrol agents with guns. The men searched his car, and asked him a couple questions about Juárez, and checked his I.D. Over and over. They looked inside each purse, in the back seat, looked inside the car, but it was mainly for show. Akira wanted to ask if they knew anything about a man killed near the Hotel Tulum the night before. He was afraid they'd detain him as a witness if he did, so he didn't ask. After a few minutes, he was cleared back through to the El Paso side, back to America, and he drove straight through to Albuquerque in the long shadows and silence of a New Mexico desert morning.

21

Akira woke late in the afternoon to find his father fumbling with a brand new Swiffer mop in the kitchen — a strong industrial lemon scent hanging in the air. His father was just back from Costco, and enormous bundles of paper products, and gia-normous jugs of liquor and detergent and fabric softener and lemon Pledge littered the freshly polished countertops in the kitchen and the dining room table. Hot water was filling in the sink. His father looked up from the huge plastic bottle of floor wax through a new pair of readers resting on the tip of his nose. His father shut off the water — the room silent as steam rose from the basin. "The Girl From Impanema" played softly in the living room.

Akira grabbed a bowl from the cupboard.

"Where have you been?" his father asked.
"Looking for a job."
"For three days? I hope you found one."
"I did. So you can stop worrying."

His father set the directions down, and went back to the

Swiffer — tucking the mop pad's corners into the grip area. "Ah-so!" he said, pleased. Realizing he did not need it, he yanked the plug from the sink, and the hot water drained off.

"What are you doing?" Akira asked.
"We will clean up after ourselves from now on," his father said.
"You fired Señorita Vasquez?"
"I told her we could no longer afford to her pay what she deserved."

Akira rolled his eyes. He found some milk for his Frosted Flakes. Akira sloshed both in the bowl, and ate his cereal loudly.

"We could afford a maid if you didn't buy all this stupid stuff," Akira said.
"It's cheaper to buy in bulk," his father said. "It saves hundreds of dollars."
"Yeah, well it costs hundreds of dollars too." His father didn't disagree.
"Tell me about this job," his father said, an eyebrow raised.
"It's a sales job. Women's accessories," said Akira. "I should make mad paper, yo."
"Where will you work?"

"Wherever I want. I sell high-end stuff on my computer —
sorta like mom's old store."

"That sounds very promising."

The old man was almost wistful, gazing off as he said it.
What an idiot.

"I knew you had ambition. It's only when we enjoy what
we're doing that we find out what we're capable of."

"I'm gonna sell more than anyone."

"I hope you do. Work hard. Do your very best — no matter
if you dig ditches, or are the boss."

"I will," said Akira. "In fact, I'm gonna go see how my
sales are going right now."

Akira took his cereal into his room. He logged in to check
his auctions. The winning bid was just under $300 with
still a half day to go. It didn't seem real. He checked his
Gmail, his Facebook, and his Twitter account. Still nothing
from anyone. He grabbed another purse from his closet
and prepared the auction page, using photos swiped from
the Versace website. He copied some descriptive text,
pasted it on the item page, and launched another auction
— this one for a garish red, alligator leather monstrosity.
He was in business.

Akira took a shower, dressed, and packed up his computer. With his father hanging around the house, Akira figured he'd be more comfortable at Double Rainbow, or some other place with free wi-fi and refills on coffee. He could check his auctions in peace and search for a kick-ass HD movie camera. He figured he could just write screenplays while waiting for all his purses to sell.

He decided he'd start another auction every time a purse sold so there would be money coming in every couple days — who knew how much. He still had nine purses left to sell, so he figured it would take a couple weeks. If everything still seemed cool, he'd just drive back to Juárez and buy more. Hell, maybe he'd take half a week off — just kick it at the Hotel Tulum. By his math, he stood to make at least four grand, maybe more — in just over three weeks. Hell, call it a month — no need to kill himself. Besides, he'd have to know how to take it easy when he was rich. Plus he'd have his Juárez vacation to look forward to every month.

Ginger's Burgerhaus could keep their lousy $145/week. They could keep their stupid fry machines, and store managers, and team leaders, their regional quality and sales associates, and they could keep their stupid fucking customers. Yep, they could stick it all straight up their hamburger ass!

22

Akira refilled his coffee and went back to picking at the last of his cold fries. On his MacBook, he cycled from the eBay auctions, to Facebook, to Gmail, and occasionally to Twitter, or YouTube. It had been hours. Zoë wasn't working and everything was dull.

He also had iPages opened to a new screenplay. So far he'd typed UNTITLED by Akira Nakimura, and inserted his address and copyright down in the lower right-hand corner of the title page. On the first page he had a scene heading: Int.-Police Station-Night. Otherwise, his cursor just blinked. He tried to think of something that started in a police station. It seemed like an interesting place to start a cool, new movie. After ten minutes or so, Akira thought *If I had Final Draft, this shit wouldn't be so hard.* Akira was thirsty and wanted some beer. He'd forgotten his fake ID, so he was basically screwed. *Fucking iPages,* he thought, *it's shit for screenwriting.* He got tired of looking at the damn screen, so he saved his untitled movie, x-ed out of the program, and flipped back over to the web.

He trolled link to link, page after page, forgetting to return to previous pages to finish whatever it was he'd started reading. His head was a mash of half-read, half-finished tidbits. It felt like being drunk. He didn't know anything, couldn't know anything, and knowing things didn't even really matter anymore. He looked at other people on their laptops, all staring intently at things no one would ever remember in any productive or meaningful way. Even remembering shit wasn't necessary anymore. If you wanted to know when something happened, you just checked Facebook. Or your iPhone. Or Gmail. You didn't need to know anything anymore.

He tried searching movie cameras again. *Top of the line*, he thought, *only the best*. He Googled HD cameras and found one: A RED camera. It cost twenty grand. *Too many purses for this hombre*, Akira thought. Akira figured he'd have to settle for a Canon or Sony, probably. He looked at specs and stats, and tried to compare cameras to one another even though he didn't really understand them. He found a new Black Magic Cinema Camera for a few thousand dollars. He checked out a few videos and they all promised that using it was easy, and all the footage was beautiful. He decided that was the one he'd get when he'd sold enough purses.

Akira started watching trailers for new, independent art-house movies coming out. *The pinche competition*, he thought. He watched a handful and decided the secret was making movies about shit people understood but never would think up themselves. Then it was just a bunch of references to more famous books or paintings, and crazy visuals — anything shocking or memorable. It all seemed easy enough. If only he could make movies, he knew he'd be rich.

He tried Gmail, Facebook, and Twitter again. Nothing — just a bunch of spam for fake watches and boner pills. He checked his eBay auctions. The first was set to end in a couple hours. Soon he would know just how well it was all going to work. Akira figured most buyers would be so happy to have a designer purse, and the fact they paid so much while still saving some money would make it real for them. Believing made anything real, and that's all the convincing it took. There were still only a handful of bidders, though some more people were now watching the auction. It occurred to Akira that he could reach out to all the second place bidders, and offer them a purse at their final threshold — even though eBay frowned on such things. If he could get a few people to buy, he'd have his money even faster, and could make another trip to Juárez. He thought maybe he'd even hire some friends to drive him, or even just go to Juárez for him. *No, no* — Akira thought, *they'd just steal my idea, start doing it too — because people fucking suck.*

Akira ordered a thick slice of chocolate cake and a glass of milk. He asked the dude at the counter about Zoë.

"Who?" the dude said, as if he didn't know.
"Pretty girl, dirty blonde hair," Akira said. "She usually works afternoons."

The guy fed Akira some more bullshit. He figured the guy was probably just trying to get with her too, so he took his milk and cake and stiffed the dumbass on the tip.

He gave it a few more minutes. When Zoë didn't show at shift change, Akira decided to go pack up the purse.

23

Akira confirmed that the first buyer had made their PayPal payment in full — $359, plus $4.95 Priority shipping. He packed the purse up with some of his mom's old bubble wrap, taped and addressed the box to the winning bidder — some chick in San Diego. He dashed off a small form that supposedly claimed $360 worth of insurance, for effect. It was something his mom had taught him. Rigging up a fake insurance slips made buyers feel safe about larger purchases. Nothing ever came of it. It was just something to dress up the box.

He sent the winner a quick email, saying the package would ship out immediately, and thanked her for the prompt payment. He'd wait on leaving her feedback until the package was there, and there were no goddamned problems. Akira launched a new auction and, before logging out, checked on the others. They all looked pretty good — early bidding wars, eleven people watching one of them.

At the Post Office, Akira mailed the box off with help from a clerk in a red wig and grey cloak, wearing blood-red contacts he could hardly stand looking at.

"What are you supposed to be," he asked.
"I'm a Banshee," replied the clerk. Akira acted like he
knew what that was.

He then drove to the I.C. Food and Liquor Mart to
celebrate. He grabbed a sixer of Negra Modelo, and a
bottle of Tanqueray. He threw in some peppered beef jerky,
a Hundred Grand bar, a bag of Doritos, and some jalapeño
cheddar cheese dip. At the register, the man asked Akira
for his I.D. He checked his wallet. He'd forgotten to grab
his fake again.

"She knows me," Akira said, pointing to a woman who
also worked there. "I'm here all the time."
"Good for her," the man said, "I.D."

Despite wanting to argue with the guy, Akira figured he
couldn't burn his best liquor store. He had been coming
here since getting his fake, and they'd never really busted
his balls. He choked down a couple of insults, and told the
man he didn't have his I.D. with him. The man said he
couldn't sell the booze. Akira said no sweat, that he
understood, and paid cash for the rest. The fuckhead rang
it up.

"I'll just run home and get my I.D.," Akira said, again choking down his rage. It was miles out of his way — running back home, and grabbing his I.D., and it meant maybe even having to hear some more bullshit from his father — but it was worth it.

Akira was relieved to find the house quiet and his father napping. He grabbed his fake I.D. from his desk drawer, and snuck back out.

Back at the I.C. Food and Liquor Mart the man said, "Thanks for getting your I.D., you know how it is." "Yeah," Akira said, "someone's rules always fucking with working men." "The fucking government," the clerk said. "Total bullshit," Akira said.

He had no idea what they were talking about. But the man seemed to agree and would probably remember him now, so it was fine. Akira chatted with him and the woman a bit more before finally leaving with his beer and gin.

Akira drove toward the volcanoes jamming some *Leeches of Lore*. He started texting everyone — trying to get a little party together. No one was up for it: saying they had to study, or saying it was too cold, or *what-fucking-ever*. Akira always went to the volcanoes when he wanted to disappear. Cell reception wasn't for shit out on all that slag, and he could pretty much just sit out there and drink beers with the stars. He parked and sat in his front seat, eating his junk food, and drinking. Then he gave up on the eating.

He put on Snoop Dogg, bumped that shit. He got out, pounded his beer, and danced in his headlights. *This is more like it,* he thought. *I don't need anybody.* When he got tired of dancing, he promised himself he'd buy a chair — something he could carry in his trunk.

He looked out over the city and thought of his auctions, of the dumb girls bidding all over America. They wanted these overpriced purses to feel special. They were idiotic, and selfish, and ignorant. He thought of his mom, how proud she'd be of him — of his ambition, his creativity, his straight-up balls. "Customers are stupid," that's what she always said, "not smart enough to get what they want at a good price." His mom loved getting everything on the cheap, and re-selling it for top dollar. Akira told himself there was no way his mom wouldn't be proud.

"You bunch of marks!" Akira screamed at the city, then

slammed the last of his beer. "$360 for a filthy Chinese purse? From Juárez?! Just so you can be someone?"

He cackled — hurling the empty bottle at Albuquerque. It shattered somewhere in the invisible igneous black crags of the dark below. Akira worked another bottle cap off with his car key, and turned it up for a few long bubbles. There was no one and nothing else anywhere. He cranked the volume and rapped along:

> *"...He is I, and I am him —*
> *slim with a tilted brim,*
> *what's my motherfuckin' name?"*

He bounced his hand like he was hitting switches, like he was slapping a fat Latina ass, swigging beer and laughing as he stared out over the burning orange lights of the city — blinking and seething like dying embers in a fire. He downed the last of his beer.

The desert answered him only in wind.

24

Akira woke — freezing. The windows inside the Skyline had a thin sheet of frozen condensation. He ran a fingernail along one and a little snake of soft ice unraveled, and dropped near the door lock. Akira promised he'd start carrying a blanket and some pillows in the trunk of his car for nights like this. The ugly, warm musk of stale beer sat thick in the cabin. He thought he might be sick.

Akira opened the door and stumbled out into the frost. There wasn't a cloud in the frozen night sky, and the moon was a sliver surrounded by tiny, distant stars. The urge to throw up passed and he took a piss instead. The hot acrid stink of it almost steamed on the cold black rocks as it poured out of him, his guts draining. Back inside, he checked his phone. The battery was dead. He found his keys in the ignition, turned them, and fired the engine. The clock on the dash read 3:37 a.m.

His forehead hurt. In the rearview he noticed a red lump. He tested it with his fingers — sucking air back in through his clenched teeth as he did.

Pieces of the evening began to come back to him: Handfuls of chips stuffed in his mouth; jalapeño cheese sauce caked on his pinky knuckle; beers and beers and beers; peppered jerky; then gin, straight gin. He found the bottle in the back seat and thankfully it was still pretty full.

Then, other things: thoughts of girls; girls in magazines; girls at his old school, at the mall, in Mexico — talking shit about Akira. Girls and makeup and jewelry and pantyhose with seams up the back. Girls' bodies, lips and hair. Girls in porn. Girls licking pinching biting nibbling cupping crushing rubbing...

He remembered thinking about his mom, about what she'd say, what she'd think. He remembered crying a little, then hating the fact that he was fucking crying. He remembered trying to stop, trying to be tough. And, when he couldn't stop, he remembered trying to bust a beer bottle over his own silly, stupid, crybaby skull.

Akira laughed a little. *At least I know where I got this,* he thought, testing the red lump again before driving back home.

25

Zoë was working. And she was delivering food to tables, not stuck behind the register. She'd have to talk to him.

He figured if he could just spot something, get some indication, a clue about something she liked — a book she was reading or something — then he could Google it and pretend he knew and liked it too. He watched her run food out to other tables, always smiling, always helpful. She was terrific. Akira tried to think of something really clever to say to her. *Yo, what's up shortie? How you doin'?* It would never work. He was rocking a do-rag, a black Yankees cap chillin' to the side, black Adidas tracksuit, and his brand new Tims but he still had no game.

"Turkey jack with fries?" she asked, holding his plate.
He stared at her.
"Um, did you order a turkey jack and fries?" she repeated.
"Yeah...yes, sorry." Akira said. "I just was gonna say something..."
She looked at him with a crinkled brow as she set down the plate. Akira realized he was talking gibberish. In a panic, he tried to save it: "I was just trying to Google

something cool to say to you."

"Oh yeah?" she said, smirking. "What'd you come up with?"

"Nothing."

"Oh, well…I guess I can come back," she said, pretending to pick up his sandwich and leave.

"No, that's okay," Akira said. "It probably won't get any better than that. I'm too hungry anyways."

"Do you need anything else…ketchup?"

"No, I'm good." As soon as Akira said it, he realized he needed ketchup.

"Okay, well my name's Zoë."

"I know. I'm Akira."

"That's a cool name. Where's it from?"

"Japan."

"Oh-Em-Gee! That's so cool!" she said, but Akira had no idea why. "Anyhow, just holler if you need anything else."

He watched her ass switch back and forth as she walked away, and thought about how stupid he was. Then he tried to figure out how to get some ketchup without her knowing.

He watched her over the top of his MacBook as he ate. She ran orders out to tables, and seemed to have pleasant conversations with everyone. A table full of guys in the corner kept her chatting for a full two minutes with all their stupid yakking. Akira was sure she was annoyed, but just being nice. When she finally walked away, all the douchebags ogled her ass. Two of them high-fived, and pulled faces at each other. One even reached out for her ass after it was half way across the room — his palms up, tickling his fingers while his stupid fucking friends laughed. Akira thought about trying to fight them all. He'd march over, all slow-mo cool, and say, "Okay, which one of you fucking bitches gets their ass kicked first?" They'd all think he was insane, then he would destroy them, one by one, as everyone in the restaurant looked on, happy someone was finally doing something about these loud-mouthed, disrespectful punks. But there were too many of them. That wasn't the way the world worked. Assholes like that never got what was coming to them.

Back on Facebook, a picture of a super-hot chick flashed on the sidebar. Under it read: "Thousands of single girls are looking for guys like you on True!" He clicked the picture, and it took him to a sign-up screen for some dating website. He x-ed it out.

In his chat list, he saw that Kurt was online. Akira started chatting, bragging about Zoë.

"Seriously?" Kurt asked.

"Full on, man," Akira typed. "She's all the way into my shit, *vato!*"

Akira then told him about the table full of douchebags.

"They're disrespecting her. You should come down here, we'll start some shit..." Akira said, but Kurt didn't respond, his lame brain probably buffering. His chat icon switched to unavailable.

Akira spent the rest of the afternoon there, not really doing much of anything. He'd taken to streaming bootlegged movies on YouTube, and after a couple, he was surprised to see the sun had gone down and a screaming moon had crawled out from behind the Sandias. Some time during the second movie, Zoë had left without saying goodbye to him. He wondered what kind of work schedule she could have where she was barely ever there. He figured it was because she was hot, and hot girls always got to do whatever they wanted, so of course she had it wired at work.

Akira figured he better go home, if only to keep his father from freaking out. He'd definitely been cooler since Akira started selling purses, but still it was just easier to get home at a decent hour. *Besides,* Akira thought, *I'm sick of this fucking place* — meaning the Double Rainbow without Zoë.

Akira was surprised to find his father wasn't home. There was no note and he had no idea where his father had gone. Akira thought about going back out, but he couldn't really think of anywhere to go. He dozed off on the couch watching a Ninja Warrior marathon and slept there most of the night.

26

Akira was a half-day late sending out the next purse. The auction had ended, payment had cleared the previous day, and all he could hear was his mother's voice prodding him to do better. Akira fired off a quick e-mail to the buyer, saying the purse would be *en route* by tomorrow at the latest. He boxed up the purse, and decided he had to mail it off before he did anything else. That seemed to please his mother's nagging voice.

At the post office, the line was long and ridiculous. There were eight windows, but only two people working, and everyone fidgeted and sighed and pull faces of frustration and disgust at each other. One man, a few people behind Akira, said, "Government at it's finest!" and stormed out, rattling the glass door as he left. A third worker opened her window, and people seemed a little relieved. But then one of the original workers went on break, and another groan rumbled through the frustrated crowd. There was nothing for it. Akira got close to leaving three or four times himself, but ended up staying. He spent twenty minutes on line before finally making it to the window. The transaction was relatively painless, and Akira's frustration turned to indulgent, satisfied accomplishment.

He decided he'd reward himself with lunch and a little shopping. He went to California Pizza Kitchen, and was able to use his fake I.D. for a couple beers. The workers there were, on average, attractive — and he figured it must be some kind of unwritten corporate policy only to hire beautiful people. He ate his entire pizza, despite promising himself to take some home, and afterwards he wandered around the ABQ Uptown mall — looking at clothes, and bedroom sets, and flatware, and all the couples shopping together. There was something about it, about watching a guy follow his girl around, store to store like his father used to do, looking at all kinds of stupid stuff. Akira decided these poor saps were all broken lapdogs — that their women had brow-beat them into mall shopping and he promised himself he'd never be one.

He went to the Apple store, and looked at all the filmmaking stuff. He decided that when he started making movies, he'd need a MacBook Pro, and Final Cut Pro — editing software that cost over thousand bucks. *I can rent the rest,* Akira thought, *as long as I have a good camera, a computer, and that software.* He put together some rough prices, and was shocked at the expense though still determined to buy it all someday. The 15-inch started at

$1999, and could easily hit three grand with all the necessary software and storage. Whenever any of the Apple store employees talked to him, he told them he was a filmmaker. The girls were attractive, but none were really interested in his bullshit, so Akira got mad and decided that he'd buy all his gear online — no commissions for haters!

Akira tried the Barnes & Noble at the Coronado Mall, where he thumbed through a bunch of digital filmmaking books. The shit was seriously technical, and Akira decided that he was more of an idea man, and that he'd have to find a good cinematographer to help him shoot his movies. He wondered how to find and hire people for a project, and how much it would cost him, but quickly dismissed the thought. *Once I have a badass script*, Akira thought, *motherfuckers'll line up to be part of the production*. He looked at the Criterion Collection DVDs, seeing as how all kinds of famous actors and filmmakers said Criterion was *the shit*. He didn't really recognize the movies, so he just bought a couple random titles, and went home to watch them.

The first one he opened was some crazy French movie. A married couple was cheating on each other, and the adulterers were each plotting to kill the others somehow.

But not before they killed the woman's parents — as they apparently had a bunch of money or something. Mainly it was a bunch of car crashes and wacky shit. There was this insanely long traffic jam filled with every kind of French car and everyone was pissed off at each other, and a bunch of kids walked faster than the cars went, and at the end of the gridlock there were bodies strewn all over the road. Later there was a gunfight, and a girl who sang a little song before she died, and a guy acted like he was gonna smash a baby frog before he and a woman supposedly ate some human meat. Akira had no idea what the hell he was watching and decided it must be brilliant, and was probably the best movie he'd ever seen.

As far as he could tell, it wasn't really about anything, and he immediately decided he'd make a movie like it someday so everyone would say he was brilliant too. He fell asleep with the DVD stuck on the main menu screen — a staccato percussion repeating as he slowly drifted off.

27

Akira ate at Outback Steakhouse — Alice Springs Chicken with garlic mashed potatoes and a Caesar salad. The ridiculous room had recently been updated with dark wood, and what he assumed were Aboriginal hieroglyphics instead of a bunch of goddamned neon Foster's Beer signs, boomerangs, and kangaroos. He ordered another Wallabedarned with his fake I.D., but drank it too fast and gave himself a brain-freeze.

He'd mailed off three more purses in the last few days and, between shipping costs and ATM withdrawals, he'd actually lost track of how much profit he'd cleared. He hadn't seen anyone of his friends anywhere, and couldn't catch Zoë at work. He told himself he was focusing on gettin' that cheddar, yo.

Everyone at Outback sat staring at giant TVs with guts so big they could hardly wedge in to the remodeled booths. They jammed Bloomin' Onion strings and Aussie Cheese Fries into their gaping maws, getting fatter and fatter with each fucking bite. They disgusted Akira, and he told himself he was nothing like them. He sat for a couple hours, drinking and people watching. A girls high school soccer team arrived in a big, loud, beautiful crush of noise and sweat and perfume and giggles, and Akira sat peeking at them over the top of his iPhone. He tried to act all cool, and uninterested, but they were too gorgeous, and he was nothing and no one, and felt fat and ugly and ashamed. One table of girls seemed to notice him, and maybe they were even talking about him — peeking over at him every now and again. But no, he wouldn't believe it. He wished he could send them all a round of drinks, and invite them over — but he knew it would never work. In the end, he watched them eat and leave, and when he was sure they were gone, he paid his check and left too.

After dinner, Akira didn't want to go home. It was just before nine, and without even really knowing why, he decided to go to Fantasy World. It was just across the street, and if he remembered correctly, there was no cover until after 9 p.m. He rushed over, parked, and hustled inside.

Cover was $5 before 9 p.m., a Veteran's Day Special "honoring our troops," — not free like he thought. At the ATM, he pulled a couple hundred from his mom's account, paid the cover, and tipped the cashier five bucks. He was ushered in past the drawn red velvet curtains by a silent muscle-head bouncer. Inside the main room, it was dark, with neon, and rope lights lining a makeshift walkway between tables. He sat near the main stage, sinking in the thick black seat.

"What can I get you?" a waitress asked. She was lean, wiry, with limbs tangled with veins and a few tattoos. She seemed annoyed he was there.
"You have Dr. Pepper?" Akira asked.
She left, saying nothing either way.

Akira glanced around the room. It was early yet, and only the main stage had a girl on it. It was near the end of her song — some mopey-ass, tortured emo-rock shit about how hard life was or whatever. She was naked, but from his angle Akira couldn't see anything. There were a few people sitting near the stage, staring like serial killers into the poor girl's crotch. The place was dead. The waitress returned with a plastic cup of lukewarm Dr. Pepper.

"Six dollars," she said. Akira fished out a ten and paid her, tipped her $2.
"Can you break these for me," Akira said, handing over two $20s. "Singles."

The waitress pulled a gangster-wad of bills from some

hidden pocket in her miniskirt, counted out a stack of ones. "Here's thirty," she said, then handed him a couple fives, and walked off.

On stage, the girl was gathering up her clothes and a few wadded-up dollar bills — crushing them against her naked chest as she scurried off. A new song started, but no girl was dancing. When the song was half-over, a drug-dulled goth chick wandered on stage, shook her ass a little, and writhed around like she was stuck in tar. Her tall, clear plastic heels thacked against the linoleum stage as she brought them down — a bit too late to keep time with the drums. She worked her bra loose, then her panties, and one of the guys on the other side of the stage cheered. Everyone else sat back staring, stone-still but for the occasional sip at their $6 soda pops.

The whole goddamned scene started to depress Akira. The music. The girls. The waitress. The lonely, terrifying customers. Akira wondered how long he'd have to stay to keep from looking like some prude who'd paid before realizing he'd made a terrible mistake.

Despite it all, he couldn't stop looking. He felt jealous. The girls all seemed to realize that they had some kind of power over the poor saps in the crowd. He watched their bodies move, saw the flesh bend, and stretch, and fold, and unfold — the hot pull of it was both wrenching and alluring. One girl, a doughy Latina, was littered with hickies, all spackled-over with thick make-up. He imagined some goddamned boyfriend and hated him — wanted to save her. He gave her a few dollars. She took them, and disappeared to the back when her song was done. He watched for her, thought maybe he'd even talk to her, but she never came back out. Akira was instantly disgusted with himself. How had he ended up at Fantasy World anyways, giving away his money like a stupid fool? Again he looked at the dingy, uncomfortable fucking chairs, the linoleum, and the whole sad, stupid goddamned world. He had to get out.

He drove towards home in the sick yellow glister of halide city lights thinking of the girl's hickies. That bastard boyfriend of hers, he got to have her, but Akira got no one and nothing. He tried to think of anywhere to go but home, but there was nowhere. He didn't want to see anyone, or be bothered with appearances and stupid drama. He wanted to disappear, and for someone, anyone, to worry about him.

His father was asleep in his favorite leather chair, a Sonny Rollins record still spinning rhythmically even though the music had ended. Akira cradled the needle arm back in its slot, and turned the record player off — then tossed a blanket over him as he snored. Akira drank the last of his father's watery Scotch. In the kitchen he rinsed and refilled the glass to water the calla lily.

In bed he pawed at himself, trying to remember the girls from Fantasy World. He dug his brain for clear images of their bodies and Brazilian waxes, but all he could see were the hickies, and all he could think about was his mother's money. Everything else was stuck buffering — pixelated and pointless. He gave up.

28

Akira went, day after day, to the Double Rainbow to sit and eat and drink coffee, and watch after Zoë. She had these two front teeth that stuck out ever so slightly when she smiled and her lips pouted out even when she wasn't and it slayed him. She was constantly putting on this pink lipgloss, a little tube with a wand attached to its lid. Dip dip, smear — dip dip, smack. He loved watching the ritual. He took to writing her little notes while pretending to be really busy on the phone. The more calls he faked, the more she wanted to chat.

"Dig that smile!" he'd write. Or "Love that lipgloss!" Followed by: "Sorry — big buyer down in Mesilla."

He'd point to his phone, and clap his fingers together, as if the imaginary buyer wouldn't stop talking. She'd giggle and write back: "Tell that dumb ass to shut it! I haven't talked to my Japanese friend all day!" She drew little hearts under her exclamation points instead of dots. Akira saved the notes.

He'd watch other guys talk to her, and he'd sorta get mad,

but hide it — play it cool-like by making up his own mad rhymes about these fucking chumps. He usually went with something about how old they were, or bald, or fat, or broke and worthless — and he'd feel better. Or he'd rap about how he'd bust the fools up: *"I'm leavin' Tim-tracks / across your skull cracks,"* he'd spit at all these douchebags trying to push up on his boo.

He'd watch Zoë work and imagine their relationship — how she be friendly for her job, sure, but would shine off all the losers because she was his girl. He'd watch her curly, dirty blonde hair with salon high and low lights, watch her lean, taut, athletic body slink around the restaurant, always on about some damn cause or another.

"Oh my god," she'd say first thing, "did you see what happened in…" *wherever.*

She'd preach about some miscarriage of justice somewhere, some blatantly racist thing someone said, or how mad she was about a third world regime and disenfranchised people in need of liberation and freedom. Akira would nod along and agree, then, when she left to expo more food, he'd Google it all — read Wikipedia so he'd have something intelligent to say about it when she returned.

Otherwise, he'd just sit there, chat with friends on Gmail, check Facebook, and Twitter while tracking his auctions. Every other day an auction would end and eBay would confirm it was a done deal — and the money, usually between three and four hundred dollars, would land in his mom's divorce account. He'd hit ATMs almost every day, pulling out the max, and even still he could barely keep up. He'd spread out his gangster wad on his bed — take pictures and post that shit to Instagram, #baller #chedda #paper #skrilla. He'd list another of his remaining purses, copying the information from Valentino or Prada or Louis Vuitton or Christian Dior, and launch his next auction. He'd box up the bidder's purse and head to the post office. Waiting in line, he'd think about all the girls out there, on laptops, laying in bed in their tight panties, all wanting what he had. Some days Akira would wear a suit, pretending he'd come from a meeting — but mostly he just wore his gangster shit: Ecko, Timberland, or an Adidas track suit — matching Yankees cap over a do-rag, sometimes his chain. He wanted everyone to know he was serious about his paper, yo — *a genius, with no bullshit uniform, and a five-hour work week.*

It'd been almost a month and, towards the end of a double, Zoë was sitting at Akira's table even though she wasn't supposed to. "If he sees me," she'd said about her boss,

"I'll get in trouble. But I don't give a shit…I'm *hella tired!*"

She started talking about everywhere she wanted to go, and everything she wanted to do.

"I'm just interested in things…in people, and I wanna, like, go places," Zoë said. "New Orleans, Paris, Transylvania…"

Akira sat, watching her mouth move. It was the soft, pink curve of the lips, her pretty white teeth — just crooked enough to have character.

"You know, I do all kinds of business down in Juárez," Akira said, "I go there once a month."
"See, that's what I mean! That's super interesting. Is it so crazy down there or what?"

Akira complained about the roaming fees on his phone when there, but realized she meant 'crazy' like 'really cool' — so he dropped it.

"I'll take you sometime, if you wanna go…" Akira said. "What's your number? I'll send the link to the hotel I stay at…"

And just like that, they were texting.

29

Akira returned home to find his father in his favorite chair, drinking bourbon, and listening to Miles Davis. *So… another pointless talk then,* Akira thought. Akira figured he'd try for his room all the same.

"Akira," said his father. Akira stopped at his bedroom door — rolled his eyes. "I need to talk to you, son."

Akira shuffled into the living room, plopped down on the couch, and waited for his father to say something. The ice cubes in the glass tinked as his father set it down — as always — precisely on the waiting water ring. "I talked, today, with your grandfather. You and I must make arrangements for *Obon*." Akira said nothing. "Your mother did not want to be…your mother always wanted to go back to Japan."

"What's it even matter now?" Akira said. His father's eyes narrowed.
"Son, I made a promise to her. I will keep it."
"I don't get any say?"
"Of course. I want you to go with me."

"And if I don't?"

"I'd like it if you did. It could be good…for both of us."

"And if not?" Akira asked.

"If you don't go, I think you'll regret it."

Akira said nothing. The air was still between them as Miles Davis filled the room.

"Maybe not now," said his father, "but someday."

Akira looked around. The dark TV screen, the living room windows and the cold night outside them, the ice cubes melting in his father's drink. Akira stared at his feet, at the scuffs on his new Timberlands.

"But," his father said, "I cannot make you go."

"Good, 'cuz I don't want to," said Akira, getting up from the couch.

"Son," his father said. "Just think about it for a few days."

Akira thought of the awful clack of chopsticks on bone, and the deep, lonely silence of the crematorium, of standing there with no one but his father. Again Akira's eyes swept the room, everything tightening in his chest.

"Fine," Akira said as he stared at his father. "I'll think

about it."

"Thank you," his father said. That settled, his father tried to shake the last few drops of liquor loose from the cubes. He sucked at the glass, then set it exactly back down on the wet ring again.

"I've got work," Akira lied.

"That's good," his father said. "'As a cure for worry, work is better than whisky.'"

Akira went to his room. He turned on his iTunes and logged in to check on his auctions. Everything looked good: early bidders, lots of people watching, and a purse set to sell by morning was already at $388. He decided to build a playlist for his next drive down to Juárez. He got about halfway through it before getting distracted by Zoë's Facebook wall, then finding some porn. He watched a couple of lesbians, hoping to learn a few tricks — if ever he got the chance. His mind boiled over thinking of the sights and smells and tastes and sensations. In bed he tugged at himself until he was almost home, then rushed to his bathroom to finish. Afterwards he rinsed the sink and the spigot down with cool water, washed himself — which felt tremendous — and toweled off before drifting to sleep thinking of Zoë's mouth and that pink lipgloss.

30

Akira finished the last of his meal so Zoë would come back to pick up his plates. She seemed to be taking her sweet time getting back to him this afternoon — spending a lot of time blathering with some olive-skinned Mediterranean type sitting near the magazines. Akira tried not to be annoyed. *She probably thinks you're a psycho,* Akira thought. *'It puts the lotion on its skin or else it gets the hose again…' you fat, ugly, stupid fucking monster…*

He hated to leave town, even for a few days, when things were going so well with Zoë — but he knew he needed more purses to keep the money train rolling. His last purse would go live Tuesday, so by Thanksgiving he'd be tapped. There was no way around another trip to Juárez. He told himself shit he figured he'd hear in business school — "you gotta strike when the iron is hot," "no product, no profit," and "if you fail to plan then you plan to fail." Just a quick trip — a there-and-back kinda deal, he decided. The sooner I go, the sooner I'll get back. Maybe he'd even leave tonight.

He watched her taut frame move in a kind of slow-motion,

watched her body push at her shirt, and was sure when he left town she'd flit off after someone else. Then he'd slip into "just friends" territory. A girl like that — you gotta make damn sure you keep other fuckers from sniffing around. The whole situation was impossible.

But then, a thought: *maybe she'd go to Mexico with him.* Akira felt the hope and dream of it bloom, and he'd soon built it all up in his mind — how impressed she'd be with the Hotel Tulum, everywhere they'd go, all the great stuff they'd do. He'd splash around a bunch of cash, impress her. Then she turned, just a few tables away, and he could tell she was finally heading back over. He tried to think up some smooth line, some cool-ass way to ask her, but before he could stop himself, he said —

"I've gotta go to Mexico tonight."
"Oh-Em-Gee! For what?"
"Merchandise. Inventory is mad-low."
"Isn't that, like, a long-ass drive?" said Zoë.
"Not too bad. I just throw on some tunes and jam," Akira said. "You could come with me…"

Zoë stacked up the empty plates.

"…if you want…"

The clatter hung between them.

"I'd totally wait for you to be done here," Akira said.

In her silence there seemed a certain curiosity about the possibility — but no, she couldn't. Of course she couldn't. A bolt of shame and panic tangled up and clinched in his chest. *You idiot, you fucking idiot...* his head thundered. It was too soon. He was fucking it up. He had to get out — anything to keep him from tanking it even worse.

"Anyhow," Akira said, "think of it as a standing offer," and after some mindless chit-chat he was able to finally get the hell out of there.

Akira sat in the parking lot, his seat reclined back, and staring up at the cloudy sky — trying to figure his next play. He searched his phone, punched a name, and dialed.

"Dude," Akira said when he got through, "I have to get the fuck out of here, man," pretending to be at home. After a few pleasantries, Akira said, "Listen, I've got an idea — a way we can make some serious scratch. Let's chop it up over dinner — my treat. I know just the place..."

Akira picked up Kurt, and drove towards the North Valley. He talked about Zoë, how maybe they would be a thing or whatever, before pulling in to the dirt lot in front of N&P's Lounge and Packaged Liquors. The place looked ancient, and the ramshackled outsides probably hadn't been changed since the 1970s. Akira parked, and killed the engine.

"Dude, I can't go in there," Kurt said, "I lost my fake."
"Relax," Akira said, "we aren't here to drink."

Akira opened the metal-grated door, shuffled sawdusty steps past a few haggard regulars nursing pints, to the thick metal door by the package liquor counter near the back. There Akira banged three times and waited. The little door behind a speakeasy grill opened, and a man's eyes appeared, saying nothing.

"John sent me," Akira said. "Told me to '*Ask the Dust…*'"

A heavy bolt unhitched, and the door swung open. The place was a cross between a 70's Playboy photo shoot and a Pottery Barn catalog. Thick black velvet drapes were tacked over windows and the tables were set with white linen, and heavy, polished flatware. A man sat playing Billy Joel on a polished grand piano. They slid into a red leather, high-backed booth, the cocktail glasses gleaming with the light from a kiva fire crackling in the corner.

"Dude — this place is pimp." Said Kurt.

"Shit, son…you know how I do," Akira said. "I'm seriously jonesing for one of these filets."

"Evening gentleman," the waiter said, welcoming them with menus, and a bread basket. "Can I start you with a couple drinks?"

"Jack and Coke," Akira said.

"Certainly," the waiter said, "can I see your ID…"

"I don't have it," Akira said. "But I'm in here all the time — ask anyone."

Akira argued a little, but there was nothing doing. The waiter offered to bring a manager over.

"Forget it," Akira said. "Dr. Pepper."

"Coke," said Kurt. The waiter went for the drinks.

"Dumbass," Akira said. "Just means the bill and the tip will be smaller."

Akira looked around the restaurant. It was slow — only a couple people at tables, all out of earshot.

"So what's up, man?" Akira asked. "Where you been at?"

"Just trying to get through a couple online classes at CNM," Kurt said. It was okay, better than the fucking Burgerhaus, he said. Plus he'd been doing some side work for his dad instead of finding another shit-job. "Just been busy, I guess."

"Yeah, me too," Akira said, explaining the fake purses, his mom's eBay Powerseller account, how much money he'd been raking in — all of it.

"Purses from Juárez?"

"Yeah," said Akira. "Shit's crazy, right?"

Kurt agreed that it was. The waiter returned with their drinks, and took their dinner orders. Akira asked for a refill, and some more bread.

"So, you want in? Next time I go?"

"What do you mean?" Kurt said.

"We buy as many as we can. Split it all 60/40." Kurt sat thinking. " Easiest money you'll ever make, dawg — I swear. "

"I don't know..."

"We stay at this kickass hotel I know. A suite," Akira said. "They treat me like fucking royalty down there."

Kurt still wasn't sure. They were silent for a while or talked about some other boring shit. The waiter returned, setting their bacon-wrapped filets before them.

"Yo, can we get that bread?" Akira said, and the waiter scurried off. "This dude sucks."

The steaks were decent. Not as good as Paul's Monterrey Inn, of course — but few things were. Every time the waiter checked back, Akira had a new request: another refill, an extra side of ranch dressing, more butter, some steak sauce. Once he had them, he hardly remembered to use them. Akira was disappointed — he figured Kurt should've been more grateful. The more he thought about it, the more Akira decided it was probably just jealousy. Kurt chewed huge bites with his head down, not saying much, and mainly just checking out the few girls in the place.

"Fine — 50/50," Akira said. "But I need to go this week, like tomorrow."
"Cool," Kurt said, though Akira had no idea what "cool" meant. The waiter interrupted before Akira could ask.
"Can I get you guys any dessert? Coffee?"
"Just the check," Akira said.
"I'll be your cashier when you're ready — no rush. Thanks for dining at Nana & Papa's Speakeasy…see you again."
"The hell you will," Akira said once the waiter was out of

earshot. He checked the bill: $76.37. "I got this," Akira said, dropping four twenties in the case and snapping it shut.

"You want me to leave the tip?" Kurt said.

"Don't need it," Akira said. "I'm rolling deep, dawg. Check this shit out."

Akira pulled a wad of bills from his jacket pocket, fanned it out like a gangster.

"Holy shit."

"See what I'm saying?" Akira said. "*Rollin' deeeeep, son. You will be too.*"

Akira slugged down the last of his Dr. Pepper and got up. "Gotta drain the lizard."

When he was sure Akira was in the bathroom, Kurt stuffed another $10 in the bill.

Back in the car Akira tried again.

"So, when should we go?" Akira said.

"I can't, man."

"I thought you said 'cool' — what the fuck?"

"It's not right," Kurt said. "It's a lie."

"A lie?! Man…" Akira said, "This whole goddamned world is a lie."

There was nothing from Kurt. Akira jammed the keys in the ignition, and fired the engine.

"Fine, sorry. Forget I said anything," Akira said. "Where should we go now?"

"I have to go home, dude."

"Jezus, I thought we were hanging out?"

"We did," Kurt said. "I haven't done any reading, and I still have math...sociology. I'm way behind."

"C'mon — dessert at the Gay-bow. I can show you my new chick."

"I can't, man. I promised my parents I'd be back by, like, now."

Akira gripped the steering wheel tight, stared past the dappled raindrops on the windshield.

"So, should I find you an ATM?" Akira asked.

Kurt looked at him, blinked a few times, and bristled — trying to figure out what to say.

"Jezus...relax, man," Akira said. "I'm just fucking with you."

They talked about of bunch of meaningless shit — movies,

music, where Kurt was spending the holidays, and how a guy they knew already getting married and having a kid — as Akira drove Kurt home.

Akira cursed at his so-called friend as he watched Kurt walk back to his parents' house. Everyone fucking sucked. Akira checked the clock on the dashboard — it was just after 5 p.m. The gray, rainy sky had made it seem much later all afternoon. As Akira neared the highway, the sun broke through at the far western horizon. The sky blazed in a dazzling, sun-setting orange haze — one that seared the underside of the dense clouds as he jumped on I-25, and headed South.

31

The sun was just down out his passenger side window —
the horizon blank and cruel — as Akira drove and the cool
night sank down around him. The sage and scrub oak
mesas slid by and the sky went purple then black as his
tires slapped out a cadence over the tarred seams veining
the New Mexico blacktop. Just beyond the reach of his
headlights, in the yawning night, was the desert — pitiless
and harsh. He tried not to think about how bad he'd
fucked up with Zoë, tried not to think about what an
ignorant, horrific fool he was or how terrified she must be.

But by the time he stopped for gas and a sack of flaming-
hot Cheetos in Truth or Consequences, he'd decided he
was actually cooler than *the gang*, that by leaving all
nonchalant-like, he had actually saved it with Zoë, and this
thing he had going with her was still *on like Donkey Kong*.

32

It was late when Akira finally made Juárez. He fumbled with the GPS but his phone was already crapping out. He told himself to be more careful with the phone anyway — that he didn't want to get hit with too many of those goddamned roaming fees like the last trip. Everywhere police lights flashed, and all but the busiest streets were blocked by armored vehicles as Mexican Police in black face masks yelled and peeked inside cars — fingers on their machine-gun triggers.

Akira had no idea how he would find the Hotel Tulum. Whatever the city pretended at when the sun was up — this was something else. Akira decided this — with sirens flashing, and armed cops worked intersections on high alert — was the true, dark heart of Juárez. He knew going anywhere but the hotel would be foolish. The police sent traffic on dizzying detours, farther and farther from where Akira thought the hotel should be. He tried asking a cop, but the man just waved him on like a cow to slaughter.

Akira x-ed out and re-loaded his GPS app. Nothing. Tired of waiting, Akira tried a small side road, then another.

There were more homes and traffic seemed much lighter. He made some headway. When he could glimpse between buildings, it seemed cars still packed the parallel avenue he'd abandoned. Then his side road suddenly ended at a crumbling cinderblock wall, one graffitied over a thousand times. He backed up and tried another small road, but it too ended in a graffitied wall.

Just to the left of the wall, at what looked to be the blank edge of a large swath of empty desert, Akira saw a fresh pair of tire tracks had climbed the curb. The tracks eased over a long-buried knocked-down fence, and Akira felt sure that getting across the field would get him closer to where he needed to be. There were some city lights on the other side, on what he imagined was another busy road. His headlights stared out over the yellow dirt. *What's the worst that could happen?*

Akira nosed his Nissan up the dirt-sloped curb — and followed the tracks in the sand.

The tracks slalomed between sandy berms that Akira figured were plants blown over in a sandstorm. He followed along, going further right than he wanted to, passed more berms. He was stuck going forward — unable to abandon the tire tracks and afraid to turn back. At the

edge of one of his headlights, Akira thought he saw a
descanso.

Cresting a sandy hill, Akira happened on a small pickup
truck — the vehicle that made the tracks. It was parked,
headlights shining off into the black void ahead. Its tailgate
was down and there was something in the truck bed
covered with a sheet. The edge of it swayed in the cold, dry
wind. Next to the truck was a startled man with a shovel.
He had stopped digging, and was now shielding his eyes
from Akira's headlights. A yellow dust passed between
them — kicked up by the desert night. The man planted
his shovel with a sharp, knifing noise, and began to walk
towards Akira.

Akira looked at the man, who was curious more than upset
— *a clever ploy, surely!* Akira looked at the sheet, at what it
must be covering. He could hear only his own racing
heartbeat and imagined the man's slow, deliberate steps
crunching in the sand. The man's lips moved, but Akira
heard nothing — just sat staring at the truck bed.

It had to be a body under that sheet…a small body. *What
else could it be?* Not a sheet, a *shroud*… Akira knew it had to
be a body…

The man got closer, hiding his face as he pretended to shield his eyes. *He's not curious…he's upset.* The man was at Akira's bumper, walking slowly, slowly, still saying something Akira could not hear. He was right there.

Akira jammed the Nissan into reverse and stomped on the accelerator. The man stared for a moment, then waved his arms wildly. Akira tried steering backwards, but could see nothing in the desert night. The back left tire ran up and over something, followed by the front. Akira was tossed around in the driver's seat. He turned the wheel. Again his tires found a berm, then another. Akira thrashed violently about, hitting his head against the roof. He stamped the brakes. In the distance he imagined the man, arms still flailing, this time wielding a machete. Akira yanked the shifter into drive and turned the car around.

Before him, again, were the berms. Only on this side lay crude, handwritten signs at the base of each. *Graves — they could only be graves.*

With no tire tracks to follow, Akira aimed for a vanishing point in a familiar direction, looked for any combination of light poles and streetlights he might've seen before. He swerved between graves, his engine whining. He watched the mirror — sure that lone pair of murderer's headlights would come darting over the black horizon and split the night. He steered and steered, settling on some old tire tracks to follow back towards the city. Akira found a crashed-open hole in a crumbling cinderblock wall and scraped the Skyline through a tangle of barbed wire and over the curb — back to the soft, naked glow of a street light. He rode past small houses on a quiet, empty street, desperately looking for a traffic jam, for policeman, for an armored vehicle and men with automatic weapons — anything to hide behind. His rearview was still empty, but Akira was convinced that meant nothing. The man was obviously an ice-cold, calculating killer. A man like that, who could keep his cool as he approached, keep his awful existence a secret — surely he'd be closing in any moment. Akira caught sight of a tall gas station sign between the dilapidated rooftops and immediately yanked the wheel towards it.

A flood of lights and cars and police and traffic appeared, all stuck and honking in gridlock — beautiful fucking gridlock. Sirens wailed and lights whirled. A masked policeman yelled at him to move. Akira was delighted.

"The Hotel Tulum?" Akira said to the cop. "I can't find my hotel..."

Annoyed, the cop stopped traffic in both directions, and pointed Akira straight ahead. A few lights and detours later, Akira saw the glorious hotel sign glowing giant on the cityscape-horizon.

He pulled in, tossed the keys to the valet, and checked the back of the car. There were scratches in the paint and a small dent. On top of the back bumper sat a yellow pile of soft, wind-blown sand.

33

Akira woke from horrifying and restless dreams. He couldn't believe the field, the graves, and sat staring through what he realized must be an exact copy of the same goddamned palm tree painting. *Are you fucking shitting me?* he thought, insulted by the idea that last time he was at the Hotel Tulum the painting had meant something to him. Now it had been cheapened. He decided the only way through the disappointment was a dip in the pool.

In the elevator down, he looked at his bare feet and fantasized again about a life lived in strange and beautiful hotels, in exotic places, full of interesting people having interesting conversations. And, every few days, they'd leave or he would, and there'd never be any pain. It seemed perfect.

On the gate to the pool, Akira found a sign, written in Spanish and English. The pool was closed for regularly scheduled maintenance for seventy-two hours, and the management was sorry for any inconvenience. *Seventy-two hours from when*? Akira thought.

"What's wrong with the pool?" Akira asked the girl behind the desk. She was on her cell phone, on a call that clearly seemed personal. She rolled her eyes a little, twisted the phone from her ear, and asked how she could help him, though she obviously didn't mean it.

"The pool, the pool — what's wrong with it?" he said again.

She made what must've been a joke, because the bellhop laughed — something about *mocos y piojos, señor*. Akira didn't know what the hell that was, and he certainly didn't laugh.

"Sorry, they did put in the chemicals. For cleaning." She tried to go back to her phone call.
"Seventy-two hours from when?" Akira said. She gave him a confused look. "It doesn't say from when." Still she looked at him. "The sign! It says seventy-two hours...but it doesn't say from when. Seventy-two hours from when?"
"I'm sorry, sir. I don't understand..."
"Goddammit, seventy-two hours from… When did they put the chemicals?"
"Oh — *cuando*. They put it, um," she looked at a bellhop. He didn't know either. "A day, maybe? Two days?" She

talked to the bellhop in Spanish. The bellhop rattled on a bit, finally stopping at a, *"No sé."*

"No sé?" Akira said, "Yeah, no shit *'no sé,'*" looking at the girl and then the bellhop. "Great. That's great."

Back in his room, Akira decided that so far the day had been a real shit sandwich, so he'd better just get the purses — why spend any more time in this shithole? And if, while he was gone, he got a message or an email or a text from Zoë, he might even head home in time to catch her at work. Of course, if she didn't call or text or email — well, she pretty much didn't give a shit about him and he should just stay at the hotel for a few more days. Yes, this was an important test for Zoë — it would decide a lot about their early relationship. Akira phoned the front desk and told them to bring his car around.

34

The air was yellow and still. Akira just wanted to get the goddamned purses and get back to the hotel. He sat at a stoplight trying to remember how he first found the purse guy. The shop wasn't too far from the old, famous church, half a mile tops — but he wasn't sure which direction. The late morning promised something of a warm day and the sun-drenched surfaces were starting to heat up as he found the church and circled the nearby streets. When it began to feel familiar, Akira grabbed a parking spot, and decided to look on foot.

"Hey!" said the man with the purses, through the crowd. "You come for bags, yes?" He grabbed Akira by the arm, hustling him past the screaming sales pitches of neighboring hucksters and back to the purse shop.
"Purses," Akira said.
"I save many purses for you, *señor*," the man said, digging out his Chinese box near the back. "Best price!"

Akira asked again why the bags were from China. The man explained they were factory rejects, made in the same place, by the same people, and with the same materials that all those over-priced bags in the shopping malls were made from. That they were supposed to be destroyed, but he knew a man who would steal them to trade for good bottles of mescal.

Akira paid the man $275 cash for another fifteen purses. The man surprised Akira by sticking out a hand to shake. Akira looked at the hand for a moment, smiling, and then shook it. It seemed silly, like Akira was some kind of real businessman, but if he was honest, he felt sorta proud. Akira told the man he'd probably be back in a few weeks, and to be sure to save him all the best purses. The man assured Akira he would.

Akira looped the purses on his forearm like grocery bags, six on each arm, and clutching the rest to him as he made his way through the crowd. He got a few laughs from folks he passed as he looked for his car, but Akira didn't care. *Laugh it up*, he thought, *this is probably five grand right here.* He finally found the Skyline, popped the trunk, and dumped his cache in back. He tried driving back towards the old church, hoping to really get his bearings — but got lost, and gave up.

At a stoplight a short time later, a dirty little street urchin begged at Akira's open window, selling chicle. The kid had a lop-sided, mischievous smile and two crooked front teeth. Akira bought a flat of chicle for $2 U.S. The sun was high and warm, and Akira turned up the volume on his stereo, rapping along with Public Enemy. The light turned green and Akira rolled on into the dusty afternoon, pretty sure he knew where he was headed.

35

Back at the Hotel Tulum, Akira checked his phone. There was no message from Zoë. That's if the phone was even working — no real way to be sure. He went down to the business center to check Facebook, and Gmail, and Twitter, and everything else, searching for some kind of clue as to what she was up to. No recent updates anywhere. *Probably just working,* he thought. Akira had to keep himself from posting something on her wall. It was a test, he reminded himself and he couldn't go back until she asked about him. That would prove she liked him.

Or maybe she just didn't give a shit. That had to be it. Most people didn't give a goodgoddamn about anyone or anything but themselves. He felt sure that if he could just matter, *really matter*, in Zoë's life, and if she would just like him, *really like him*, then that would be enough. But the more he thought about it, the more obvious it became: she was out with some other dude — maybe one of those guys from work, or a customer or whatever. He really hoped she was just working.

After leaving the business center, Akira decided he'd stop

in *El Acueducto* for a drink.

Four hours later he was refused further service. The bartender politely but sternly asked Akira to leave the pool area and one guest actually clapped, saying, "*¡Lárgate de aquí, chinche apestosa!*" Akira, in his drunken haze, promised himself to figure out what the hell that meant. The wait staff did not care that, as punishment, Akira would no longer let them be in his movie, nor did they care how much business they were potentially costing the Hotel Tulum by cutting him off. They were not heartbroken that Akira would no longer have his entire film crew stay there during his $3 million dollar production, most of which he'd already raised, meaning it was green-lit and pre-production was in full-swing. The hotel staff was also not disappointed that Akira now refused to shoot most of his interiors in the hotel, and they didn't mind that he would basically blacklist the hotel with any of his powerful Hollywood friends who wanted to shoot something on location in a Mexican border town. And as security and the staff fished a fully-clothed Akira from the chemical-laden pool with a hook, blood dripping from his split chin, they weren't the least bit bothered that, mark his goddamned words, Akira would never be caught dead in the Hotel Tulum ever again.

36

In the morning Akira woke naked and cotton-mouthed, his head itching and chin throbbing. The best pillow he had was dappled brown with dried blood and strands of hair. The night before was nothing but a long, scratchy black reel with brief flashes of memory. He had no idea how he'd made it back to his room. Under the ceiling fan, he stared at the damn palm tree painting, head pounding, trying to piece it all together.

He remembered getting the purses — and was pretty sure they were still in the trunk of his car.
He remembered drinking at *El Acueducto*, starting to get drunk.
There were people maybe, a girl with an atomic bomb on her T-shirt?
No, no — that was way before.
Anyhow, there was some sort of problem.
At the bar.
The bartender.
Yes, he got cut off.

He went to the bathroom to piss. The sting of chemicals hit

his nose as the door thumped into his lump of wet clothes. A buck of nausea rocked his guts, then passed — he was empty and had nothing to throw up anyway.

The pool — yes, he was in the pool.
He remembered breaking the surface of the water…
…looking down at drips of fresh blood as they swirled.

He peeled the BAND-AID from his chin and pushed at the raw edges of a gash. He wasn't sure how much more he wanted to know. Akira tried a shower, but the hot water stung his cut chin, and made his body itch even worse. He turned the tap to cold — stood shivering in the frigid stream, watching a few loose thatches of hair fall from his hands. He rinsed his mouth, tried a swallow of water, but threw it right back up. He wasn't sure if metallic taste was the water or his mouth. The Mexican mouthwash the hotel provided stung his teeth and made him gag. There were no dry towels, so Akira wrapped himself in the bed sheet.

He had the purses. He knew he should just go. But he couldn't, he just couldn't. *Not until she cares*, he thought, *not until she wants me back.* He put his fake Ray-Bans on, drew the blackout curtains shut, and punched the red button on the heater — then poured himself into a chair.

He spent the rest of the morning napping, or on the crapper, or watching *telenovelas* — mainly just itching like a fiend and hiding behind the DO NOT DISTURB sign on his locked door. He fell asleep watching a soccer game: Germans dismantling the Mexican team.

37

Akira woke to a soft knock on his door. At first he thought he was just hearing things, but then the knock came again — gentle, almost designed to keep from disturbing him. Akira tip-toed across the room and looked through the peephole. A woman stood waiting, head tilted, almost listening. The fish-eye lens bent her out of proportion, but she was curvy, professionally dressed, with a small gold name tag, and what looked to be a very pretty face. Clearly she worked for the hotel, but Akira had never seen her — he felt he would remember. Akira stood, debating over opening the door. He watched her as she leaned in, listened even closer. She checked her watch and made to leave. Without knowing why, and even though he was sure she was there to throw him out, Akira opened the door.

"Hello," she said, "I hope I didn't disturb you?"

"It's fine," Akira said, "I'm fine."

"You don't remember me?" she said.

"Remember you from where?"

"My name is Senorita Juanita Espinosa. I'm a manager and

concierge here at the Hotel Tulum." She stuck out her hand to shake. "Call me, Nita."

"Akira."

"Yes, I know," she said with a smile. "This is your second stay with us, yes? You're in Juárez on business?"

Akira had no idea what to say. Was he being thrown out — if so, where was security? He shook his head.

"I wanted to stop by and check on you this morning," she said, furrowing a her brow with a wry smile as she looked him over. "You had quite a night last night, no?"

"Sure feels like I did," Akira said.

"I just wanted to make sure you were okay," she said. She seemed genuinely concerned, and Akira noticed a small heart tattoo near her thumb.

"I'll live."

"And your chin," she said pointing, "it's okay?"

"It hurts."

"I'm sure."

The same flash of memory came back to him, only this time there was more to it. He was arguing with the bartender. Someone was between them, security maybe, trying to grab Akira's arm. He remembered diving in the pool to get away. He felt the instant thud of crushing his chin into the bottom — surfacing, watching the blood swirl. This time he saw the bright red spatter in his palm after cupping his chin, and felt himself being fished from the pool like a dead marlin.

Then, a woman's face…pretty…Nita's face.

"You helped me," Akira said, "last night."
"Ah, you *do* remember me," she smiled.

She told him that she helped him to a restroom, that she cleaned his chin, covered it with ointment and the big BAND-AID, then made sure he made it back to his room.

"I have much practice," Nita said. "I have four brothers. Every holiday they get drunk and fight each other."

Akira felt a pang of tenderness wash over him, and his insides well up. He wanted to hug her, to thank her. Then another flash of memory — good Christ, did he try to kiss her last night?! He didn't…he wouldn't…

She looked at Akira's red, flaking skin. She explained about the pool chemicals, how the pool staff sometimes had similar problems. She scribbled out a short list of items on the hotel stationary, and an address — then explained that the *Farmacia Bto. Juárez* was nearby. She told Akira to take the list, that the man would give him those things, and bill the hotel. He said he wasn't sure he'd find it.

"You will," she said. "Just make sure you go to the *Farmacia Bto. Juárez* — not the *Farmacia Juárez* across the street." Akira decided that having two places named almost exactly the same thing right near each other made perfect sense — in a Juárez kinda way. Nita told Akira that she was glad to see he was okay, and if there was anything he needed, to just call down and ask for her. He closed the door and, through the fish-eye peephole, watched her go — especially the seams running up the back of her stockings.

He checked himself in the bathroom mirror — hardly recognizing the face staring back. His scalp flaked and itched like mad and his skin was burning. Akira even found a couple of pus-filled boils at the back of his neck, probably from his wet head. His black hair seemed patchy and in sunlight he could see that the tips had turned slightly orange.

"Another fucking day in paradise," he said to the mirror.

38

After a few minutes walking, Akira found the *Farmacia Bto. Juárez*, just as Nita said he would. It was the kind of place Akira would've passed by, nothing in English, with a counter that opened straight to the street. A giant steel grate rolled-down over the merchandise at night and, on the outside anyways, it seemed to cater unapologetically to locals.

"Hello. How can I help you?" a young man behind the counter asked in perfect English.

"I was told to look for this," Akira said, handing the man Nita's note.

"Ah, Señorita Espinosa," the man said. "Tell her I said hello." He looked at the list. "Sábila? You have a sunburn?"

"I'm itching like a meth-head," Akira said, pulling back his long sleeve. "From pool chemicals, I think."

"That's probably no fun."

"True dat."

The man wandered to the back. Akira searched the shelves, all the boxes, mostly small, all similar, and wondered how anyone ever found anything. On another shelf he saw what looked like hair dye kits. The American looking ones were all expensive. Akira decided that was some kind of capitalist racism, and looked at the cheaper Mexican brands. The man came out from behind the shelves, carrying a box.

"Here we go," the man said, handing it over. "Anything else?"

"Yeah, that *Deseado*…it any good?"

"They're all pretty much the same," the man said, handing Akira the box.

"Can I see that Vidal Sassoon one?"

The man handed it over. Akira tried to compare the text on

each — *tinte para el cabello* — without much luck. He pretended to keep reading for what felt like long enough, then settled on *Deseado* and the small box of *Dolprofen tabletas*, 800 mg — also on Nita's list. He asked the man about ecstasy, if people could just buy it in any old Mexican *farmacia*.

"Not that I know of," the man said.

"I knew it," Akira said, deciding he'd tell Darius he was an idiot if he ever saw him again.

Back at the Hotel Tulum, Akira felt sure he needed to keep a low profile, so he didn't bother with the business center — just went straight back to his room. He bolted the door and stripped down, slathering himself with the gel. He felt instantly better, the burning cooled, and for the first time all day he felt semi-normal. He got the sheet damp, wrapped himself in it again, and washed back one of the pills with a swallow of water.

He opened the *Deseado* box, and quickly realized he was out of his element. There were pictures, but all the instructions were in Spanish. There were plastic bottles, and surgical gloves, and something needing to be mixed, and closely timed, then rinsed and possibly conditioned with *botella numero tres*. Akira said, "fuck it," and got started.

He mixed the stuff according to the pictures, cackling to himself like Dr. Jekyll. Akira painted his skull with the stinky, pasty mix, and set the alarm on his iPhone. On TV, a game show blared, full of wacky hilarity. The crowd really got a kick out of some fat guy in a furry giraffe costume. Akira had no idea what the prizes even were, or how the game show worked, but it hardly mattered to anybody watching. His alarm went off, and he rinsed the filth from his head. He massaged the conditioner in, and waited. He couldn't tell if his scalp was itching more or less, but felt the dye job was gonna look pretty boss.

He rinsed everything out, and when he looked in the mirror, it seemed his hair was both thinner, and had turned lighter — a kind of orangey-brown. He decided he looked like an evil villain's henchman in some comic book movie. After yesterday, he knew room service would probably spit in his food, so he was stuck with whatever he could scrounge in his room: a few Slim-Jims, some other gas station leftovers, and the last of a bag of Funyuns he'd bought on the drive down. They didn't sit well on his stomach and he had to lay down.

It was dark when Akira woke — disoriented and confused.

He found loose orange hairs in the bed, and the way the curtains moved in the blast of stale heater air terrified him. *To hell with Zoë*, he thought, he had to get the hell out of Juárez as soon as he could gather himself up. Akira put on a skullcap and went to a the front desk to check out.

There were a few unexplained charges on his bill and he asked to see Nita to get it all straightened out.

"She's gone for the night," said the man behind the desk. "Just forget it," Akira said.

The man behind the desk explained that it was silly to leave now; that Akira had already paid for the night, that it could not be refunded, that he'd be better off leaving after a good night's rest. Akira felt like it was some kind of trap — like the cops would be coming for him if he didn't get out of there. There was no reason why the cops would be after him but Akira still insisted on leaving immediately.

At the border crossing, the Mexican side waved him back to America, *no hay problema*. The U.S. Border Patrol wanted to know what he was doing in Juárez, why he was traveling so late, when the last time he'd been to Juárez was, and what the hell all the purses were about.

"I sell them to rich girls at my school," Akira said. The head officer just laughed, while he thought he heard another call him a Jap-Fag. Still another officer asked if Akira was trying to hide his identity by dying his hair. Akira made a joke about Sherlock cracking the case wide open, and the officer threatened to take the whole car apart searching for contraband. Akira waited and waited to be cleared. He felt sure the asshole was just dragging his feet. When they'd grown bored with Akira, Border Patrol finally cut him loose.

Akira drove home through the black New Mexico night. The dotted highway lines and sad tungsten lights of every little dusty New Mexico town flickered by like a Zoëtrope. Akira imagined the lives of all the people asleep and dreaming as he pressed on under a dark, spinning sky.

He made Albuquerque by dawn, and, near his house, he saw a man driving a truck-sized outdoor vacuum across a Wal*Mart parking lot, sucking up McDonald's garbage and plastic shopping bags. It made about as much sense as anything else ever did.

39

He'd been back just over a week, and still no word from Zoë. There was no way he was going to turn up at the Double Rainbow looking like he did, so he had been staying home, running his auctions, and selling two purses every few days instead of just one.He only really went out to mail off purses, get more packing tape or bubble wrap from Office Depot, or to grab a quick bite. He wondered how long it would be until she missed him — if she ever even would. With each passing day she failed the test again, and it became harder and harder to pretend that she gave a shit about him. To hell with her, he thought, what makes her so goddamned special?

At least his father was nice enough not to mention a single thing about the hair.

Running auctions, two at a time, meant Akira spent more time at the post office. He'd managed to find pockets of down time and always tried to go then to avoid the lines. But the closer it got to Christmas, the worse the lines became — everyone mailing multiple boxes, and bitching up a blue streak. Even eBay seemed inundated. And despite it being prime time for shopping, the purses seemed to be selling for less. Akira figured it was just a saturated market, that he'd picked the wrong time to double up on auctions. He decided his timing was off because everyone was shopping for other people — so of course they were cheap. It's only when people are buying stuff for themselves that they splash around some serious coin.

To top it all off, there was *divapink1989* — and her endless string of complaining fucking emails. She bought a black Jackie soft leather top handle bag, and was increasingly displeased with her purchase. Apparently she had nothing but time to bang out lengthy missives. Akira had responded, outlining the 'no-returns' policy on each of his eBay auctions. Still she insisted on more emails, which Akira decided to ignore.

Akira was tired of XBox, tired of Gmail, Facebook, Twitter, YouTube. He was tired of sleeping, tired of eating, tired of *divapink1989*, tired of boxing and mailing out purses. He was tired of his father, tired of him when he was home, and tired when he wasn't home. He was tired of his skin itching, tired of his stupid hair, his stupid gut, and especially tired of his stupid fucking face. He was thinking of everything else he was tired of when a text message came through on his phone. The notification was almost jarring, and Akira realized that he barely even needed a phone, seeing as it never rang, and no one but his father ever texted him. He checked it.

It was Zoë.

She said she had just seen some Clint Eastwood movie about WWII and Japan — that it made her think of Akira. The next text said that if he hadn't seen it, he totally should because it was really good, and ended her text with a few emojis.

He waited as long as he could, then texted her back, telling her he'd have to check it out, asking her what she was up to, then told her he was thinking of shaving his goddamned head.

She texted back that he shouldn't shave his head, that most guys who shaved their heads looked ridiculous.

He texted that maybe he'd see her later, that then she'd see why he was thinking of cutting his hair off.

She texted back: LOL! kewl.

40

He figured the day wouldn't be a total waste after all. He knew Walgreen's carried a bit of everything, so if he could fix up his stupid lid, then maybe he could catch Zoë at the Double Gay-bow. On a health and beauty aisle Akira found the hair dye products — a few of them were even for men. Grecian Formula. Touch Of Grey. He remembered commercials about unconfident men who couldn't get jobs, Corvettes, boners, or beautiful women because of their thin, greying hair. Yep, the old and impotent apparently had no reason to go on. He thought of his father while grabbing a package of black dye from the manager's specials rack — dropping it in his handheld basket.

He wandered the store aimlessly, looking at all kinds of shit he didn't want or need. He put pink lipstick samples on the back of his hand, and looked at air fresheners to hang from his rearview mirror. He slid his fake Ray-Bans on top of his orangey-brown mop, and tried on a bunch of women's sun glasses like his mom always wore. He took four pieces of white poster board, a pack of thumbtacks, and a three-pack of permanent colored markers — to storyboard his movie. He tossed in some Jalapeno Cheddar dip, some Salsa Doritos, and a four-pack of Starbucks Vanilla Iced Cappuccinos. At the register he asked for a can of chewing tobacco, and chucked a beer can koozie that read "The Cops Never Think You're As Funny As You Do" on top — imagining all the laughs he'd get when drinking from it. He bought it all.

Back home, Akira found a note from his father: he needed to talk to Akira about the Japan trip; needed to know if Akira had changed his mind about going; and if not, could Akira take him to the airport — to call him right away. Akira crumpled it up, trashed it, then dragged his Walgreen's bags to his room and shut the door.

Akira grabbed the hair dye kit, assuming it would be similar to the Mexican one. Turned out, you needed an advanced degree in the salon arts to make it work. In this one, there were activators, reducers, separate directions for highlights and lowlights, and step after dizzying step. Akira followed the directions as best he could. His bathroom stank like hell. For dark black, with no high or low lights, the directions said leave it in for 40 minutes. Akira covered his head with the goofy plastic shower-cap and dumped out the rest of his Walgreen's stuff.

He took a chew of tobacco, and thumbtacked the poster

board up. He tried imagining it as a movie theater screen showing his films. He imagined tough-guy heroes, and shootouts, and stunt sequences, and explosions. He saw hot, topless women who'd suck him off for a part in his next blockbuster. Akira started crudely sketching some storyboards. Despite trying pretty hard at it, his pictures looked childish and stupid. He decided it was better to just pay someone else to storyboard, that he was the idea man, and didn't have time to piss about with storyboards and niggling details.

He was suddenly violently ill from the chaw. He ran to the toilet, and vomited. The spell passed, and he washed his mouth out, threw the chew away, and drank an iced coffee drink. It seemed like maybe it would stay down.

His laptop finally charged again, Akira logged on to Facebook, Gmail, and then his other accounts. Nothing was happening anywhere. On eBay, he scheduled his last four auctions. He felt like he spent too much goddamned time answering annoying questions from potential buyers: Yes, these were real; he dealt directly with the factories producing them; he had a Powerseller Ranking. He explained over and over again about using stock photos in his listings for standardization, and ease in posting multiple auctions, but that he did his best to make sure they were accurately described and represented. He reminded everyone that the sheer number of sales necessary to become a Powerseller meant buyers could bid with confidence.

The work was slow and tedious. He reminded himself of how much money he was making, and how little work he was actually doing — especially compared to ol' Ginger and her Burgerhaus. Sure, the work was dull, and the stupid customers were annoying — but it was way better than anything else, and it really only took an hour or two every day to keep it humming.

Then Akira logged on to Facebook, and then to Twitter, posting, "Who got weed? Hit me up" in both places. Finally someone rang him back.

"Well, I don't know nothing 'bout weed. I'm talking 'bout *lecture notes*. From class…" he said, trying to speak in some kind of drug code to trick the cops.
"Notes…right," said Akira, and they both waited for the other to speak. "Well, I've been missing a lot of classes!" Akira asked how much for a sack.
"One," the dude said.
"One what?" Akira asked.
"Bill."

"One bill?"

"Jesus…one hundred dollars."

"Right, okay…so. How much, for, like just *a few* notes."

"Fuck, dude. How much do you want?"

"That's what I'm trying to figure out, motherfucker!" Akira said, but the guy had already hung up.

Akira wanted to give the cops the number to track or whatever. Except that shit was never anonymous and Akira figured the dude might come after him somehow. He decided he should probably just forget it, that he didn't even want weed, that it was just something to do. Life was super dull unless you were doing something — anything was better than nothing. He turned on some music, drew the curtains in his room closed, and laid down to sleep it all away.

Akira woke, realizing he'd left the goddamned dye in. He ran to the bathroom to rinse it as fast as he could. It was terrible. Instead of shit-orangey-brown, it had turned a hideous, wispy, unnatural ginger red. He decided he looked about as stupid as a Japanese fucking Carrot Top, and wanted to smash his own stupid face in. He could stand on the sidewalk out front of Ginger's Burgerhaus, flipping and helicoptering the "Get 'Em While They're Hot!" sign — he wouldn't need the goddamned wig.

Akira couldn't see Zoë like this. He stuffed his head into a beanie, and went back to Walgreen's to complain. The manager apologized while stifling a laugh, and gave Akira a refund. Akira decided to buy an expensive hair dye kit and try again. The manager gave him a 20% discount on the purchase.

It didn't work either.

He tried peroxide next, mainly hoping to bleach out the tips — to disastrous effect. He stuck his head under the tap to stop the burning — tried to wash it out, but it was too late. His scalp now burned like Napalm, and the hair, when dry, had turned shock white with bits of dark gray at the roots. *Chemotherapy-chic*, he thought.

His phone beeped. He checked the text and sure enough, it was Zoë, wondering where he was.

Akira texted back some bullshit about having to help his father with something, that he couldn't get away. On a whim, Akira texted, "Buy you dinner some night?"

To his shock and amazement, she texted back: "Sure. Saturday?"

He re-read the text a bunch of times just to make sure it said what he thought it said. Dinner. Saturday. Yes, she would have dinner. With him.

When he could hold out no longer, he texted back trying to play it real cool-like, saying they could, "figure out a plan later."

She texted back "kewl."

Akira spent the next few hours in a stunted kind of awestruck bliss. He took a cold shower then slathered his stupid gray hair with the last of his Mexican healing gel. He put 50 Cent on constant repeat, rapping along while boxing up a purse for a buyer from Tucson, Arizona.

"If I can't...do it...homie, it can't be done..."

He googled "white haired cool dudes" and discovered Jim Jarmusch, an independent filmmaker who was supposedly pretty great. He figured he's say he was going for the Jarmusch look, that he'd done it all on purpose. Akira knew Zoë would probably want to talk about all kinds of political shit on their date, so he figured he'd better start reading some news websites. He found a few, saving each link in his "favorites," and promised himself to read them everyday between then and Saturday night. When that was done, Akira Googled "dating tips" and scoured blogs, anything that would tell him the right things to say and do on his date with Zoë. Half the articles told girls to be whores, the other half told them to be prudes. Akira tried men's magazines: Maxim, Details, Men's Health. They didn't help much. He did learn about a thousand ways to do sit-ups though — the kinds Marines do. Every magazine, men's or women's, agreed that everyone must be hot, muscular, and enjoy an outdoor lifestyle. The articles said girls didn't want to be told what to do, they wanted to be involved, wanted to decide for themselves. Akira made a mental note of it. He tried a few Marines sit-ups, but stopped after six, worried he'd pulled a muscle in his side.

41

Akira topped off his Nissan Skyline at a Love's Gas Station right off the highway. An article he'd read said that if you run out of gas on a date, the girl thinks you planned it and that you're trying to rape her. He couldn't have Zoë thinking that. Inside he paid, and tried, again, to piss. He wanted to get it all out, so he wouldn't have to leave her at a table alone. Cosmo said that guys who did that were jerks. He stood there not peeing for at least two minutes before someone else came in and Akira had to pretend he was just finishing up.

He stared at the condom machine as he washed and dried his hands. There was a crazy-green-colored condom called the U.F.O. — the Unidentified Fucking Object — with ribs and some kind of tendril-like tickler at the tip. It was supposedly guaranteed to "send your date into orbit." It was $3 — twelve quarters in the machine. Akira decided on the regular old latex job, which was a dollar cheaper. He bought some gum, and asked for his change in quarters so he could buy the rubber.

Akira was to meet Zoë at the Double Rainbow when her

shift ended, so they could go eat at the Olive Garden. "The one on San Mateo," Zoë said, she knew someone there and would totally give them the hook up. After that — a movie, maybe dessert. Akira told himself it was cool, that she was this ultra-modern girl, that she knew what she wanted — she was in charge, like Cosmo said. Still, it didn't much feel like she needed him to do anything but sit there, do what he was told, he thought. He tried to ignore it. She unlocked her car and they both climbed in. When she turned the key, the radio blared. She turned it down, apologizing, and explaining that she just liked to fucking rock. Around her gearshift was a red-thread wristband with a medallion that read "Kony 2012." Akira promised himself to figure out what it was, not to forget.

"Oh-Em-Gee!" she said, crushing out her cigarette and flicking it out the window. "You totally changed your hair!"
"I was shooting for Jim Jarmusch," Akira said.
"Who?"
"A filmmaker I dig. But I just ended up looking like some futuristic albino."
"No," she said, "it looks cool."

Inside he relaxed a bit, sighing. Okay — so I'm not a total fucking monster then, he thought. She was already busy talking about work: how she had all these tables, and no help expo-ing, and the kitchen kept running out of things and people were getting mad at her, like it was her goddamned fault or something. Akira listened, trying to find a good spot to jump in. He'd been reading up about this insanely crooked election in Eastern Europe, how the party in power was doing all this shady shit, fixing ballots, keeping people from voting. He figured it was right up Zoë's alley. He asked if she'd heard anything about it.

"That sounds pretty terrible," she said. "I'll definitely have to check that out."

Way to go, fuckhead, he thought, so much for that. What are you gonna do now? Akira tried to think of something, anything else he'd read — but his brain was vapor-locked with loathing. She's gonna know, he thought, she's gonna figure out you're a dull, stupid, boring fucking asshole. He went back to questions about work, about how she'd done on tips.

"I mean, you know me," Zoë said, "I'm, like, totally the furthest thing from a racist or whatever…but, Indians — they're, like, the worst tippers!" She continued, "Worse than gang-bangers. And poor-white-trash too."
"Totally," Akira said, happy to be off the hook.

"First, there's always, like, fifteen of them, but they wanna split the check…or sit at three different tables so you can't auto-grat them — even though they're totally all together! Then they all want their special orders, and shit on the side, and extra ranch dressing, or A-1 sauce for their steaks. And they always want separate checks. Plus they make a huge mess and leave you, like, three dollars — on a hundred dollar tab!"

At the Olive Garden, she parked between a dumpster and what seemed like employee spots — not really a spot at all. Akira tried to run out and open her door for her, but she was already out of the car by the time he rounded the trunk. She looked around the lobby, asking a hostess she clearly knew and clearly didn't like about Steffan. He was there — that's all the info the hostess offered. She pouted, looking around, before finally just putting their names on the wait list. The hostess handed Akira a numbered plastic pager with flashing red lights, and they sat down together on a nearby bench. Akira couldn't think of anything to say, so he looked around for someone to make fun of, trying to ignore the fact that Zoë was continually looking across the room at something or someone.

There were people sitting, and waiting, but no one seemed to be particularly happy about being at the Olive Garden

— they just sat and stared. Akira figured people were there more out of habit than desire. It's just what you did: you went to the Olive Garden; you ate too much bread and salad; you ordered a big, stupid plate of food that you couldn't finish and barely wanted to take home. You did it because everyone else did it, because you could afford it just like they could, and it felt comfortable to be among equals. Everyone at the Olive Garden was making sure no one had better lives than each other…and no one did.

"Quick! - What's that guy's voice like?" Zoë asked.

Akira didn't know. Zoë explained the game: you looked at someone, and made up a funny voice for them, and pretended to talked like they talk, about whatever was happening in their pathetic lives — making them the butt of the jokes. Akira liked it. He pretended to be the frumpy guy who was eating alone, reading a book. His jokes weren't very funny, but Zoë laughed anyway. She, of course, was really good at her game — pretending to be the voice inside some old woman's head who was sitting silently nodding her head while her husband just talked and talked at her. Zoë pretended the woman was plotting to kill him, like she'd poisoned his pasta and was waiting for the no-good, cheating cooze-hound to die so she could finally be rid of him. And when he died she was gonna take one of those singles sex cruises — get fucked by a bunch of dark-tanned deckhands. Akira cackled, delighted.

"I didn't make that up. My Aunt Joan did that," Zoë said. "Just the cruise thing…she isn't married."

And then, out of nowhere, Akira's guts were bucking and roiling — hot and ready. *No no no no no,* he thought, but there was no way he could ignore it. He had to shit. Akira excused himself, and barely made it into the handicap stall before shitting as fast and as hard as he could — rocking back and forth on the toilet. It felt like gallons drained out of him, and the stink hung like mustard gas. He tried to hurry.

The plastic pager flashed and vibrated — their table ready. He pushed and fought, working up a light sweat. When, mercifully, he was done, he spent another couple minutes cooling off, dabbing his forehead with paper towels, and wiping his armpits dry. He told himself it had probably only been a few minutes, that it was fine, everything was going to be fine. He checked the mirror once more. His hair gel was already going limp.

When he came out, he couldn't find Zoë. At the hostess stand, the girl ignored him. It was only after showing his pager that some stupid assistant manager guy said, "She's over there," with a smirk. Akira found Zoë in a booth near the kitchen.

"Everything come out okay?" Zoë asked. "You were seriously gone for, like, ever."

Inside he reeled. He wanted to make a joke of it, but nothing came — just shame and disgust about all the things she must've been thinking.

"Found her, huh?" said the same assistant manager dude, sidling up to her in the booth. Before Akira could answer, the guy said, "'Sup, Zoë?"
"I can't believe you made us wait — you asshole!" she said, playfully slapping the dude on the arm.
"Don't come when we're totally slammed next time, you dippy blonde!"
"Steffan, this is my friend, Akira," said Zoë. "Akira — Steffan."
"'Sup, bro," Steffan said, giving Akira a 'hang loose' hand gesture.

She explained how she used to work with Steffan a million years ago, that he, "totally hooked her up with a table." He was a smaller guy, maybe mid 30s, good looking, fit — a gym rat, probably. Basically everything you're not, Akira's brain said. Zoë ordered a couple beers. Steffan said that even though she was a total fucking lush, he still loved her, so he'd hook it up just this once.

"So, how are things?" Steffan said. She went into all of it — school, thinking about taking a gap year to just, like, travel or get spiritual or whatever, and work being stupid-crazy.

"Tell me about it," Steffan said. "I had two no-call, no-shows tonight and had to cover a damn ten-top until we could get someone in. Ran my dick off getting refills…" Steffan paused. "Six bucks."
"I know, right?" Zoë said, "Wasn't I just telling you— I was just telling him in the car about this table I had!"

Oh goody, this again, Akira thought. This time it was, like, twenty of them, at, like, four different tables — a $99 tab.

"And they left you a hundred," said Steffan.
"A hundred dollar bill!" Zoë said. "I shit you not!"

Akira got the feeling they could trade horror stories all night — and might, if he didn't jump in. But with what? Regale them with tales of the Burgerhaus? He was tempted — the self-involved pricks. *Oh, that's nothing*, Akira would say, *I worked the drive-thru at Ginger's — which is basically a million-top — and at the end of my shift, I actually owed the Burgerhaus eight dollars for giving someone the wrong change!* He imagined saying it, imagined them both of them looking at him like his face was melting.

Nearby a table full of old people spilled a drink. Zoë laughed, and clapped a little sarcastically.

"Wooooooooooooo," Zoë said, "just put that anywhere!" Akira thought it was charming. "That's what we say at my work, whenever anyone drops a tray." Akira didn't care. It was enough to get Steffan back to work and the hell away from them.

"Steffan's Belgian," she said. *Hmmm, like the waffle,* Akira thought, wanting to waffle-stomp Steffan's face. "He speaks, like, perfect French."

After they finally ordered, Zoë asked him about his background, and where he'd lived. He told her about New Jersey, the laundromat his folks bought when they first moved to Albuquerque, how he'd been in the city most of his life now so it was pretty much home.

"What about Japan?" Zoë said. "Isn't Japan home?"

Having never lived in Japan and having only visited twice, he wasn't sure what to say. "It's so great that you're Japanese," she said. "I want to know exactly what it's like!"

Akira tried to tell her what he thought she'd like to hear — things about Buddha, and Zen rock gardens, and lotus blossoms. He mentioned temples, and vast bamboo groves, talked about Mt. Fuji, Shinjuku, about the Sumo tournaments. She thought it was all so great.

"You're the first Japanese friend I've ever had," she said. They clinked their beers, and started on the salad and breadsticks.

Zoë grabbed Akira's phone and went through it, asking who certain people were — the girl's especially. Akira pretended they were chicks from all over town. He figured, for a hot girl like Zoë, he needed to seem like a player, otherwise she'd be bored, or think she totally had his balls in a sling. In truth, most were just girls he used to go to school with and somehow still had numbers for, even though they hadn't talked since graduation. He wasn't even sure the numbers were any good any more.

Akira grabbed her phone and did the same. There were all kinds of guys in her phone, too many, actually. Akira hated it, but tried to be cool. "Just a friend," she'd say, no matter who he asked about. Most were from work, she explained, or "guys that, like, asked for my number or whatever." She said they were all interesting guys, from all over the world — from all kinds of backgrounds. He tried to go through her text messages, but she freaked out, and took her phone back.

The food arrived, and Akira ate his Chicken Parmigiana — trying to think of something cool or clever to say. The conversation's falling flat, he thought, it's going to shit! Akira kept thinking about all these guys, from all over the world. Zoë ate very delicately, fork pinched perfectly between two fingers, constantly wiping away crumbs she imagined on her lap or the table as she looked around the room.

"You're a really clean eater," Akira said. He instantly regretted it, *A clean eater?* — *you fucking idiot*, he thought. "Oh thanks," Zoë said. "I'm like hyper-aware of that stuff ever since being a server, you know? Like, filthy people who leave huge-ass messes or whatever are so totally disgusting."

Akira agreed, it *was* totally disgusting. Zoë's gaze lasered across the room. Akira turned to see Steffan loosening, then re-tightening the dress tie on a young waitresses' uniform, whispering in her ear. The waitress giggled, and Steffan watched as she walked away to check on her tables. Zoë saw it all too.

"So," Zoë asked, "do you have any, like, terrible stories of racism or whatever?"

Akira tried to think up some terrible stories of racism. He told her what he could think of, but it didn't seem too different than what he figured other people experienced. Some name calling, misconceptions. Usually people weren't really sure what to call him because they didn't know if he was Chinese, or Japanese, or Korean, or whatever. Sometimes someone made a crack about karate or said something in a crazy *ching-chang-chong* language that they seemed to think all Asians spoke.

"That's so ridiculous," Zoë said. "It's like 'hello, I'm just Japanese, people...deal with it already!'"
"Totally," Akira said. "You don't act weird about it though."
"Yeah, I know —" Zoë said, "thanks."

Zoë grabbed her phone and said she had to pee — that Akira should get a couple more beers from Steffan. Akira grabbed their empty bottles and walked towards the faux-fresco on the wall near the front bar. Near it, just around the corner booth — with it's bunches of dusty, plastic grapes hanging out of a lighted bowl on top of a fake Renaissance column — he heard someone say:

"You try to call that booty, you gettin' a busy signal, son!"

Akira found Steffan, a bartender, and a bar back — all stunned and giggling like schoolgirls. Laughing, he asked Akira, "Yo, what's up, playa?"
"Zoë said to ask you for a couple more," Akira said, sliding the empties across the bar top.
"Oh, for sure, man," he said. "I'll have your server bring 'em on over."

Akira sat back down. He couldn't say shit, because he wasn't sure they were talking about Zoë. But they were. He didn't even know what he'd say if he did — something about disrespect, or whatever. The beers came, and Akira pounded half of his, trying to decide what to do. He decided her honor must be defended somehow — that he couldn't let it slide, that this fuck Steffan shouldn't get away with it. He was gonna say something…he had to.

Akira pounded his beer, and went to the hostess stand —

trying to think of what he'd say. When he got there, there was no one. The hostess was off wiping down an empty table and talking to a busboy, and who knows where Steffan had gone. Akira started grabbing the flashing pagers from their charging dock — three, six, eight of them. He had them clutched and cradled to his chest, walking away as nonchalantly as possible — getting away from there. He ducked down the hall to the restrooms, and into the men's room — unseen as far as he could tell. Fuck you Steffan, Akira thought with a smile…

When Zoë got back, Akira asked if she wanted to check out the movie times, and decide on something. Zoë preferred *Love Drunk*, a goddamned chick-flick about a magic bottle of wine that revealed your true love if you drank from it. Akira thought they should see *Bachelor Paddy*: small-time grifter Colin Farrell is furloughed from prison to bury his mother — only to be mistaken for a European prince. They couldn't agree.

"Honestly," Zoë said, "I'm pretty cashed. I'd probably just fall asleep anyways." Akira thought how great it would be, her snoozing on his shoulder as the movie lights flickered.

The waitress brought the check and, even though one of the articles he read suggested going Dutch so the girls didn't feel any pressure to repay you with sex or a handjob or whatever, Akira reached for it. Zoë grabbed it before he could — running off to again talk to Steffan. Akira watched as they talked. Zoë seemed to be laying it on pretty thick flirting-wise and Akira thought that maybe he should be pissed. Just be cool, don't be an asshole, he thought, don't be yourself. Zoë went from flirty, to indignant, to really annoyed — finally tossing the ticket at her "friend" and storming back to the table as he laughed with a co-worker.

"Honestly," she said, "he's acting like such a prick!"
"It's okay," Akira said, "I can pay."
"Fuck that," she said, "I've hooked him up *soooo* many times. He can just deal with it."

Sooo many times, Akira's head said. *Yeah, what else has she done sooo many times.* He told himself he didn't care, that it was saving him money. *Yeah, I bet she's hooked him up,* Akira's brain said, *hooked him up plenty…* Akira almost forgot to tip, but caught her looking, so he threw down $20.

On the way out, Akira felt his pockets, making sure he had his keys, wallet, phone, and his rubber — just in case. It was chilly outside, but not terrible out, the crisp bite of fall in the night air. The beers seemed to be working on Zoë, or she pretended they were. She stopped next to a newish looking red Dodge Dart.

"We should totally fuck with his car!" Zoë said.

"I don't know…" Akira said.

"C'mon, don't be such a pussy."

"I'm pretty sure he'll know it was you," Akira said.

"Damn right he'll know! That's what he fucking gets!"

Zoë tried stabbing the tire with one of her keys — but her wrist gave out, and it didn't work.

"You do it," she said.

"What? Why?!" Akira said.

"Just forget it," she said, pulling out her lipstick. Dip dip, smear — dip dip, smack. She swirled the pink wand around and around, covering each crevice like frosting. She walked to the passenger side of Steffan's Dodge Dart, wiped the dust off the window with the butt of her hand, then planted a big, fat, pink kiss right in the middle of it.

"There," she said. "Explain that, douchebag."

Akira's head swirled. Whatever the hell that was all about, he could only guess. She blathered on about something as she drove back to the Flying Star, but Akira just nodded

along. Visions of Steffan short-circuited any attempt at
responding.

"Should we get dessert?" Akira asked.
"Pffff, I'm stuffed," she said. "Besides, I'm not supposed to,
you know, hang out with customers here," she said.
"Company policy."
"So," Akira said, "you're pissed at that Steffan guy?"

Zoë didn't say anything, which Akira took to mean yes.

"This'll make you feel better," Akira said. "I heard him
talking shit, I think about you…"
"Steffan? What'd he fucking say?"
"I don't know," Akira said, "something about a booty call,
and how you were a whore or whatever."
"That fucking asshole!"
"Well, anyways…don't get mad, but…."

He pulled out his phone, punched up the media gallery.
He brought up a video: a tight close-up on a mess of Olive
Garden guest pagers, some flashing, others fizzling out.
The video pulled back to reveal the toilet bowl they sat in,
a little chuckle from Akira on the audio as he flushed —
the pagers spinning in the bowl.

She looked at Akira, and after a few long moments with her mouth agape, she said, "Badass." She leaned in a little, kissed him on the cheek.

"You're sweet," Zoë said.

They stood for a moment. Akira told himself he should go in for the kiss. But he couldn't — he just couldn't make himself try. She stretched up both arms, wrists bent funny, saying, "Okay then — I better get going…" She gave him a little hug, letting go a half second before Akira — giving him a tiny little pat on the back of his shoulder until he did.

As Zoë walked into the Flying Star, he climbed into his car — waiting to wave at her if she looked back. She didn't.

42

Jazz was playing loudly through the front door, and Akira knew his father must be into the Lagavulin. Akira's father, sitting with eyes shut and his back to the door, didn't hear or see Akira come in, and Akira didn't see his father. Akira found his way to the stereo, and twisted the dial down a few ticks.

"Akira," his father said, "come visit with your drunk ol' dad."

His father had been looking through some family photos. Akira avoided looking at pictures of his mom.

"I'm tired," Akira said.
"How's your job going?"
"Good. Gotta make another sales trip down south soon. I'll probably be gone a few days."
"Do you have enough money?" His father fumbled for his wallet.
"Does anyone?"
"Some. Not many." Akira's father smiled, finally dragging his wallet free from his pocket. He pulled $20 from it.

"Here."

Twenty whole dollars, Akira thought, *adorable.*

"You can stop for a burger at the Owl Bar," his father said. "Play some Johnny Cash on the jukebox." Akira remembered doing exactly that with his mom and dad each and every time they were near San Antonio, New Mexico.

Akira reached for the money. His father's hand grabbed hold of Akira's arm and the old man stood, as if to say something else. A small noise even built in his throat, but never made it out and his father hugged Akira instead. Akira reeled, smelling the sweet stink of booze on his father. His father released him so Akira made for his room.

"Son," said his father, stopping Akira once more. "About our trip to…"
"I'm not going," said Akira.
"Akira, please —" His father searched. "A child must bury his parents. It's the natural way of the world, part of becoming a man."

There were additional reasons and advantages, even vague promises of closure, of feeling better, as if there were some kind of magical redemption sent back across the void. It was all so fucking idiotic, such Dr. Phil bullshit.

"I believe it will bring us some peace," his father said, swallowing the last of his Scotch.
"Are you drunk or just stupid? I said: I. Am Not. Going." Akira said and once again started for his bedroom.

His father stepped in front of the door — eyes gone wide and lit at the corners. Then Akira's father grabbed him by the collar, and yanked him down eye to eye.

"Is that any way to talk?" his father said.

Akira thrashed about, his arms flailing against his father's steel grip. Despite being shorter, Akira had always known his father to be powerful. He remembered years ago, a run-in his father had with some young punks at the laundromat. He remembered actually being afraid for his father — at least until it started. Akira had seen, in his father's eyes, a kind of eerie calm — control even. It seemed his father enjoyed beating those kids. The memory of it had always both terrified and impressed Akira.

But his eyes weren't like that now. They were still calm — but they tracked a half-tick off, clouded with drink.

"Get off me!" Akira said.

"You little shit..." His father said.

Akira felt his face flush — his breath both shallow and rapid. He stared into his father's face. A long second passed before his father came back to himself. He let go of Akira. They stared at each other, breathing, with nothing between them.

43

Akira avoided his father over the next few days, and his father avoided him — which was fine by Akira.

And there was no word from Zoë. Akira hadn't had any luck lingering around, drinking too much coffee, hoping to catch her at work. He couldn't stop thinking about the stupid fucking friend hug…the little pat on the back.

And fucking *divapink1989*. Her incessant emails hadn't stopped, and Akira decided he would send a final reply, and that was it. After that, he'd let eBay handle her crazy ass.

Dear divapink1989,

If you're unclear about the no-returns policy, please carefully read the FAQs in my store info. If you are worried about authenticity, or have questions or concerns, the easiest thing to do is <u>not bid on my auctions</u>; I'd truly prefer you didn't. There are plenty of customers looking for my awesome deals and every bid you put in is money they could save. You can see my Powerseller Ranking; you can see that I've been in the eBay *business a long time and that I've had very few problems.*

Having said that, they have almost all been with buyers like you. It's not worth making the sale to me if there are going to be problems that affect my eBay storefront. If you can find a better deal, please feel free to bid on them.

This is the final email I will write you. Please stop emailing me. If you continue to contact me, I will ask the eBay Dispute Resolution Team to get involved.

It was a trick he'd learned from his mother. "Customers are either like friends, or like cattle — big, fat, dumb, and chewing cud," she'd say. "Sell nothing to complainers — it's never worth what you make." She taught Akira that listening to one complaint, was listening to a million — because as soon as you did, you would never stop. "Better to hear none." He copy/pasted his mother's signature at the bottom of the email, and clicked send. Just as he did, his cell phone buzzed — a call from his father. He let it go to voice mail. The phone beeped with a message, so — annoyed — Akira checked it. He had forgotten that, last week, he had agreed to drive his father to the airport today — right now. Akira swore at himself as he stuffed his gear in his backpack. He called his father from the car.

"Hey," Akira said, "are you ready?"

Of course his father was ready — he'd already been waiting twenty minutes.

"It's not my fault," Akira said, "the guys at the Jiffy Lube took longer than usual."

Akira knew his father would be impressed, that taking care of routine maintenance on his car was exactly the kind of thing his father advocated and admired.

"I'm just around the corner," Akira said, and they hung up.

Akira drove like mad, red-lining the engine, and screaming at all the stupid fucking assholes on the road who obviously had nowhere to be and no goddamned idea what the hell they were doing! He rounded the corner on their street and found his father waiting, luggage on the curb. They loaded up, and — save a quick conversation about how it looked like the oil change guys had forgot to give Akira a new reminder sticker — they drove to the airport in relative silence.

"I'll count on you to look after the house while I am gone," said Akira's father, opening the car door. Akira snapped the hazard lights on, popped the trunk. Akira's father pulled the suitcase from the back, and the crash of the trunk being slammed back shut set Akira's ears to ringing.

"I should be back in a week," his father said.

Akira nodded.

"Akira..." his father began.

Akira did nothing to make it easy. They simply stared past each other for a few long moments.

Finally his father said, "Please water your mother's flowers. Call if you need anything."
"Okay," said Akira.

From the front seat Akira grabbed his father's carry on before realizing *she's in there, she's in there...* It was all Akira could think. Around them, other people got out of cars, grabbed suitcases, hugged each other, laughed, cried. *She's in there...* Skycaps tugged bags, hustled for tips as families who loved each other teared up, parted. *There she is...so small.* Akira had to get away.

"You can't park here," said a security man with an airport

badge. The man was old and grizzled, with a Marine flattop.

"I'm not," said Akira, "I'm just dropping off..."

"Yes sir," said Akira's father, "we were just saying goodbye."

"You've been idle sixty seconds. That's a violation..." the man continued on. Parking was, apparently, serious business. Akira looked at his father.

"I love you, son," Akira's father said, extending his hand.

They shook like two men haggling over veal.

44

As he drove away from the airport, Akira decided he'd throw a big house party — yes, a big social thing so he could get some time in with Zoë. He figured he'd invite all his friends over, and they'd be jealous. But not at home. Those amateurs would all get drunk and stupid, and break shit and embarrass him. Akira decided a hotel was better, easier. And more gangster too. A hotel suite like in Mexico, and someone else would clean it all up. Yep, the Navajo Hotel and Casino — like a motherfucking baller.

At home, Akira rifled through the stack of his mother's unread mail, and found some promotional mailers from the Navajo. His mother used to get all kinds of promotional rates on rooms because she played the slots like a fiend — free play, and special coupons, discounts, and sometimes even free stays for Platinum Members. They were just trying to get Akira's mom to piss away more money, but the joke was on them. He called up, gave them her Platinum Membership number from the flyer, and was connected to her "Personal Hospitality Host" at what was supposedly his direct line. He introduced himself as his mother.

"It looks like it's been a while since we've seen you," the Hospitality Host said.

"Yes, I had some very important business," Akira said. "in Japan."

"Welcome back. What can I do for you today?"

"I'd like to cash in some Platinum Player Points for a room tonight," Akira said. "A suite."

"I'm sorry — we only have discounted rooms tonight — nothing free as it's the holiday season. But how about a free upgrade to a suite?"

"Now you're talking," Akira said.

They worked out the details. Along with the room was a double food credit — an apology, the Personal Hospitality Host said, for being unable to accommodate the room request on such short notice.

"I'm gonna send my son Akira to pick up the key," Akira said, "I can't close my shop until after 6:00 p.m."

"Not a problem," the Platinum host said, the key would be waiting for her son at the front desk — and they looked forward to welcoming Akira's mother back to the Navajo.

Akira packed up everything he could think of and drove to the I.C. Food Mart. There he bought everything he imagined Zoë might like. He filled two empty suitcases with almost $200 worth of alcohol and supplies.

He'd only been to the Navajo a few times, but the more he thought about it as he drove, the more sure he was it would impress Zoë. The stacked stone walls, sweeping covered walkways, all the wood and stone and water and sky — Akira figured all chicks went for that fancy shit. It was no Hotel Tulum, he thought, but it'll do in a pinch! He remembered picking up his mom there a few times, drunk and reeking of cigarette smoke — happy as a clam if she'd won money, or grumpy as hell if she'd lost. He remembered rolling up on the giant structure the first time, and being genuinely impressed.

He picked up the room key at the front desk, room 417, no problem, and took the elevator upstairs. The door opened into a small tiled foyer, with a little bathroom just off to the left, overlooking a giant party-size living room. On one side of the room sat a couch, coffee table, and a couple chairs — a conversation area, perhaps. On the other was a tall dresser with a safe, a DVD/CD player, and a small fridge inside. Mounted to the wall above it was a large flatscreen HDTV. Akira decided he'd upgrade to a pimp, 50", wall-mounted flatscreen in his bedroom after he sold enough purses.

Akira walked across the broad room and threw the curtains back, finding plantation shutters that opened like an accordion. Just out the windows sat the jagged, majestic crags of the Sandia mountains. Akira opened the patio door and below the mountains were the rolling hills and paths of a golf course, complete with a waterfall and a small, meandering creek. Closer to the hotel were the pool, the hot tub, and white-linen cabanas sprinkled around the outdoor bar. There were well-dressed people laughing and drinking at poolside tables and a few kids splashing about like a goddamned commercial. A group of a friends sat drinking and laughing around a fire pit. The New Mexico sun had tipped over to the southwest and was heading back down toward the horizon. The light was soft and warm, and a light breeze whistled through the opened patio door. Akira took his shoes off — swaggered around the room.

He pushed open double doors to the bedroom. A plush king bed sat facing another flat screen, and more shutters covered the bedroom's patio door. He found another small sitting area with deep cushioned chairs outside. Back inside, a bathroom the size of a small spa was attached — with a jetted tub, a walk in shower, broad stone tiles around small, polished black ones. Ornate fixtures appointed every surface. Akira decided that Jay-Z probably had a similar set-up.

He threw himself on the king-sized mattress and started texting everyone, posting about the party on Facebook, and sent out a Tweet:

Fuck whatever you thot you wuz doin!
Suite 417-Navajo Casino, 8pm 2night!
It B off da chain! Holla!

When Akira didn't see any confirmation from Zoë via text, he called her to make sure she'd come.

"A suite?" said Zoë.
"You know how I do!" said Akira.
"Can I bring a friend?"
"Only if you come early and help me set up," Akira said. It was agreed — she'd bring a bunch of lime wedges for cocktails, and be there by 7:00 p.m.

Back downstairs, Akira popped his trunk, and loaded a bellhop cart with his bags. He pushed the clinking, glugging cart slowly, hoping not to arouse any suspicion.

Akira unlocked the room and rolled the cart in, unzipped

the first suitcase, and got to it. He hooked his iPod up to his BOSE docking station, plugged the whole rig in, and picked "99 Problems" on the touchscreen. The music blared. He set up his computer on the table, then realized he'd forgotten his cell phone charger.

Next he wrestled both suitcases into the bathroom and lined the tub with two cases of PBR for the fucking hipsters, some forties of Hi-Gravity Steel Reserve, three six-packs of Corona from the suitcases, and some Smirnoff Ice Green Apple Bite for the girls. He set a sleeve of red plastic Solo cups, and bottles of Bacardi, Stoli, Jack, and Tanqueray on the sink countertop. He made trip after trip to the ice machine with the plastic wastebasket, filling the bathtub and one of the sinks.

Akira cracked open a PBR. He thought about Zoë, about how they'd been talking a lot, and how he was pretty into her, how awesome it was she was coming. *Maybe tonight was the night.* Akira imagined all kinds of scenarios — booze, fun — all ending with him and Zoë in the king-sized bed in the master suite. He tapped his pocket, once again finding the rubber he'd been saving since their date.

Akira's beer wasn't cold, and he could only get half of it down. Akira re-checked the ice, the iPod, the room, the clock, his email, his Facebook, and Twitter over and over. He tried texting Zoë, tried to get her on the phone. Every time it was her chipper voicemail greeting saying, "Hey guys, it's Zoë — at the beep, tell me how much you love me!"

Akira jumped in the shower, then sat sweating and watching the clock as the light against the Sandias went all pink and purple with sunset. He grabbed a sandwich from a small cafe downstairs, and 7:00 came and went with no Zoë. Akira tried everything he could to not over post about the party, or brag it up too much. He knew that some of his friends had seen the fucking posts because they'd been online, or got notifications on their phones but no one had said anything about it. It was fucking infuriating. Akira looked on Zoë's Facebook, her Twitter, and checked for her on Gmail, for a green "available" dot. Nothing. Just before 8:00 some people showed up…folks he sort of knew, friends of friends and immediately started helping themselves to everything.

At 8:20 Zoë finally texted she was on her way.

There were more people Akira barely knew by then, and it was massively annoying: the elevator required a room key to get to any hotel room floor. At the front desk they explained to Akira that it was to keep uninvited guests out of the hotel room halls — that it was for his privacy, security, and protection. Akira requested an additional key, and had spent the better part of the evening thus far shuttling people to and fro, all the while getting more and more pissed that none of them were Zoë. It was a quarter after nine when Zoë finally showed up - without limes, and with some goddamned guy in tow.

"Where the hell are the limes?" Akira said.
"Whoa whoa whoa, take a chill-laxative there, Gangnam Style," said the guy with a snicker.
"Oh, fuck — the limes!" said Zoë swatting her friend on the arm. "I totally told you I was forgetting something!"
"Ow, slut!" her friend lisped, pretending to be hurt.
"It's your fault! You were supposed to remind me!" said Zoë.

Akira didn't know what to say. His head swarmed with rage. He tried to breathe, take it easy. In the reflection of the polished metal Akira studied the guy and stared at Zoë's body. The lust and fury swirled each other, and for a moment Akira was simply overwhelmed. He knew he dare not say anything, for fear of what might come out. Zoë was oblivious, listening intently to her friend yammer on about some new band.

Up in the room, there were some quick introductions. Akira was relieved to hear her say this was her "gay bestie," who worked with her. The guy was already too busy spilling his Smirnoff Ice Green Apple Bite everywhere to bother shaking hands. He'd been there all of eleven seconds, and already he was holding court on the subtle differences between *The Real Housewives of Atlanta* and *The Real Housewives of Beverly Hills* — who was the biggest bitch, who he was most like, et cetera.

"He's so courageous," said Zoë. She said that Akira had met her friend once before at the Double Rainbow. He vaguely remembered Zoë blathering on about how courageous her friend was then too. "I mean, it's like, with his being gay, and coming out and everything…and his parents like totally hating him, and being, like, all hella-religious…"

Akira apologized for not being able to sit through the whole sad ballad of her gay bestie again — unfortunately, he had to fetch some goddamned limes from somewhere, and bring up more stupid people who were downstairs dashing off angry texts.

"No worries," Zoë said, and then started telling someone

else how courageous her gay co-worker friend was.

Every time Akira would bring a group up, some dumb ass at the party would need to go back down — to get their cell phone charger, or smoke some weed, or go find their fake I.D., or gamble on the nickel slots, or meet up with some guy they ran into and sorta knew from Red Robin. Akira spent his evening not nuzzled up with Zoë on the couch in his gangster hotel suite, living large like a pimp, but riding the goddamned elevator up and down like a fucking rube — getting nothing and going nowhere.

Akira found his way to the bathroom, and grabbed one of the few remaining beers from the ice. A gutterpunk had a foot up on the toilet lid, preaching like a evangelist to a couple girls perched on the edge of the tub.

"So I told them, I said 'That dude stealing! He just stuffed something down his pants!'" The girls giggled. "And the security is all, 'So?' And I'm all 'So?! So go stop him!' And the dude's all 'Can't. We have a Non-Interference Policy.' Can you believe that shit? Dude said they got big checks from their insurance company for 'inventory degradation — so who gives a fuck — why risk his ass,' he said!" The preacher pulled a face, and again the girls laughed. "I mean, shit, the dude's robbing them blind — and this pig is busting my balls for skating…not even on the fucking sidewalk!" The girls were enthralled, all of them baffled by the great injustice of it all.

"Beer's not gonna do it," Akira said to himself, tossing the can back in the ice. "Better go with missiles," he said, packed a cup with ice, and poured himself a huge Tanqueray and tonic. He looked around. *Who are these fucking people?*

"You look bummed," Zoë said. Akira explained how bored he was with the party.
"I might as well be a fucking bellhop."

Zoë decided to totally help him out. She agreed to take people to and from the party for him.

"Just give me a room key. Easy-peasy Japanese-y!" She put a hand to her mouth and said, "Oooop," like Betty Boop. "Oh. Em. Gee. — I am such a retard! I totally did not mean to insult you!"
Akira cracked a smile, and said, "No worries."

Akira gave Zoë a room key, and she hopped to it. "So you can finally have some fun too," she said, hurrying off to fetch her first wave of guests. It was no better. In one corner of the room, someone was bitching about the party not having the right booze. In another corner a group of people were arguing about who had the best pot, which was the best Vin Diesel movie, and who was the best rapper. Out on the patio a few people smoked cigarettes while a guy tried to get a game of quarters going. They all seemed to be buzzed and happy.

Akira found a quiet corner and sat there, getting slightly drunk. Zoë was off elsewhere, doing whatever, with whoever — with anyone and everyone but him. Every now and again he'd tell someone to quit fucking with his iPod, or quit throwing bottle caps off the balcony — but mainly he just walked around, looking at all the people he hardly knew, and feeling old, feeling apart, feeling separate. The Tanqueray helped, but only for a while.

Finally Zoë sat down near him.

"This is a goddamned nightmare," said Akira.
"People are, like, totally loving it," Zoë said.
"I just want you to have a good time."
"I am. I totally am having fun!"

Probably it was the booze, but it all sounded patronizing to Akira. He grumbled and drank while Zoë talked more about her stupid fucking friends: her gay friend, her Mexican friend, her Belgian friend, her Canadian friend, her fucking Ethiopian friend. He wanted to tell her he loved her, that he wanted her, that she was everything... tell her he wanted to take her to New Orleans, to a 2nd story room with a balcony overlooking the French Quarter, but he couldn't. He couldn't say anything because somewhere deep down he knew she didn't fucking care.

Zoë got up to take a couple of girls back down to the lobby. Akira followed her out. As the door to the elevator began to close Akira said, "Promise me you won't leave. I really just want to hang out with you..."
"We'll totally hang out!" said Zoë as the door shut.
"Obsess much?" snarked Zoë's gay-bestie, and Akira could hear the gaggle of giggling idiots as the elevator dropped out of earshot. He walked back, and — having forgotten his goddamned room key — knocked so someone would let him back in to his own goddamned party.

Akira had a few more drinks. For lack of anything better to do, he propped the door open with the security bolt, and took enough trips to refill the ice in the tub and the sink, even though few beers remained and the liquor was running low. Some guy gave Akira two tabs of what the guy said was ecstasy, saying as he left, "Thanks for the kick-ass party, bro-heim." Akira chewed out someone for fucking with his iPod, and he ran a half-naked couple out of the bedroom. Everyone except Akira was drunk.

A couple of guys started wrestling, and the crowd said "which one of you wears the rubber?" and "girls, girls, you're both pretty!" and "whoa whoa whoa, this ain't Foxes Booze-n-Cruise!" Then a few had sober conversations about how all that macho, insensitive shit was "so totally not cool." Some stuck-up bitch kept ashing on the carpet despite it being a non-smoking room, and another smart-ass ordered 24 hours of porn on the pay-per-view. Ripped, muscled, shaved, and tanned flesh writhed and jiggled and mechanically thumped and pumped, blaring on the unwatched screen. Akira just wanted to see Zoë, and of course she just flitted from one place to the next — bussing the party and flirting with everyone as if she was at work. Akira caught himself taking another shot almost every time he went looking but did not find her.

Finally, the booze ran out and the party started to break up. Akira tried to pick up, but all the trash cans were full. Red plastic cups sat everywhere — piled up on tables, countertops, floating in the melted ice of the tub. Akira chased off some guy who was clearly hoping to pass out on the couch. Akira searched the room, found Zoë through the crack in the back bathroom door. She was helping her gay bestie who was throwing up. On the TV, some tattooed guy in socks was mechanically thrusting at an upside-down Asian girl, plastic tits knotty as fists, splayed out on a staircase. Akira's fingers traced the outline of the condom in his pocket.

"I'm sorry," said Zoë, "he's really fucked up. I should get him home."
"Come back," said Akira, " — after. We can hang out finally.".
"I'll try," said Zoë.
"I haven't seen you all night."
"I said I'd try," said Zoë, as she helped her gay bestie stumble out the door and down the hall to the elevator. Akira knew he should follow her but he just couldn't make himself — and instead stood in the hall, one heel propping his room door open.

"My god, that Greek guy you were talking to," yelled her friend. "Holy Baklava! You should hit that, girl!" Zoë shushed her friend as the elevator doors closed, and just like that Akira was alone again. He went back in.

The door to the room slammed shut behind him, and Akira looked around at the mess. *To hell with this,* he thought and shut off most of the lights. He plunked himself in a comfortable chair, and told himself he'd sit up waiting for Zoë to return. She would find him sitting up waiting for her, and then she would finally see and appreciate his loyalty to her, his devotion. Akira caught himself nodding after a while, so he got up. He opened the patio door to the cool desert night, thinking it might keep him awake until Zoë returned. It didn't. As soon as he sat back down he dozed off.

* * * * *

The key card beeped in the hotel door, and a rush of excitement ran through him. *She came back,* he thought, his brain flush with joy and dread. He decided to pretend he was asleep, the way he used to when he was a kid. He remembered his mom would find him supposedly sleeping on the couch and sweetly rouse him awake. He wanted to see what sweet and gentle thing Zoë would do to wake him up.

But it wasn't Zoë. They were two voices, male, obviously drunk. They stumbled through the dark and into the bathroom. One giggled and took a piss saying, "Shut the fuck up, dumb ass!" while the other could be heard fishing through the ice water in the tub. Akira couldn't make out the voices, and peeked through his nearly closed eyes, staying deathly still, hoping to get a look at them. One of the guys emerged zipping up, and the other had his T-shirt kangaroo pouched with what proved to be the last of the beers. Both remained silhouetted in the muted yellow bathroom light behind them.

At the door between the bedroom and living room, the pisser said, "Fuck that fuckin' gook," knocking over the cans and bottles next to the TV. Akira knew he had heard the voice before, but was too drunk to place it. The two figures stumbled out the hotel room door whispering and giggling, their footsteps even breaking into a sprint as the hotel door rattled back shut.

45

Akira woke, cheek to the tiled floor, and gagged at the stink of his vomit. The soft orange lights of the city filtered in through the night and the opened patio doors. The desert air came in too — cold and terrifying. It had rained. He surveyed the wreckage: all the beer was gone, the ice near melted, and his iPod had been stolen. Snatches of memory flashed back — Zoë late; Zoë without limes; Zoë off fucking about with her gay friend all night; Zoë leaving; Zoë lying about coming back, Zoë abandoning him just like everyone else.

He hated everyone and every thing. None of them had half the creativity and guts he had. Which of them could make the straight-up bank Akira was raking in right now? Or throw a gangster-ass-party at a gangster-ass-suite at the Navajo Casino? No one, that's who.

Akira packed up his laptop and whatever was left of his stuff, and left the Navajo Casino at 4am without checking out. He needed food, but the only things that were open served garbage. He drove around for a while, light after light, hardly anyone on the road. He found a McDonald's just off the highway, parked, and fell asleep.

* * * * *

Banging on his window.

"What?" Akira said as he rubbed his eyes. He turned the key, and rolled the window down a couple inches.
"You can't park here," said the guy — a rent-a-cop.
"I'm waiting for them to open. I need breakfast."
"You can't park here."
"I'm a customer, man. I'm totally gonna order the whole menu when they open…"
"But you can't park here," the voice said, again, identically.
"Man…c'mon," Akira said.
"But you can't—"
"'—park here.' Yeah, I got it," Akira said, zipping the window back up.

Akira drove on in the cold, still dawn. After a half hour or so, Akira parked at Double Rainbow, Zoë's Double Rainbow, in a spot close enough to catch the Wi-Fi. In the trunk he found a blanket and a couple pillows. He crawled in the back seat, locked the car, and fell asleep.

* * * * *

Akira had been squatting on Double Gay-bow's Wi-Fi since waking up. He told himself finding Zoë was the easiest way to get his iPod back. Whoever took it, he'd simply explain, it had to be with the keycard he gave her — so she just had to tell him who she gave it to. Honestly, it wasn't a big deal. He just needed his iPod back — that's all this was. This wasn't a fishing expedition to uncover why she left, where she went, or with who, and certainly wasn't an attempt to find out why she didn't come back after promising him she would.

With nothing better to do, he checked his auctions. There was yet another goddamned bitching comment from *divapink1989* on his new Louis Vuitton auction. After his email, she'd taken to posting "questions" on all his new auctions. In truth, they were little more than thinly veiled threats and negative comments, and were costing him who knows how much action on sales. Akira spent portions of each day trolling his own auctions deleting her negative comments. Akira asked that she be blocked as a troll who was terrorizing his business but eBay didn't seem like they were going to do anything. Annoyed, he screen-captured the comment, deleted it, and sent the screenshot with yet another eBay Dispute Resolution Report to eBay while watching for Zoë through the windows. He tapped out the last few sentences and fired off the email — looking up just in time to see Zoë coming outside, walking straight for his car.

Like a boss, he thought.

But no, not his car…in fact, she didn't even notice him as she instead walked to a Jeep Wrangler, California plates, in a spot the two rows back. Akira watched in his rearview as she leaned in to kiss Jeep Wrangler, on the mouth, twice, then smiling and chatting a while. Apparently Jeep Wrangler was in some kind of hurry. He handed her something, they talked a bit more, then she kissed him again. She watched as Jeep Wrangler pulled out, barely giving her a wave, then she went bouncing back to the building with a smile. At the doorway she stopped and again looked back, but Jeep Wrangler was on his phone, busy running his hands through his stupid hair and admiring himself in his mirror. She shook her ass back inside — probably to expo more food and have more fake conversations with people she'd pretend to care about just so she could say everyone loved her.

Akira saw his hand pushing through the glass doors and into the Double Rainbow — tracked her as she carried a small tray to a table of customers. Hot blood flushed in his cheeks, and only the muffled murmur of conversations and the far off plink of silverware against plates registered. His brain sizzled and popped, trying to hear what she was saying in the deafening static of his pure white rage. She was smiling, the fucking cow, smiling, as if nothing was wrong at all. Then she was at a table full of hipster kids. Akira knew he should go back to his car and go. He knew he should get out of there, and not come back for a few days. *Just go...*

He marched at her, met her as she returned to the expo counter — a customer's empty cup in one hand.

"The fuck was that?" he said.
"What?" she said, startled — as if she didn't know.
"California?!" Akira said. "That fucking Jeep?"
"He's just an old friend...from high school. He's in town for the holidays. He said I could drive — "
"Does he know we went out?"
"Uh, we *hung* out."
"We *didn't* go out on a date?" Akira said.
"Well...it was more like just friends, you know?"

A nearby table noticed their conversation.

"Just friends?!"
"Getting to know you and stuff."

"You just 'getting to know him' too?"

"I've know him for years. We're friends..."

"Oh, you kiss your friends?"

She was quiet for a moment.

"Yeah," she said, "sometimes."

"But *we're* friends...isn't that what you just said?"

"I did..." she stammered. "We are…"

"So where's my kiss?"

"That's different…" she said.

No further explanation was coming.

"Look, I have work to do," she said, turning to walk away.

Akira didn't know what else to say. Blood crashed hot into his ears, his cheeks. His throat and temples pulsed. He followed her.

"Pick," Akira said. "Him or me."

"That's not fair."

"Pick."

"I'm not gonna—"

"PICK!"

"Fine," she said. "Him."

Akira grabbed a stainless steel napkin holder — smashed it against the blue tiled wall. He felt tears welling, and knew he had to get out, just get back to his car — knew he might murder her if he stayed.

46

Akira pulled over at an old park, one he recognized from his days playing soccer. He walked among the kiddie play land, and the huge, leafless cottonwoods. He couldn't get a good breath, like he was under water, and couldn't make the surface. His heart pounded, and the last of his air was dying in his lungs.

He found the men's room. He turned on the cold tap — splashed some water on his face. He tried some more, then shook off his hands as he looked in the polished metal that passed for a mirror. He found a raspy old paper towel — blew his nose. Coughed.

"Him," he thought.

The faucet dripped.

Then Akira was punching. Again, again, again, until his fists hurt, then with his elbows, bang, bang, bang, the screws pulling powder from the cinder block walls, the metal stalls caving in. Akira yanked at a door, pushed the hinges the wrong way. Then he was kicking, kicking,

kicking until the door was loose too. He grabbed a toilet tank lid, smashed it on the bowl below. In the next stall he kicked the aluminum toilet paper dispenser from the bent stall wall. The last tank lid cracked the front of a urinal, and water, piss, and the urinal cake tumbled out. Akira stepped back, slipping on the flattened door and the wet tile.

He sat there, back to the wall, the destroyed bathroom silent and still but for the trickle of running water. He heard a tiny whine coming from somewhere deep in him, the light spidering in his watery eyes. He sniffed up his running nose. The skin of his knuckles was a bloodless white, with small stipples of red seeping through abrasions. He remembered hearing, amidst the racket, the squeak of his skin as it tore between bone and the metal stalls like basketball shoes on a polished parquet. Dead, scraped-up skin was burred up into tiny tufts at each splintered knuckle. His hands throbbed. He found a trickle of blood and a fresh gash at his elbow.

Back in his car, Akira thought *fuck it*, found the Interstate, and punched it — stopping only to gas up and buy snacks in Socorro. There he discovered he'd forgotten his mother's debit card. Still he had almost seven hundred in cash on him. *Plenty for a bunch of purses*, and continued South.

47

At the Hotel Tulum, Akira waved off the valet. "I'm just checking in, then going downtown." The fool nodded, but didn't seem to understand. "Don't park it!" When that didn't seem good enough, Akira yanked the keys from the ignition. His Cheeseburger Doritos and peppered beef jerky were strewn about the passenger seat, along with what remained of his six-pack of Mountain Dew Code Red. He didn't want the valet to see it, so he gathered it up, along with all his electronics from the party and stumbled inside.

At the counter, Akira explained that he needed to book his room with the debit card they had on file, that he didn't have the actual card itself — he'd accidentally left it at home. The girl didn't seem interested in helping him.

"I've stayed here twice in that last couple months," Akira said, that surely his production debit card was in the system. "Just get Nita, she'll fix everything."
"I'm sorry, sir — Ms. Juanita is in a meeting."
"I've been scouting for a major Hollywood film," Akira said. Akira took his Ray-Bans off and stood there as she

tapped her keyboard and stared at the screen. "I mean, c'mon, how can you not remember me?!"

She said she remembered seeing him before, that she would ask her manager. She disappeared in the back for a while. Akira dreamed up an explanation, just in case. *Ms. Mayumi Nakimura is the producer of the film*, he'd say, *I'm an authorized user on the account, I'm her son — that some fucking P.A. forgot to pack the card.* Akira figured that was good enough, that it would work. If they kept giving him shit he'd say something like: *I don't get the problem here, we've used the same production credit card for our last two stays…*

She finally returned. She'd left a message for Nita regarding using previous billing information for a new guest visit.

"It is more easier next time to bring the card," she said. Akira was tempted to say something, but decided that, until Nita sorted it all out, he shouldn't push his luck.

"A suite?" she said.
"I don't care, as long as it has good pillows."
"Yes sir, pillows — very good."
"I want more pillows. Extra pillows."
"Yes sir, extra pillows."

Akira said, slapping $5 on the counter. "Lots of pillows. As many as possible."

She pretended to resist, tried to slide the money back. Akira grabbed his room key, and left the money. Looking down from the glass elevator he checked again. His $5 was gone.

Upstairs the suite looked the same as his last room, only it had another chair, a small fridge, and two sinks instead of one. The goddamned palm tree painting was there too. He threw all his junk on the bed, and stuffed what he'd bought from the Allsup's and the sodas in the mini-fridge. He checked his phone, again realizing he'd forgotten his charger. His battery was at 47%.

"Motherfucker," he said, stuck the phone in his pocket and headed back down.

Out front the valet tried to tell Akira something about not parking in the loading zone. Akira nodded *yeah, yeah,* then threw $5 at him too.

48

Akira fought with the familiar street names and the few landmarks he could remember while he drove, hoping to stumble back. He set out in a familiar direction and, a couple streets later, found the church near downtown. He made the turns that felt right, and just as he began to feel lost again, spotted the shop's sign. The miracle of finding the shop instantly faded — as it was closed.

"Hey," Akira said to the shopkeep next door, "where's this guy?"

"What do you need, my friend? I have best in all Juárez."

"This guy. The guy right here, this shop. Where is he?"

"*No está*...He no here today."

No shit, Akira thought. "Well where is he?"

"His daughter, she haves a...has a...how you say, *Quinceañera*." The man rattled off something in Spanish to someone unseen in the back. The answer came: 'Birthday. Special birthday,' followed by what sounded like swearing. "Ah, his daughter haves...has a special birthday. They make big party. *Muy importante*."

"When will he be back?"

"*No sé*. I sell to you, my friend. Whatever you want."

"Where are your purses?" The man found a few dusty old ones. They were no good. "When does the big party end or whatever?"

"Maybe all the weekend," said the man, "Or maybe he is here *mañana*."

"Great," said Akira, "that's just great." But the man had stopped listening. Akira thought about asking after a cell phone charger — but decided the man was rude and not worthy of the business.

Akira looked around. The furious yellow sun baked everything and every one. A dusty haze kicked up from the slow-motion bustle of bodies walking, waving, or passing on scooters or rusted-out, old jalopies — burning his eyes. He realized his Ray-Bans weren't on his head, or in his car — he didn't know where they were. Great…just another terrible day in Juárez, Akira thought.

Staple-gunned to a nearby telephone pole, next to missing girl flyers, Akira saw an ad. It read *'Rento Toro Mecánico'* and had a phone number next to an angry, poorly drawn bull's head. Akira had no idea how or why that flyer had been made, nailed up right there — what kind of logic led to the decision. Who would buy a mechanical bull in hopes of making a fortune renting it out, and what kind of nut-job would rent one off a Juárez flyer? Akira could only laugh at the silly, stupid heavens.

49

Back at the hotel, Akira found a stack of pillows on his bed, with a note:

> *Mr. Nakimura,*
> *The billing issue has been resolved.*
> *Thought you might like some extra pillows.*
> *~Nita*

He popped downstairs, hoping to thank her — but she was already gone for the day. He went to the business center to check his Gmail and Facebook and Twitter and YouTube. It was all dull. Dull dull dull. He tried a few drinks at the *El Acueducto* then decided he'd try the pool. There was a hot girl, 16 maybe, baby-fat curves, with Ray Bans — probably his — and a pouty pink mouth. She texted with one hand while leaning back on her other, puffing her tits out in her neon green bikini. Her two chubby friends tried to talk to her but she only half-listened, pretending to be bored by them, bored by everything. Akira immediately knew she was a bitch, and that he hated her. He thought about going over, demanding his sunglasses back, but went to the poolside bar for another beer instead.

"So, you did change your hair cut, eh?" the bartender said.

"Huh?"

"Your hair. Is different, yes?"

"Oh, right," Akira said. "Gotta keep that shit fresh, yo."

The bartender nodded.

Akira ordered, then watched Neon Green for a while. The bartender popped the top, handed him the beer. Akira paid, tipped him a buck.

"Like Justin Bieber, eh?" the bartender said. "Is cool, yes?"

"Naw man," Akira said, "not even a little bit," and regretted giving the guy a tip.

"Terrible," said some fat man with zinc sunscreen on his nose, staring at the news on the TV. "Just Terrr-iiib-blllle," the man said again, stretching out every syllable. It was some sort of natural disaster in *where-the-hell-ever*. Apparently he thought Akira gave a shit. "They say there's probably no way to know how many died."

"Pfff," said Akira. "Who cares?"

"Excuse me?!" the man said.

"If I had to live there," Akira said, taking a pull on his beer, "I'd rather be dead too."

The man was horrified. "You kids today," he said and stomped off.

Akira sat under some huge palm fronds in a booth near the pool. He peeked through the ferns at Neon Green, her taut breasts bursting at the strings. He imagined cupping them, kissing them. The sun slanted down through the skylights atop the cavernous hotel and it was all so impossible, and he hated her and himself and the world.

"'You kids today,'" Akira said in his best fat white man voice. He made his fingers into a .45, put the imaginary barrel in his mouth — pulled the trigger. He imagined his brains all over the leaves, the sacred idol cubbies made from the charred white stone tiles behind him. He pounded the beer then let his corpse slowly slump down in the corner of the booth.

Neon Green and her fat friends gathered their stuff and left the pool. Akira decided to follow, maybe figure out which floor she was on, which room. He tried keeping an eye on her from the glass elevator, but lost her in the waterfall. He saw nothing but the vast carpeted balconies overlooking the jungle atrium — the aqueducts and palms and indoor pool below staring back up at him. Akira was sure she was back in her room, probably sending sexts to some fuckhead in a Jeep wrangler.

At the gift shop downstairs, Akira bought some cherry

Nyquil and some swim trunks. He drank a couple glugs on the way upstairs to change. He yanked the tags from the new shorts, and sat on the toilet. He figured Neon Green's parents wouldn't let her out of the hotel, so she'd probably show back up at the pool after dinner. He was gonna sit in the hot tub waiting, demand his sunglasses back if she did show.

But before he could, the Nyquil took hold, and he went out-cold for what ended up being eleven-hours.

50

Akira had been awake since 4am, but there was nothing to do. With no auctions to follow and no friends messaging him, Akira couldn't even make himself go to the business center. Goddamned *divapink1989* had taken the joy out of even that. It was the first time he'd been up early enough for the free "Continental" breakfast they offered downstairs, so at 6am Akira went to check it out. It was a bunch of pre-made pap. He ate four sticky buns that could've been from a gas station, some coffee, watery orange juice, and a plate of rubbery bacon.

He checked the pool for Neon Green, then bummed around the lobby for an hour, hoping to see Nita. He tried the TV, tried looking at the yellow city out his window, tried laying around on the bed and not checking his phone, or his computer, or any of that techno-shit that barely worked anyway. *I don't need self-important twats posting about their goddamned breakfasts or relationship status or whatever.* Akira was practically glad his battery was running down, and that he could only use his phone for emergencies. When he finally got tired of trying everything and nothing working, he called the hotel valet for his car and headed out.

Downtown, Akira found the purse shop — still closed.

Akira asked around, and managed to turn up a phone number for the shop. He turned his phone on, punched the number into his contacts and shut it off. He checked the battery: 19%. He figured he'd call from the hotel phone once, maybe twice a day, until he got hold of the owner. Once he caught the man, he'd get another load of purses, and get the fuck out of Juárez. Until then, Akira figured he'd simply hang out around the Hotel Tulum — just enjoying himself for a change.

Back at the hotel, he valeted his car, went upstairs and tried a bath. The hot water stung all the fresh cuts at his knuckles and elbows, and nothing was good like before. Akira found a pen stuck in with the hotel stationary. He chewed the cap as he chucked the pen up towards the ceiling over and over, trying to get as close as he could without actually hitting it. Satisfied he could throw it no closer, Akira stood on the bed in front of the palm tree painting — scribbled *Akira, 1959* in the corner. He smiled, deciding he'd tag the painting in every room he stayed in...maybe even the entire hotel.

Down at *El Acueducto*, after a few margaritas, Akira got wrapped up in a conversation with a long-haired hippie-type guy who was "bumming around Mexico" because he was "sick of the American War machine" and he was trying for some "spiritual kicks." He could almost hear all of Zoë's religious crap: how the Koran was just as true as the Bible; how they were both — if you really looked — basically the same book; how it was all proof of god, and proof that god was everywhere, and that he gave everyone a path to salvation. *Yeah, yeah — but what about every terrible fucking thing in the world?* Akira always wanted to ask her. Murder, rape, war, famine, disaster — of course she wouldn't have an answer for all that. But the hippie-guy was just blathering about terrorism now — nothing about god, so Akira agreed that war was never going to work but there was nothing they could do to stop it.

"Does it really matter? They'll kill us, or someone else will." Akira said. "I really don't even see what the big deal is about dying. We all have to die…so who cares how?" "What about, like, your soul, man?" the dude asked.

Akira said he didn't know and didn't care, that religion was all just some giant kind of trick to get people to behave.

"That's like, pretty pessimistic, man," the guy said.

"I mean, c'mon…72 virgins? That's the prize for blowing up infidels?! Who the hell wants 72 virgins? *Maybe* I'd sign up for, like, 72 filthy whores…who knew every trick in the book…"

The hippie-guy about choked on his beer.

"But virgins? Man, you'll be talking to your gaggle 'til rapture…for *maybe* a little side-boob action?!" Akira was rolling now, and the dude was laughing.

"That's some funny shit, hombre," the hippie-guy said getting up to leave.

"You're going?"

The guy said yes, that he had stuff to do. Akira wanted him to stay. It was the best conversation he remembered having for some time. He was all set to hate the guy and argue over Islam or whatever…but the dude ended up being pretty cool.

"C'mon, one more beer. My treat," Akira tried.

"We'll have to take a raincheck."

Akira had no idea how that could ever happen. He'd never see this guy again. A raincheck was pointless.

"Guess you gotta rush back to your room…to pray to Mecca, huh?" Akira said.

"You know it," the guy said. "Gotta get my 72 whores! Good luck with your movie," and with a handshake, left Akira sitting at the bar.

Akira sat for another hour or so drinking. It was dull. He was pretty sure the bartenders talked about him in code, calling him *"espina"* or *"pedorrito,"* and he'd heard some bellhop call him "Scorsese." He watched people come and go. He wanted to make someone else laugh with his hilarious rant about religion — but no one would talk to him or listen, so he just gave up. Eventually it was just Akira and the bartender — *El Acueducto* was quiet save a sad woman softly singing through the speakers hidden in the ferns.

Then Akira saw Nita, the shadow of tumbling water reflecting on the wall behind her. Nita had a highball in her hand as she walked over on her high heels.

"Señor Nakimura," said Nita, surprising Akira, "another drink?" She turned to the bartender, "A margarita for my guest."

The man snapped to it, mixing the drink quickly. With a wave and a silent point, Nita made sure the bartender used the top-shelf tequila.

"What's that you're drinking?" Akira asked, sitting down.
"Scotch," Nita said.
"My father drinks Scotch."
"I bet. A man's drink," Nita said, making a fist as she did. She was a little drunk, but didn't seem to care. "How's business?"
"It's been better."
"I know this feeling," she said.

The bartender set the margarita in front of Akira. He wanted to ask Nita what she meant, but didn't — something about it almost seemed like a violation. The staff stood by on full alert, almost terrified.

"Relax!" she said to the bartender, who flinched, smiled, but still remained rigid. "*Pobrecitos*...they're all afraid of me."
"Why?"
"Because I'll kick their asses if they keep making me look bad!"

Akira laughed, but the frosty edge to Nita was every bit

unnerving for him too. She asked why his business was bad.

"I haven't been able to get to the shop where I buy my purses. The owner's daughter is having her *quinceañera*."
"Purses for your movies?" Nita asked, smiling, pretending at confusion.
"Well...maybe," Akira said. "I don't know yet."
"I'm sorry," Nita said, patting his arm. "Not my business."

She drained off her glass then called the bartender over for a refill.

"Him too," she said, even though Akira had hardly touched his drink.

The bartender went to it. They sat silent as the water tumbled around them. The bartender slid their drinks across the bar, and went back to polishing glasses.

"I've been working in hotels now almost twenty years," Nita said. "I am twelve years here at the Hotel Tulum."

Akira said something about her looking too young to have worked for twenty years.

"*Oh, qué suave,*" she said. "Aren't you sweet?" She took a deep pull on her Scotch. "I'm the only woman in management — did you know this?"

Akira shook his head 'no.' She said the bosses give her all the "*pinche mierda*" to clean up.

"'You're good at it,' they tell me — just so they don't have to do it!" Nita said. "And for this, they pay me less. There is no justice for a woman in a man's world."

She said that she'd learned she wasn't getting a pay raise and the other managers were.

"So tonight," Nita said, "I will drink myself a little bonus."

Akira said that he was sorry. He tried to make her laugh with his 72 virgins bit.

"But virgins?" Akira said. "You'll spend eternity talking your head off for nothing!" Nita chuckled.

"You men," Nita said, shaking her head. "You're so easy. Figuring out what men want isn't hard — usually they yell it at you in the street! Then you decide — if you give it, they are happy…if you don't, they are mad."

Akira smiled, finishing his first drink.

"Ah, but women," Nita said, "sometimes even *they* don't know what they want. And when they do, they are made to feel shame for it."
"That doesn't seem fair," Akira said.
"It's not! You see, even when a woman gets what she wants — maybe it does not make her happy."

Nita said she thought that maybe women weren't supposed to be happy, that the gods wanted to make it harder for them.

"One minute, you are a pretty thing to look at, use, and ignore," Nita said. "The next, you are a hard, ugly thing to use, to fear, and to ignore."

Akira didn't know what to say, so he said nothing.

"Why are you all the time moping around this stupid hotel?" Nita said. "You are young. You should go out, embrace life — indulge yourself! You worry too much. Try to be happy!"
"I'm too goddamned smart to be happy," Akira said.

She laughed, louder now, and didn't care. Akira smiled, said it was late — that it was probably better if he just went to sleep.

"Ah, very wise," Nita said. "But don't sleep through your youth!"

Nita shook her head, climbing up from the bar stool. She apologized, though he wasn't sure what for, then said she needed to go to the office for something. Before leaving *El Acueducto* she turned back to Akira.

"It's like my Mema used to say: '*Tienes el toda la vida para perderse en arrepentimientos.*' This means, 'You have all of life to lose yourself in...' — oh, how do you say it — '... regrets.'"

Nita killed the last of her Scotch, set her glass on the lip of the bar, and sauntered off — the bartender lunging to catch the highball just before it fell.

51

Akira woke early, hoping to call the shop, find them open, and finally buy more purses. He checked his phone — dead. Akira realized he hadn't written the number down anywhere — just typed it in his phone. *Idiot.* Akira would, once again, have to physically go to the goddamned shop just to see if it was even open — even though it probably wasn't. Akira rang the valet for his car.

The shop was still closed, and it looked like nothing had changed since the day before. Everywhere the once-vibrant yellows and oranges and blues and greens of painted walls had been sun-baked and soiled over by dust-blown mud and years of traffic exhaust. The occasional smells of burnt meat and rotting fruit wafted in through Akira's cracked window as he chewed on an unlit cigarillo. He figured it made him look a little tougher — maybe keep all these bastards from messing with him. At a light, Akira watched an uninterested man standing at a giant, steaming vat, selling some sort of boiled meat. The man made a sale and resumed staring into his phone.

Heading back to the hotel, Akira recognized the street to

the dog track, and on a whim drove there. Another day was on its way to wasted — so he figured a couple drinks, a few races might be a decent distraction. The thought of more dull hours at the hotel was enough to make him brave. He parked and found the entrance, paid, and found a corner where he could drink, bet, and be alone.

After a few races, the crowd started to get bigger — apparently some big event was scheduled for 1pm. Soon the place was overrun by taco hats and these outlandish nippled boots — ostrich or crocodile or some damn thing — and a bunch of sketchy guys with knives, pearl snap-button shirts, and gold teeth. Akira overheard a group of fratboys laughing and carrying on. *For once*, he thought, *I'm not the biggest asshole here.*

The frat boys regaled each other with stories about the world famous donkey shows…and Akira found himself again wondering if it was real. The 1pm event came and went — a drawing for some sort of free trip — and the crowd immediately began to thin out. Despite preferring fewer people, Akira had grown weary of the whole place — losing every bet he made.

Back at the Hotel Tulum business center, Akira hopped on a machine and checked all his accounts. Nothing much was going on. There was a message in his mother's eBay account, and Akira new it was more trouble from *divapink1989*, so he avoided it. He caught himself hoping for some kind of Zoë news...then again, maybe he didn't want any.

He logged out of everything and went to his room, unsure if he could even sleep.

52

He'd slept like hell, waking in the middle of the night.
Unable to fall back to sleep, he wasted two hours at the
business center, accomplishing nothing. The eBay message
was from Pam, a D.R.O (Dispute Resolution Officer), who
was part of the Dispute Resolution Team assigned to this
incident in re: *divapink1989*. The email was professional,
but mentioned potentially downgrading his Powerseller
Ranking if Akira couldn't resolve the "Jackie Soft-Leather
Top-Handle Bag issue" to the mutual satisfaction of all
parties involved. Akira needed more goddamned purses
and he needed them now.

Doesn't this fucking shopkeep want money? Akira thought,
sitting in his car, staring at the clapboard sign and the rusty
old garage doors bolted shut. *Doesn't he need extra money for
his daughter's special birthday party?* For a second Akira
thought he could just smash through the doors — grab
some purses. It was a stupid idea, but he didn't have a
better one. He knew he couldn't do it, that he couldn't
possibly risk any kind of trouble in Juárez. *They'd dump me
in that corpse field without a second thought.* Akira gave up
and drove back to the Hotel Tulum.

53

As the elevator door was closing, a dripping wet inner-tube was jammed in the way. The doors opened again and a cute little girl with swim-floaties on her arms climbed on — followed by her mother. Clearly they were headed back up to the lazy river entrance on two, even though the signs said, "no inner-tubes on the elevators." The mom was sorta pretty, holding half of the little girl's inner-tube, and fighting with her phone. She hardly acknowledged Akira's presence. *People and their gadgets*, Akira thought, *blind to the whole fucking world…*

"I'm swimming," said the little girl.
"Yeah you are," Akira said. "Don't forget your Grecian formula for after."
"What's Gee-zann form-a-la?" the little girl said, then repeated it to her Mom.
"What's what, honey?" the mom said, still frustrated and tapping at her phone.
"What he said," the little girl said.

The mom glanced up long enough to measure Akira. She started at his feet, then panned up the rest of his corpse, past his fresh cuts and busted knuckles, stopping at his mangled, chemical-burned mop. She gripped the girl closer, smiling politely.

"I don't know, sweetheart."
"Just a smokin' joke, ma'am," Akira said. "I woke up in Juárez, Mexico with grey hair…" Akira said, pointing to his head. The woman smiled a fake smile, gave up on her phone, tucked the little girl behind a leg, and stared at the elevator numbers — waiting for the two to ding. As the doors opened, he said, "You enjoy that pool, now!" Mom scurried out. Akira made a silly face and the little girl — looking back over her shoulder as mom dragged her off — smiled.

In his room, Akira tried opening the patio door, tried a nap, tried some telenovelas. The show was a kind of Mexican western, with a young and beautiful girl who was nursing a wounded *vaquero* back to health. She dressed his bandages, brought him some coffee, and worried about him. Maybe he had almost died the night before. He thanked her, and said something serious about what it meant to be a man. A tear fell from her eye, and she kissed him softly as the camera panned to the tattered rags strung up like curtains over the broken window — the setting sun coming in as it pulled out of focus. Akira clicked it off.

He wanted to get drunk, maybe stoned. Actually he wanted to be drunk without having to do the goddamned work of drinking.

He wanted to drink a bottle of codeine cough syrup, and sit in the hot tub, pissing himself. He disgusted himself and he was disgusting. Yes, he wanted to sit in his own piss and laugh at everyone who got in his piss-tainted hot tub.

He wanted to walk around insulting people, whatever was obvious about them, whatever first came to mind.

He wanted to be invited to the goddamned *Quinceañera*, wanted to dance with the daughter, and tell her nice things, and promise to take her to America.

He wanted to go back to that terrible strip club — find that fucking dude who talked shit to him.

He knew he couldn't stand his room anymore. Or the pool. Or *El Acueducto*, or maybe even the entire goddamned Hotel Tulum. He wanted to go somewhere, find something. Do something. Indulge. Maybe he'd find some Mexican girl, and get drunk with her.

Akira decided he would go out.

54

"Take me to where the pretty girls are," Akira said to the cabbie. The cabbie did nothing, just sat there. *"Las chicas, muchas chicas,"* said Akira.

"Chicas, sí," said the sad-eyed man completely uninterested. He might as well have been discussing taxes or balancing a goddamned check book. "You like drink? You like watch?" Akira thought, *watch?* "Maybe you like fuck, eh?"

"Uh, drink, drink," said Akira, "yeah— a bar…" overwhelmed by options he'd hardly considered.

The cab rolled off into the dusty afternoon — a bloody haze over the city as the sun dropped red. Akira looked at the back of the man's head, his shirt, the stuff on his cab's dashboard. There were bright colored trinkets, religious looking, maybe the Virgin de Guadalupe. There were photographs on his visor — a woman, a young girl, and a fat little boy with glasses. He wondered what it was like to live this man's life.

"Is that your family?" Akira asked. The man nodded. "You all live here?" The cabbie cleared his throat, annoyed.

Akira let it drop. They drove on in silence.

Traffic got bad near downtown, with cabs turning in from all directions. No one was moving. Horns honked, and occasionally the cabbies yelled at each other, but mostly they all sat, meters running, resigned to their fate. There were what looked like army guys directing all the cabs to take a different road in. Everyone inched along.

"You have a nice family," Akira said. The cabbie looked long at him through the rearview.

"You are here visiting?" the man asked.

"I own my own business. I came to get some inventory for a good price. I come down about once a month."

"A business? So young? Very good."

"You live here in the city?"

"I come only for work. City is too expensive."

"You wouldn't think so with how dangerous it is."

"Cartels are always killing," said the cabbie. "They make big war on each other. Military lets them kill each other. No place left to bury the dead."

"That's messed up," said Akira.

"People are trapped. We work, and pay for life. It's not as bad outside the city."

"I live in Albuquerque."

"Ah, yes. *Breaking Bad*."

"Right. *Breaking Bad.*"

"I take my family to see balloons once. Very nice."

"Yeah," Akira said. "Everyone drives bad. The balloons go into the powerlines and catch on fire. People jump out and break their legs…it's pretty great."

The cabbie laughed a little. Akira imagined this man and his family at the Balloon Fiesta, walking around, and looking at everything, eating churros. Maybe it wasn't so bad.

"You have kept Obama for another four years," said the cabbie.

"Yeah," Akira said. "He's cool."

"I think this is a good thing," the cabbie said. Akira agreed.

The traffic seemed to finally be moving ahead of them.

"The man I do business with, his daughter had her big, special birthday. The *Quince*…"

"*Quinceañera.*"

"He asked me to go, but I couldn't make it."

"Big party. Very fun."

"Has your daughter had one?"

The cabbie did not answer. Akira thought maybe the man

hadn't heard him. He was about to ask again.

"No," said the man, reaching up to adjust his visor against the late day sun.

The cab finally broke through, and they were moving again. The cabbie said nothing more and Akira started to wonder if he'd offended the man somehow. A few turns later they were at a bar, *Colitas*. It was basically a Mexican Hooters, split level, with an upstairs deck overlooking the street. What sounded like *Tejano* music being murdered by some bullshit dubstep blared from above, and without looking Akira knew there were very few bodies up there absorbing noise from what must be huge speakers. It had all the makings of a mistake. Akira paid the man and climbed out.

"*Buena suerte,*" said the cabbie, "with your business."
"Yeah, you too," said Akira, realizing too late that he didn't know if that made any sense.

He closed his door. Taped in the back window was a piece of paper — a handmade sign. It was the same picture the cabbie had on his visor, his daughter — along with a date, a phone number, and what looked to be an offer of a reward.

55

Akira drank and drank — cheap tequila shots and a bucket of Coronitas as people slowly started to filter in. He laughed at all the ads — outdoor banners pinned up indoors, filled with hot Latina girls in bikini tops next to what must've been Mexican soccer players or TV stars he'd never seen. Akira loved that in Mexico you could be fat and ugly and still be famous. He looked at everyone in the place. The few locals were sad, silent drunks probably just off work and broken down from the struggle — there to stare at pretty young waitresses in tight, ripped t-shirts and short-shorts. The rest were tourists, college kids, a few even younger than him — all getting even drunker and acting stupid. The guys tried to chat up the waitresses and the normal girls pretended not to care. Akira tried a few conversations, and out of habit, kept looking at his phone — even though it was dead. When he had a chance, he tried telling girls that he was down scouting locations for a movie he was gonna make, but no one cared.

"What's it about?" asked one girl who finally took the bait. Shocked, Akira stammered. He hadn't expected it to work, and hadn't bothered to think that far ahead.

"It's kinda hard to explain. It's about this young guy…a drug dealer," Akira said, still flailing. "He's a dealer, and is making tons of cash — but it's not very, like, rewarding, you know? It's actually work. So he wants to quit. Then a rival drug dealer kills his mom. Anyways, it's sorta like an art-house, revenge, action thing."

"Sounds pretty cool. An action movie with heart."
"I'll put that on the poster."
"That'll be a million dollars, please." said the girl.
"Sheee-it. You've got a lot to learn about how Hollywood works, girl!" Akira said. "How about a drink?"
"Yeah, okay," said the girl, looking over her shoulder at her friends. Akira got the bartender and bought the girl a drink — a margarita. She sat for a little while, *long enough to be polite*, Akira thought, *before her stupid friends make her leave*. Akira thought he should ask what she was doing later, or maybe ask for her number, but he couldn't — he just couldn't get it out. He imagined her laughing, or lying, or being stuck for what to say and admitting that she didn't think he was cute or funny, that she just wanted to take his drink and be done with it — just wanted to take free drinks all night from the biggest losers she could find, get drunk, and then find some good looking guy to go fuck. Akira felt it was just better not to say anything at all. They talked

about pointless shit and she drank as she checked her phone, so Akira checked his dead phone too.

The girl excused herself to the restroom, taking her drink with her when she went. The bartender noticed that she took her drink, and joked with a waitress in Spanish. They went on and on, back and forth, laughing so much that each had to stop their work to recover. Akira felt sure they were laughing at him, that maybe the girl thought he was gonna roofie her or something.

He was no one. He was nothing. He was all alone in a cold and ugly world and no one would ever love him. Everything is big, and empty, and pointless, and nothing would ever matter. The real world was a place where people were hit by trains they didn't see coming, where they step on mines and are vaporized, where moms go off cliffs, and cab drivers hang xeroxed posters of missing daughters, and nothing ever fucking works out.

Akira found the restrooms. He went into the ladies just to make sure — she wasn't there. In the men's room he pissed, and looked at himself in the mirror. He searched his stupid face for answers. There were none. He turned...just goddamned tired of it all.

Back in the bar, he looked around again, but saw neither

the girl or her friends. A tussle started near the door, someone was mad over something someone else said. Two guys were in each others' faces, yelling, gesturing with their hands, and people were trying to get them to calm down. One grabbed the other by the neck, and they tumbled together into the barstool Akira had been sitting at. *Good thing I wasn't still sitting there* was all Akira could think. Bouncers came in from the sides, grabbing people, and yelling in Spanish. Bodies were dragged out, leaving the bar in an uncomfortable hum as the laughing waitress picked up chairs and tables and the bartender mopped up spilled drinks and broken glass. *That's what you get for laughing at me*, Akira thought. He picked up his stool and sat back down. The stool cracked under his fat, stupid ass.

He swapped it for the closest empty seat. The last bits of a broken beer bottle rocked back and forth on the bar top. Akira picked it up and, for some reason, ran the glass across his wrist. He was surprised at the quick bite, and how fast it actually drew blood. He glanced around to see if anyone had noticed. They hadn't. The fight was over and done, but the room was still atwitter. Akira grabbed a wad of napkins, and pinched them to his wrist. He wanted to leave, to just get the hell out before anyone saw, before he had to explain himself. He made for the door, his wounded hand plunged deep in his pocket, pinching the napkins between his wrist and hip.

Outside he hailed a cab. In the backseat he tried looking at his wrist. Flecks of napkin had started to stick in the drying edges of the wet gash, and it seemed like the bleeding had slowed.

"*¿A dónde vas?*" The cabbie said.

The man was enormous. Rolls of fat bubbled at his jowls, and the hairline on the back of his head. He hardly fit in his cab, which stank of rotten Mexican food and sweat. Akira said nothing. He stuck the wet napkins back over the cut, hoping it would clot. He decided the cut wasn't too bad because it hadn't soaked through yet.

"Where to?" the cabbie said.
Akira said, "I speak Spanish, *amigo.*"
"¿Oh, hablas Español?"
"*Sí,*" Akira said. "*Rento Toro Mecánico,* motherfucker. Believe that shit."
The cabbie laughed. "*Estás loco,*" he said.
"*Loco y borracho,*" Akira said.

The cabbie laughed again — enough to break into a little coughing jag, before asking where Akira wanted to go.

"A whorehouse," Akira said. "Take me to a whorehouse."

56

Yes, a whorehouse. Akira felt sure it was a good idea. He told himself they were uncomplicated. You just picked the one you liked…paid…and that was that. The simplicity of it all appealed to him. There was a kind of sincerity in it. You give her money, and she gives you something in return. No games. Everything else had become too impossible.

Akira picked at bits of napkin at his wrist, but it was too caked in there. He couldn't believe how easily the bottle had cut him. He didn't even mean to cut himself — not really. It was a passing thought — "what if I just cut my wrists?" When it actually worked, it scared Akira more than anything. He didn't want to cut his wrists — not really. A scar could be nice though — something to lie about later.

Through the tiny streets, and hay-flecked stucco walls the cab twisted and turned. The cab stopped on what seemed like a small neighborhood street. Akira didn't know what a whorehouse looked like, but surely they didn't look like this. A thin man got up from a plastic chair on a small porch, leaned into the cabbie's window, started talking. Akira understood none of it, and just like that it was decided.

"Go with him," the cabbie said to Akira.

The man climbed stacked cinderblocks arranged as steps and opened the front door to what looked like a small home. Akira didn't move.

"How do I get back downtown?" said Akira.
"*No problema, señor*," said the cabbie. "I wait."
"Oh, cool, man. Perfect," said Akira, trying to act casual.
"*Sí*," said the cabbie with a chuckle, "*perfecto*."

Inside was a small living room and a couch covered in old blankets. The light bulbs in the wall sconces were shaped like candles with dripping wax, and the orange coils flickered, making a dim yellow light dance at the edges of the room. *For atmosphere*, Akira figured. Long curtains hung over the doorways. The thin man walked through one. Akira heard some conversation, arguing maybe, and thought about running back to the cab. He hadn't realized it, but he was breathing heavily, his heart pounding. The thin man came back, followed by a woman. Her limbs were lean, a small neck. She wore a black tube top and a pair of denim shorts. She was smoking a cigarette.

"*Es* beautiful *chica, no?*" said the thin man.
"Yeah, yeah," said Akira. She was not beautiful.
"Fifty dollars," the thin man said. Akira thought it seemed
like a lot. "You have gooooood time."
"Okay," said Akira. They all stood looking at each other.
"Fifty dollars," said the thin man again.
"Oh yeah, right," said Akira. "I thought...I thought I paid,
uh, paid her." Akira pulled his wallet, then counted and re-
counted out $50 before finally paying. The thin man pulled
back a red sheet tacked up over a doorway and the girl
walked in to the dark beyond. He held the curtain for
Akira. Akira ducked under and walked in.

In the room, Akira introduced himself to the woman, and
put his hand out to shake. She looked at him, a little
amused. She shook his hand. The room was small, white
plaster walls, lit only by a small lamp with a dirty shade. A
string of Christmas lights blinked behind a threadbare
curtain over the small window. She took off his jacket and
shirt, tossed them on the chair near the door. She started at
his pants but he stopped her, almost laughing.

"What is, uh, what's your name?" Akira asked. The
woman looked at him. "Name?" he said again. "*Nombre?*"

305

Still she said nothing.

She pulled her tube top off over her head. Akira stared at her small breasts, each hanging over the deep lines of her ribs. There were bruises at the backs of each arm, just above the elbows. She tossed her top on the chair. There was a small scar on her belly. Akira wondered what it was from. She dug her thumbs in to her waistband, and slid her shorts down her legs. She had no panties and was shaved bare. Akira wasn't sure what he was supposed to do. Again she went at his pants, inching them downwards. Again, Akira held them up, almost ashamed. She grabbed his cock through his clothes, started rubbing. Sparks shot across his eyes, his breathing quickened, and he felt himself slowly, terribly, give in and let go. She pulled Akira's pants down his thighs. As she did his dead phone clattered to the floor. He picked it up, tried putting it back in his pocket, now down near his knees. He couldn't manage it, so he just held on to it. She tugged down his underwear and he felt his cock spring free — no going back. She could see him and he felt worried and ashamed, hoping he wasn't too small — wanting to ask but also not wanting the answer — trying not to care, trying not to care, trying…

"I'm not sure what, um, what I—" he said, but she wasn't

listening. She had his pants to his ankles, and she had him in her mouth, her hands sliding down his thighs, his calves. He looked down at her — downy black hairs gathered at her hairline, near her ears and lean jowls. He saw her jutting collarbones, her thin shoulder blades. She ran a hand up his stomach, and back down, all up and down him and fumbling. He felt electricity quiver through him, and his insides twitch — taut as a snare drum. She led him down to the bed, leaned him back as she bobbed up and down. He writhed a bit, almost wanting to get up and run, but she held him steady, a hand on his chest. Again he relented — stared straight up at the blink of Christmas lights across the textured plaster.

She stood and pulled a condom from a small bedside drawer. She tore it open with her teeth, spitting the wrapper to the floor. She rolled it down, and was then on top of him. Akira tried to look at her. Her eyes were closed behind her hanging hair, her mouth twisted up. The bones of her hips dug into his thighs like elbows, almost hurting. She bounced bounced bounced and he heard their skin slap slap slap. All at once he felt he couldn't do this, something felt wrong, it wasn't right, it didn't mean anything. He felt a kind of sickness building in him. Akira flexed the muscles in his torso, his legs. He heard small grunts come from himself, and his breath sputtered out in little bursts. It had been all of a minute. She made noises too, but not real ones. Akira looked at the lamp, the blinking lights. His stomach dropped down, and a hot tingle swelled in him, climbing towards his back, then rising, rising… It was gonna happen, it was gonna happen, it was gonna happen… He burst, and throbbed and pulsed…his clenched muscles seized…then he went weak.

She grabbed a thin roll of paper towels from under the bed. She whipped her hand around the spool twice, and tore off a few sheets. She grabbed him, snapped the condom off — looked at it before wadding it all up. She wound her hand round the roll once more, handed him a wad to clean up with. She spooled a third wad, for herself this time. Akira wondered how many times she'd done that. She squatted down and grunted a little, though he didn't know why. Akira did his best to wipe himself off before tugging his pants back up from his ankles.

"Was I okay?" Akira asked, his pulse still pounding in his neck. There was no answer. She already had her clothes back on. She brought over a small waste basket lined with an S*Mart plastic bag — half-full of wads of paper towels. Akira threw his in. She handed him his shirt and jacket.

"Thanks a lot," Akira said, but she was already at the door, holding the curtain open for him. "I mean, '*gracias*,'" said Akira.

"*De nada*," she said, smiling a little crooked-toothed smile — her two front horse teeth pushing her top lip into a stupid pucker. He thought, for a moment, that maybe she was smirking. The curtain closed behind him.

"Yes — I did tole you, aye? You have goooood time..." said the thin man.

"Yeah, yeah. Real good," Akira said. Akira didn't know why, but he felt like he wanted to see her again. Not naked or anything, just see her, standing and smoking in her top and shorts, or talking or whatever. "Is she, uh, is she coming out?"

"No, no. She clean room. Very busy."

"Can you thank her for me?" Akira asked. "I tried to tell her, but I don't know if..."

The man laughed a little.

"*Sí, sí, señor*, I tell her." He laughed again, and looked outside. "Taxi waiting."

"Oh — okay, great. Thanks a lot," Akira stuck his hand out. The man chuckled again, then reached out and shook it. "I'll tell all my friends about this place, man...you all know how to do it up right!" Akira looked again at the red sheet over the door, then stepped out into the night. "This is probably the best whorehouse I've ever been to!" Akira said, but the thin man was already closing the door and smiling.

57

"You have good time, yes?" asked the cabbie.

"Of course," said Akira, in a way he thought people would say such things. *Typical man talk,* Akira thought. He told the cabbie where to go.

Yet, it was the way he'd said it — he just didn't sound like himself. *I'm not a virgin anymore,* he kept thinking — unsure if anything actually changed, or if it was all just in his mind. The cab bounced along under the occasional light and through the dark, dusty streets. What halide light there was shined on bombed-out buildings layered with graffiti, swirls and swatches of colors with names and what looked to be dates born and died. There were bars over every window, and every door, and tall cinderblock walls tangled with barbed wire — even a baby, barefoot and wearing only a diaper, standing alone in a dirt yard. Everything he saw made Akira feel more alone.

He had no idea where he was. The cab took turns and smaller alleys, barely streets. It creeped between humble homes, a few shops, and fewer lights. He felt the cabbie might be running up the fare. He was about to start some shit but stopped short — realizing he was truly lost. Again he tried his phone out of habit, hoping to use the GPS. Still dead.

"The Hotel Tulum is this way?" Akira asked.
"*Sí, claro* — this way."

Without the cab, without someone shepherding him through this godforsaken land, taking him where he wanted to go, without paying someone to help with everything he needed, he was stuck — utterly powerless, alone, and disgusted with his ugly, sad, and stupid life.

"Yeah," Akira said, "she told me I 'really did it,' man. World class." The cabbie laughed.

Even though it was impossible, he felt sure his mother knew…somehow she knew. Her spirit, or life force, or remnant energy was somehow aware and ashamed of him, ashamed *for* him. She was deeply disappointed on a separate, astral plane, hurtling through the dying universe and weeping. His guts shuddered, seized a bit.

Maybe just a good meal? Akira thought. *Yes, a good meal…spare no expense. Eat a fine meal, over-priced and extravagant, something to settle the stomach and calm the nerves.* He promised himself he'd treat himself to either *La Posta* or the Owl Bar on the way home — like his father had suggested.

His father. What his father would say, if he knew? Akira figured his father would be disappointed. His father was always disappointed. With everything Akira did or didn't do. He'd been young once, Akira thought, before mom...hell, he probably went to prostitutes too. Akira thought of his father, not as a soft-spoken and quiet man but as the young man he must've once been. He probably had a hard time winning over the girls too. He would probably sit at bars, alone and drinking for hours, talking to no one, no girls talking to him, before stumbling off to a whorehouse. Akira felt almost sure of it, and he had no idea what his mother ever saw in his father.

Akira finally recognized a street and knew they were close to downtown. Military trucks and soldiers with face masks and bandanas were everywhere.

"How come there's soldiers everywhere all the time?" Akira asked.
"Protection," said the cabbie, "from the cartels,"
"The people are in that much danger?" Akira asked.
"Not the people," said the cabbie, laughing. "Tourists."

The cab pulled in to the Hotel Tulum, and Akira pulled his wallet. He opened it and found all his money was gone.

"Oh fuck," Akira said. "No no no no…" He felt his pockets, more out of hope than anything. He instantly knew he'd been had. He didn't know how, or when…and he was mystified. *Must have been when my pants were around my ankles.* That was the only thing it could be. She must've slipped the bills out — that gypsy devil — and put the wallet back so he wouldn't know. *I'll go back, kick in the door, he thought, get my fucking money back.* But he had no idea how to get back there.

"That whore," Akira said. Inside his mind repeated *stupid, stupid, stupid, so stupid...*
"You have problem?"
"Yeah," Akira said, "I have a *GRANDE problema…*" His mind raced. "That whore stole my money."
"You no have money?" said the cabbie.
"Take me back there," Akira said, but didn't mean it.
"Maybe I call the police, eh?" the cabbie said.
"Will they do anything?" Akira asked. "Maybe you can take them…"
"Taking a cab without money to pay, *maricón,*" said the cabbie. "You are thief."

"What?" Akira said.

"You cheat me," the cabbie said.

"Cheat you? They stole from me!"

"The police decide."

"Wait," Akira said, his head drowning. "Don't call the police."

He stared at the back of the cabbie's fat neck, at his eyes flashing in the rearview as headlights passed. A panic twisted in Akira — his breathing shallow, his chest tightening as shame flushed red in his cheeks. He felt his bottom lip beginning to quiver, knew he had to fight to keep from crying.

"Maybe you give me your phone," the cabbie said. "For payment."

Akira saw the cabbie's fingers move from the steering wheel to the polished wood handle of what Akira figured must be a knife, hidden under a makeshift dash mat of cut carpet.

"Look, I'll get you money," Akira said, not knowing how.

"Money. Or *la policía*. Understand, *pendejo*?"

Akira spiraled. *Coward*, Akira thought. *Just roll over, why don't you…you fucking idiot,* he thought. *So stupid,* his mind said over and over.

"I have money in my room," Akira lied, opening the cab door and climbing out, looking for Nita through the lobby doors.
"You bring money here," the cabbie said, "or else."

Inside the hotel, half-panicked, Akira asked for Nita. The girl at the front desk disappeared, and Akira watched the cabbie through the glass front doors.

"Mr. Nakimura," Nita said, "what's wrong?"

He tried to explain, without saying how he lost his money. Nita instantly grabbed a bellhop, and walked outside. Akira followed, and as soon as they were all outside, Nita, the bellhop and the cabbie all started arguing. Akira didn't understand any of it. They went back and forth, rapid-fire and too fast to pick up anything but the bad words. Akira tried to explain:

"No, no," Akira said. "I need to pay him. I need money."

"This man cheated you," Nita said, turning to the cabbie, "*con la puta!*"

A valet joined in, hollering something about the police. The valet opened the glass lobby door and yelled to the desk girl before rejoining the fray. Nita told the cabbie to leave — or get arrested — everyone waving their hands wildly and swearing at each other. Akira stared on, amazed. He tried to mention the knife, but still no one listened. The cabbie swore and pointed at Akira, saying all kinds of things. Nita, the bellhop, and the valet argued back. The cabbie dropped his car into gear, and tore out of the parking lot — screeching his tires and flipping off everyone. When the cab was gone, Nita led Akira inside.

"He's gone," Nita said to the desk girl, and had her cancel the cops. Nita settled the rest of the staff down, got them all back to work. She then pulled Akira by the arm, away from the desk, to a quiet corner under the white noise of the waterfall above.

In a hushed voice she said, "You did go tonight to — um — you did visit a woman…yes?"
"Of course not!" Akira said, "I was at a bar."
"Okay," Nita said, "maybe you met a woman?"
"Well," Akira thought, "Maybe. Why?"
"The cab driver — he did help you meet the woman — yes?"

"Yeah."

"He already has his money," Nita said. "Your money."

Akira didn't understand.

"He did help the woman rob you." Nita said. "He tried for more money, yes?"

"My phone," Akira said, "even though it's dead." Akira tried turning on his dead phone, then pushed it away. "They all share your money."

She explained that these things happen, that she'd seen it a hundred times, that tourists are targets — not to feel bad. Akira flushed with shame. He'd been found out — exposed as a chump, a trick-ass mark, a sad and lonely little pervert who had to pay to lose his virginity with a skinny, bruised up whore and her fat, stinky thief-cabbie friend.

"It is no problem," said Nita. He wondered how that could be, how this could ever be fixed. "Tomorrow I will tell my boss you have lost your wallet — at HardPop. He will approve a small cash advance, charged to your room — okay?"

Akira shook his head. Nita picked up Akira's phone,

looked at it, then set it back down. She walked to the front desk, asked the girl for something — walked back with a small box. In it was a tangle of phone chargers, every kind imaginable.

"Here we go," she said, clicking one into Akira's iPhone. "People always leave these in the rooms."
Akira fought the urge to cry. "Thank you."
"Next time," said Nita, "keep your money in *tus zapatos,* yes?" pointing at her shoes with a wink.

58

Akira woke, shivering, desperate to piss and slightly hungover. The room was cold. He unplugged his phone from the new charger and checked the time — just after 4am. There were no messages, if the phone was even working. Akira punched the red square button on the heater. It hummed and coughed but spewed the same air. He went to piss then found a Mountain Dew Code Red in his mini-fridge. He cracked it, had a slug.

He slid the curtains open an inch. The city hardly moved and the streets were all but empty — maybe a haggard man milling about the closed gas station in the alley below. The noise of a far off siren seeped in, and the city lights shimmered in the cool, dry night. The heater finally started to spit out some warm air.

Akira went downstairs to let the room warm up some. At the business center, he logged on to eBay. He had one new message from a *divapink1989*. It was the exact same message as always, re-forwarded, this time with a 'Sixth Request' in big red letters — like she was some kind of lawyer or some shit . He logged on to Facebook and searched around for a profile picture of anyone named *divapink1989*. Nothing. He Googled "divapink1989," and found a chat forum about some stupid hipster band with comments by a girl with that handle. The profile photo was of a doughy little moonfaced rich girl, perfect white teeth, her profile littered with inane comments about how she couldn't wait for another album, how she always loved the early stuff, how the band had faded some but their last album was a return to form. Akira hated the band, and he hated *divapink1989*'s clichéd thoughts, life, and entire fucking existence.

The more he thought about it, the more pissed he got. Her daddy was probably a dentist, or some goddamned CEO, and her mom was probably fine, the happy little homemaker, living her precious little life of luxury. Stupid *divapink1989* probably always had the best of everything, never wanted for anything. They surely had a pool, hot tub, probably still had maids. Her family certainly knew lawyers, knew powerful business types who would tell them, over cocktails, how to get the best of Akira in this whole black-Jackie-soft-leather-top-handle-bag dust-up. He knew he was trapped.

Akira figured the only way to get her to shut up was to refund her money, or send her a replacement purse. He'd be goodgoddamned if he pulled any money from his mom's divorce account back home, so he dashed off a snippy email telling her to send the purse back — that he'd send out a replacement purse if he received it.

59

In the morning, Akira called the purse shop, but there was no answer. Nita was nowhere to be found, and Akira couldn't stand explaining it all to anyone else. He gathered what money he could find — loose change and a couple of stray ones from his jacket pocket — just over $4. He struck out early hoping to avoid seeing anyone who'd been around for the cabbie incident. Akira told himself that Nita was wise, savvy to the world, and obviously knew what was going on. But he worried the rest of the staff knew too — that they'd been laughing about him all night. He was convinced they were. He needed to avoid the hotel for a while, let the hubbub die down. He found an exit gate through the pool area so he wouldn't even have to pass the front desk.

He walked for a while, wondering just what the hell he thought he could do with $4. He hoped that the Hotel Tulum would front him at least a couple hundred — enough for purses and gas money home. If anyone could do it, Nita could. Until she did, he was stuck in Juárez, he was hungry, and he had no idea how the hell to get home.

He found a little breakfast spot. He decided his only chance of figuring his way out of it all was a decent bite to eat. He looked for the cheap section on the menu, and settled on chorizo and eggs. It was 20 pesos -or- $2 if paying with U.S. bills. It came on a paper plate, with a napkin, a plastic fork, and one corn tortilla. Rarely had Akira eaten a meal as delicious. As he mopped up the last of his plate, he felt his eyes well up a bit — overwhelmed by a quivering blend of sadness and joy. He got out before anyone could see him.

Back on the streets the sun was warm now, and the city had come to life. Shop owners were dragging tables and racks and carts and displays out on the thin sidewalks in front of their stores, and people were already haggling over whatever purchases they were eyeing. There was something heartbreaking about it, and again Akira felt stirred up and again didn't know why. Just my goddamned man-moons, he thought.

An older woman stopped him as he was passing by, asking him for something.

"I'm sorry," Akira said, "I don't understand."

She pantomimed a lifting action, flexed one arm and

pinched her muscle with the other, smiling. Akira smiled back, figuring she needed help moving something heavy. He followed her into the store. It was hardly the size of a closet, and filled with all kinds of religious figurines and tapestries and sculptures. Jesus painted on broken sticks, and in punched tin. The woman pointed to an old, metal milk crate. Stacked inside were a collection of tall glass candles with all kinds of religious pictures painted on the sides.

"*Veladoras*," the woman said.
"Very nice," Akira said, no idea what it meant and unsure if she even understood him.

She had Akira pick up the crate, and follow her back out to the street with it. She had a small table, which she patted — and Akira put the crate down.

"*Gracias*," she said, eyeing him.
"Oh, no problem. You're welcome."

She looked at him for a long second.

"You come to Juárez, you should speak Spanish," the woman said.
"I should," Akira said.

She looked at him for another long second.

"If you could have anything, what would you wish?"
"I don't know," Akira said.
"What about someone else," she asked, "what would you wish for someone you know?"

Akira couldn't think of an answer. He couldn't think of anyone except Nita. He thought about how she wasn't getting her raise, how she was mad about it.

"Money, I guess," Akira said. "For a woman I know."

The old woman rustled through the crate, finally finding the one she wanted. It was a green candle, the top sprinkled with gold glitter. Painted on the side was a grim reaper bride, and beneath that a smaller child skeleton holding a banner that read *"La Santa Muerte."*

"Offer her this," the woman said, handing it to Akira. "It will bring some riches."
"Oh, I can't" Akira said. "I can't afford it."
"You take it," she said, "for helping a poor old woman."

Akira took the candle, thanking her as she settled down in

a chair in front of her shop and looked as if she was instantly asleep. The more Akira looked at the candle, the more terrifying it seemed. Maybe it was a big joke, Akira thought. If I give this to Nita, maybe she'll think I'm giving her some kind of death candle. Still, the old woman seemed nice, and Akira didn't think she was trying to be mean to him. He decided he would give Nita the candle. It was the least he could do for her, he thought, *for saving my ass*. Akira decided it made perfect sense after all.

He walked the streets some more, but nothing was as good as the chorizo or the nice lady at the candle shop, and everything was too expensive anyway. He smiled when he realized that some people re-used the *velodora* glass from the candles to drink their *horchata*. Akira made his way back to the Hotel Tulum, and asked after Nita at the front desk.

"She'll be in at four," the girl said, "do you want her to call you?"
"No, that's okay," Akira said, wanting to ask if there was any money waiting for him. But he was too embarrassed, and just said, "I'll find her then."

Akira went to his room, filled the bath with hot water, and sank in for a long soak. He went under, submerging everything but his eyes and nose — listened to the odd thumps and underwater screeches of his skin against the tub. He breathed deep, and even fell out for a short little nap a couple times during the bath. When the water got too cold, or enough had drained away, Akira cranked the hot water back on and scooched back and forth to mix it in. When Akira finally got out, his fingers had pruned up. He swaddled himself with every towel in the room then tried some TV. It was no good.

He figured a nap would help, but couldn't fall asleep. He found what was left of his bottle of cherry Nyquil and took a shot, deciding it would do the trick. He set an alarm on his phone and was out cold in just a few minutes.

* * * * *

At 3:57 Akira grabbed the candle, and headed down to the lobby. Still groggy on the elevator ride down, he searched — not seeing Nita at the desk, or in the bar. He wandered around the pool, the small gym, the restaurant, and stopped in the business center — nothing. There wasn't anything worth reading online, so Akira went back to looking for Nita. After checking everywhere again, he stopped at the front desk.

"Is Nita here yet?" he asked.

"I think she's outside," the girl said.

Akira wandered to the front, not seeing Nita until he was almost at the doors. The afternoon sun was bright through the glass, and she was hanging in the driver's side window of a cab, talking. Not a cab...*the cab*...from the night before. Akira watched through the glass. *Just a Nyquil nightmare?* he thought. Akira tucked himself behind the fronds of a big palm and stared, hoping to make certain it was the cabbie who'd tried to rob him. It was unmistakable.

Nita wasn't exactly smiling, but she wasn't yelling either. The terse conversation ended and the cabbie handed Nita something — an envelope. She took it, saying something sharp to the cabbie, then walking away before he could respond. The cabbie watched Nita's ass as she walked back toward the hotel, then drove to the back of the taxi queue.

"*Bien, acérquense todos,*" Nita said.

The valets and bellhops gathered as she pulled a small stack of bills from the envelope. She counted it out as she spoke.

"*Por el momento — ese taxista puede regresar a la fila. Si tan siquera rechaza una tarifa o sobrecarga a uno de nuestros huéspedes, se va. Puede llevar a cabo cualqueir estafa en las calles pero no lo hará con los huéspedes del Hotel Tulum. Entendido? Reporten cualqier coso rean enseguida."*

The staff nodded.

"Bueno," she said, dividing the money equally among the staff and herself. Nita crumpled the envelope, and dropped it in the trashcan near the door.

Akira hid behind the bellhop carts until she was back inside. He felt his pulse in his ears, and he was breathing hard. He walked halfway around the hotel to a side entrance, used his keycard to get in, and took the stairs to his room.

He was sweating, and winded from the dizzy climb. He struggled to get his door key to work. When he finally made it inside, he put the candle by the TV and began eating — Cheeseburger Doritos, peppered beef jerky, the last of everything he could find in his room. As soon as he was done eating he started in: *you fat, ugly, stupid fucking idiot…* He grabbed a roll of flesh at his belt line and gripped it as hard as he could, hoping to somehow yank the swollen, doughy meat from his disgusting bones. He grabbed again and again, tearing at it with his fingernails. For good measure, he punched himself a few times in the gut — his *fat, ugly, stupid, idiotic gut*. Then he punched his face — which stunned him, causing a few twinkling white spots at the edge of his vision. The Nyquil joined in, everything clawing at the base of his skull as his pulse thundered and he breathed harder and harder still. Then, despite slamming the last can of Mountain Dew Code Red, Akira passed out.

60

At three in the morning, Akira woke, his fingers orange
from Cheeseburger Doritos. He found his own scraped
flesh under his dirty fingernails, and remembered why his
gut was now raw. He pissed, looked in the mirror: the new
scar on his chin, his chemically-burnt skin, a stupid gray
slop-mop, scabs at his knuckles, bruised elbows, an
accidentally slit wrist, torn skin on his fat gut. Akira
laughed at how stupid he was…how stupid he *is*. He
looked at the ceiling, looked at the candle, the palm tree
painting, at the heater, and at the curtains moving in front
of the black window.

Akira tried, but sleep would not come. He watched the
light slowly change behind the curtain, and when he was
satisfied that it was finally morning, Akira grabbed his
jacket and all his gear — headed down stairs. He would
not be staying on at the Hotel Tulum for another
goddamned second.

"Checking out," said Akira to the manager behind the
desk.

"It is understandable," the manager said, though he never said why. The man explained they could only offer him a small cash advance — $40 U.S. — billed to the debit card he usually paid with. Akira asked about Nita.

"She is in meetings this morning," the manager said. He asked if Akira wanted to leave a message.
"No," Akira said.

Akira had the valet, a man he'd thankfully never seen before, bring his car around.

"I lost all my money…sorry," Akira said, explaining away his lack of a tip. The man seemed annoyed but said nothing. Akira climbed in the Skyline and drove away.

The garage door that fronted the purse shop still sat there, dusty and unmoved. All the nearby shops were closed as well. Apparently it was too early to be hustling their bullshit. The more Akira thought about staying, the more impatient he got. He waited in his car, doors locked, for almost an hour — wishing he could sleep but equally terrified of what might happen if he closed his eyes.

The city slowly woke, the streets building to a hum. Shop-keepers and shysters unlocked grated storefronts and unbolted doors. They dragged tables out in teams, and quickly had their cheap shit strewn about — hats, shirts, sunglasses, all unnecessary junk. Everything but his purse shop opened. He checked a nearby competitor, but even Akira knew their purses were dogshit — just like the NMSU girls had said. After waiting another twenty minutes, unsure how he could get any purses even if the man did show up, Akira said, "Fuck it," and left Juárez.

At the border, Akira was asked more annoying questions than usual — the Mexican Border Patrol agents taking extra time with his car. He answered yes or no, offered little else.. Still they made him wait. He was hungry and just wanted out of Mexico, but couldn't waste any gas money on food…not until he was sure he could make it home.

"So, it's a really serious problem, then?" Akira said. "Japanese illegals…sneaking into America…through Juárez?"

The guards ignored him. Akira answered the same questions again, for a third agent this time — he was on vacation, he had nothing to declare but his genius. They looked at his license, sent drug dogs around his car, and weren't in any hurry to send him on his way. Akira boiled inside. *No more,* he thought. *No more taco hats, or nipple boots, and no more dirty fucking kids with chicle. No more snaggletoothed whore-thieves, or cabbies, or dumb college chicks down from State. No more assholes talking shit in strip club bathrooms. No more palm tree paintings. No more Quinceañeras. No more soldiers, no more gunshots or dead legs, and no more guys barking at him to come in to their store. No more graveyards, or pictures of pretty young girls gone missing. And no more Chinese fucking Gucci. No more Juárez. No more Mexico. 'No más.'*

Finally, and without much fanfare, they let Akira go and turned their drag-ass attention to the next car in line. Akira knew it was bullshit, that they took so long to simply justify their jobs, that they could quickly move anyone through. But he was finally moving again, and the farther he drove from the border the better he felt.

On the American side, it was surprisingly breezy this time — just a few questions, a quick look in the trunk, a check of Akira's driver's license, and they waved him through. He checked his phone every few miles, wondering when any messages caught in the queue might finally get delivered. After fifty miles he just accepted the fact that there were none and no one cared. He opened his center console, looking for some tunes, and found the $20 his dad had given him. He couldn't remember ever being as happy about finding money — certainly not since he was a small boy.

With his new-found wealth, he stopped in San Antonio, New Mexico for the world's best green chile cheeseburger. Inside the Owl Bar and Cafe it was dark, and cool — just as he remembered, though the jukebox was gone. The bar's shelves were jammed with old, wacky bottles of booze with names he didn't recognize, and the sweet old women waitresses hadn't changed a bit. He felt more at home there than he had in a good, long while. He'd supped at his can of Coke, staring at a bottle of Heaven Hill — wishing he had his fake I.D. His burger came out — hot, fast, and delicious — with his fries and a side order of beans and chile.

"Wow, already?" Akira said. "That was fast!"
The waitress smiled. "Anything else?"

He did some quick calculations.

"Yes," Akira said, "I think I'll take another burger."

He devoured the first burger, but leisurely ate the second — again wondering what kind of life he would live if he lived in San Antonio, New Mexico. It would be a small life, he thought, but probably a happy one. He paid, and left smiling. He forgot to ask the nice waitress why the jukebox was gone, but even that didn't bother him much. "I'll just ask next time," he thought.

At the gas station next door he topped off the tank, and was soon back heading north on I-25. The soft, flat hills were peppered with green, and it seemed clear that while down in Juárez he'd missed some rain. Another hour passed, and the harsh desert badlands slowly gave way to the distant jagged spine of the Rocky Mountains rising on the Northern horizon. *Home.* Akira decided that he needed a break, needed to settle back in, rest up, check his finances — figure out what the hell he was gonna do next. For a few long moments he was disgusted about not getting more purses, about not finding a way to make it work. Maybe I should've broke in to the shop and just stole some, he thought. He was tired and out of ideas.

61

At home, Akira jumped on his computer and found he'd missed nothing except an email from his father with return flight information. He said the whole family back in Japan was asking after Akira, and wished him good luck with his new job.

The house phone rang, and Akira didn't recognize the number, so he let it go to his parents' old answering machine. A voice echoed through the empty house:

"Yes, hello — I'm calling from Mailboxes, Etc. for Ms. Nakimura. I hope this is the right number…I guess the cell number I have isn't any good anymore. Any-who, you've got a package here that won't fit in your mailbox — so we'll hold it at the counter. Just be sure to ask for it next time you're in. Also, looks like you have some mail piling up too. Have a good day."

At his father's desk, Akira punched the erase button, told himself he'd sort it all out tomorrow. He marveled at the precise little stacks of bills and paperwork, insurance forms, stuff from banks, credit card companies. His father had regimented notes resting atop each pile, who he talked to when, their phone numbers. It was all overwhelming. On a notebook, Akira noticed lots of figures and notes — something to do with the laundromat they used to own. *That can't be good*, Akira thought, but otherwise had no idea what to make of it. It was his father's business anyhow — *let him sort all that shit out.*

Akira found his father's Lagavulin, poured himself a measure, and sat on the couch to think. He tried not to think of Zoë, of Nita, or the *divapink1989* situation. He was home. The door was bolted safe, his room dark and cool. There was no one around, and he didn't have to give a shit about anything or anybody. Despite everything he needed to sort out, Akira decided *I'm gonna sleep until I'm done sleeping*, and after downing the last of his glass of Scotch, that's exactly what he did.

62

It was late morning when Akira woke, rested and relaxed, having spent the better part of the past sixteen hours in bed — waking only to pee, drink some water, and go back to sleep. He felt strong, powerful, and decided he was gonna sort all this bullshit out. Akira took a bath, got dressed, grabbed his computer, and headed out.

He picked up the package and all the mail that had piled up at Mailboxes, Etc. Mostly it was junk mail — coupons from Staples or Office Depot, insurance quotes, phone and computer bundles designed specifically with his mom's small business in mind. There was what looked like the monthly bank statement from his mother's divorce account. Akira couldn't make himself check the balance.

The "Priority" box was from Sandy, Utah — fucking *divapink1989*, Akira thought. The handwritten note, in purple ink and a wide, looping scribble was dismissive and infuriating. Akira wadded it up, and for a moment thought about driving all the way there now that he had her address — dreamed about what he'd say when she opened her door. He laughed at his own imaginary insults.

Akira was starving and he needed a plan. He blasted Nas'
One Mic on repeat as he drove, contemplating. He
remembered an All You Can Eat Chinese Buffet where he
and his mother would sometimes go. He drove to the
Golden Lion and ate alone, plate after plate, free refills on
his Dr. Pepper.

When his guts were good and ram-packed, Akira thought,
*what the fuck are you doing, fat-ass? You're never gonna lose
any weight if you keep eating like Marlon Brando...* He tried to
ignore it. Akira paid, and figured he'd better go — that
something had to be done about this goddamned
divapink1989 situation.

At the highway off-ramp that led to all the malls, Akira
yanked the wheel right — deciding he'd check on any
purses they had in those wacky luggage shops, or the giant
chain stores. Maybe there would be some cheap shit on
sale that he could pawn off on *divapink1989*.

At the women's department in Dillard's, Akira searched
the racks for a purse similar to the one *divapink1989*
ordered. If this didn't shut *divapink1989* up, he didn't know
what would. Akira had no idea what the difference was
between most of the purses at Dillard's and the purses he

got in Juárez. He didn't actually believe there was much of a difference. People just imagined there was so they could justify spending more and feel special — as if their purse was different or better or something. He grabbed one that looked close, one sure to impress that Sandy, Utah pain-in-his-ass. He took the down escalator and, between floors, jammed the purse into the crotch of his saggy pants.

His heart began to thunder. His pulse throbbed in his ears. He figured the non-interference policy that the gutterpunk at his casino party mentioned meant that, unless he ran right into a guard, they probably wouldn't do shit, or even try to stop him. They were insured against "inventory degradation." He scanned the other shoppers as he made for an outer exit door, looking for anyone who seemed to be looking at him. No one was. He pushed through the polished glass doors, sunlight glinting off the brass in a slow, terrifying second…

Then he was outside. He burst into a full sprint. The purse gonged around his pants and Akira clutched everything with both hands. He figured he looked like some mad, cackling buffoon hurtling through the lot, hands on his junk. He promised himself that next time he'd remember a belt. To be safe, he threw the purse into his trunk, and continued on, past his car and out of the parking lot.

He crossed traffic and made his way to a movie theater nearby. Inside he bought a ticket, then stood watching out the window — pretending to check out the video games. He could see no one following, no one looking for him, no mall security, or sirens, or police cars or helicopters. He smiled — *pretty smooth*, he thought.

He bought some popcorn, a large Cherry Coke, then went into a completely different movie — just in case some cop came asking. He shut his phone off and watched the film. It was dumb — something called *Hot Tamale!* It starred Jessica Alba, Jennifer Lopez, and Eva Mendez as three sisters who inherit a hog farm. It was so stupid that Akira got up before it was over, and went to refill his drink and popcorn. He thought about getting his money back, but decided it was better to stay off the staff's radar. Instead of leaving, Akira decided that they owed him a better movie.

He popped into the theater where *Below the Belt* — some kind of heist picture — was just about to start. It was better: a washed-up boxer caught in a web of gangsters and match-fixers. Akira thought the criminals in the movie were stupid, none as brash or clever as his expert purse heist.

63

During the final credits, Akira sat, wondering what to do. It was after 9pm, and all the beautiful people would already be off doing whatever the hell they were doing — not that he wanted to see anyone, and not that he gave a shit. He turned his phone on and found a string of texts, and a couple voicemails from his father. Akira groaned but checked them. The flight had landed hours before, and Akira had forgotten to pick him up from the airport.

Such an idiot… Akira sat until the credits ended and the lights came on. The movie theater staff came in with brooms and rolling trash cans so Akira left, hoping security wouldn't be waiting for him outside.

The mall parking lot was vast and mostly empty — the only security to speak of was a golf cart puttering along and flashing its little yellow light a quarter-mile away. Akira watched, but it clearly had no interest in him, so he walked to his car.

He had no idea what he was going to say to his father when he got home, so instead he just drove around —

hoping an explanation would come to him, something his father would buy. Of course he was gonna blow a gasket — yammer on about responsibility and priorities and keeping promises and doing the right thing. There was nothing Akira could say — any explanation about Mexico, or purses, or whatever wouldn't help. His father wouldn't stand for any of what Akira was doing. *Probably best not to say anything at all.*

The streets were quiet, hardly any other cars about, and nothing much was open anywhere — not even the Village Inn Akira tried.

"Sorry, son…we close at midnight," an old man said, "weekly cleaning."
"You only clean this dump once a week?" Akira said, but the old man had already bolted the door.

When Akira was sure his father was asleep, he went home. His father's jacket and suitcases were sitting by the couch, and a light shined under his father's door. Akira hurried to his room. He was tired, but was too worried about his father knocking to fall asleep. Akira thought, waiting up for me like I'm some goddamned child out past curfew? The more he thought about it, the madder he got. Yeah, I fucked up, Akira thought. But if he knocks on my door, I swear I'm gonna tell him I'm not some punk-ass kid. I'm a grown-ass man, Akira thought, and I don't need any lectures, or anyone waiting up on me, or giving me a look and a little talking to whenever I'm out too late!

Akira brushed his teeth, staring in the mirror, fuming. The more he looked at his face, the more he hated it. His doughy jowls. His droopy eyes. They were too far apart, and they sagged at the outer corners, and they made him look like a fucking idiot. His stupid mouth was shaped like a frown, and when he smiled it looked false, looked pained, like he was annoyed and pretending to smile. And his hair. His hair was too much. The chemical burn had made it brittle as hell, and the peroxide and the dye job left it as crunchy as old, frayed rope. He rubbed for stubble on one cheek and found almost none — like a little bitch.

He scrunched his hand up into a fist and smashed his cheekbone a good one.

It rattled his head pretty good, and immediately began throbbing. Akira figured he'd better just go to sleep before things got even more ridiculous. He laid down with his throbbing cheek, his stupid face, his barn-straw hair, and fell out in a brain-dead exhaustion.

64

The sky was slate grey and it spit a cold rain all morning. Akira woke and, seeing it through the clerestories, stuffed his head back under a pillow. He did this over and over until it was early afternoon. He wanted to believe it was the weather, and that he was just tired, but he knew deep down he was still avoiding his father. He caught himself listening to the rest of the house, hoping some noise would betray his father — who would no doubt be sitting in the living room, waiting to corner Akira. There were no noises so Akira figured it was safe to get up and get dressed.

In the living room, his father's jacket and suitcases were still sitting by the couch. *Impossible.* His father would never leave stuff laying around all night and all morning. Akira found the calla lily — the one he'd forgotten to water, the one that was probably dead now — sitting in the kitchen sink, yellowed and dry. The soil was soaked and the tap slowly dripped. Another goddamned thing Akira fucked up. In his father's room he heard the toilet flush, and — in a panic — grabbed his keys, his phone, a jacket, a belt, and bolted.

Akira was a few blocks away before he even bothered with his phone. At lights and while driving he checked Facebook, Twitter, his mom's eBay account for orders even though he hadn't listed a new auction in well over a week. Of course he found yet another email from *divapink1989*, and another from Pam, the eBay D.R.O., again referencing the "incident number," — blah blah blah.

"Motherfucker!" he yelled, "I'm handling it!" Akira back-back-backed out of the goddamned screens without reading any more of that shit.

He found an office supply store and, inside, bought some packing tape, a Sharpie, and the cheapest box he could find. In the parking lot he popped his trunk, yanked the tags off the stolen purse, and boxed it up with a note:

> *divapink1989,*
> *We cannot replace your exact order as our inventory is in constant flux. This replacement item is both newer and more expensive. We trust this closes the matter in full.*

Akira scribbled some kanji which, according to his mom, said "fat, stupid round eye" — something they used to enjoy doing together — and signed his mother's name.

He taped it up, addressed it, and took it to Mailboxes, Etc. The woman behind the counter said nothing more than was necessary as she weighed the box, affixed the postage to it, and dropped it in the outgoing bin. Akira paid, then checked his mother's mailbox—finding nothing. It was way better than the post office and he decided to send stuff this way from now on. He was hungry, but had no idea where to eat. He checked his phone for nearby restaurants and, finding only expensive places, decided to drive around until he could think of some cheap place.

Another trip to Mexico was impossible. He didn't want to see Nita, and he was sick of everyone's lies, everyone's bullshit, everyone letting him down. And as much as he hated to admit it, Akira was worried about spending money. He wasn't rich, and he hadn't made it, hadn't landed some great job like his father used to have. He sucked, and he would continue being worthless until he could get his life back on track.

He let out a long, deep sigh. Akira felt sure that, until he scored some more purses, he'd just be damn careful with money. He probably had enough to get by. He could check — he could go to an ATM and check it right now. Even still, he had no idea how long it would take to find another way to get some decent purses — keep up his hustle. He couldn't think of Mexico…not right now.

And he had no idea what his father was doing or when he could go back home.

65

Akira decided to hit California Pizza Kitchen. He drove to the Uptown mall, found a spot. In CPK Akira declined an immediate seat at the bar, instead insisting on a table to himself. The hostess gave him a pager and put his name on the waiting list and he was quietly pissed at himself for insisting. He wandered around a few nearby shops, looking at all the shit people bought. Buying things made people happy, and buying more things apparently made them even happier. Akira scoffed at how stupid the world had become.

Over at the Apple store Akira looked at a MacBook Pro, the editing software, and thought again about all the great films he would someday make. He imagined getting guerilla-style street shots on the sly so it'd look like real life. He imagined shooting on location all over the state: White Sands, Santa Fe, Taos, Truth or Consequences. Hell, he might even actually go film at the Hotel Tulum — just to show all those fuckers.

"Interested in the new MacBook?" an employee asked. It was the same guy from before, but he didn't recognize

Akira.

"Probably gonna get a couple for my production company. We're raising capital for a location shoot all over the state, maybe Mexico."

"Very cool," said the salesman, "you've definitely come to the right place."

"I'm just putting together prices now."

"You gonna need editing software, maybe some extra SSDs?"

"Yeah, man," Akira said, "all that shit. Top of the line."

"Top of the line is all we do," said the salesman with a smile.

Akira's California Pizza Kitchen pager went off.

"Right on—I gotta roll. Production lunch."

"Good luck with the movie!"

Akira thanked the guy, and left. At the restaurant he settled into his large table and laughed to himself about the Apple dude probably not working the "genius bar." He ordered an appetizer, a pizza, and a peach lemonade because it came with free refills. He looked around at everyone. They all seemed happier than him, even the ones who shouldn't be. Akira decided it was just an act everybody put on, trying to pretend that life wasn't shit. He drained off his lemonade and asked for a refill.

And the more he thought about it, the more sense it made. *Just sell the real deal,* Akira thought, *why not? No more worries, no more problems. Not forever of course,* he thought, *just a few to tide me over…until I can get back to Juárez,* even though going back sounded like hammered shit. He figured it would work, *it was easy — non-interference policy and all.*

His appetizer came out and Akira decided that all it took was balls.

Akira ate his lunch slowly, deliberately, asking for three more refills before he was done. He paid the check, then made his way to Dillard's, deciding his dreams were worth the goddamned risk.

66

Akira felt his blood pulse in his ears as he pushed through the glass double-doors of Dillard's. He'd parked nose-out next to a couple of big SUVs, in case he had to dump his cache like before. It wasn't too busy in the store, not much traffic this early on a Tuesday. The terrible Christmas music played and the woman at the perfume counter accosted Akira with her spritzer.

"Your lady-friend will love this new scent," the woman said.
"My 'lady friend' hates me," Akira said, walking away while she pretended not to believe him.

He took the escalator up to the second floor, and did a quick pass through the designer purse section. There wasn't even a sales person at the section's desk. Quiet as a graveyard, Akira thought. He kept walking, eyeing a couple of decent purses on the racks near the aisle. He did a lap around Juniors & Petites, turning back once he made it to women's shoes. No one was watching him, so he took a quick shortcut through some racks, grabbed up four purses, and started for the escalator. His arm yanked back and the rack rattled loudly — one of the purses was attached to a locked security cable. Akira dropped it and kept going, his heart thundering in his chest.

On the escalator, Akira stuffed the purses down the front of his baggy pants, cinched up his belt, and took a few quick breaths. Everything in him said run, now, just get some distance between you and everything…but he knew that was ridiculous. Just be cool, he thought, be cool…

Akira smiled at the perfume girl, and he was almost to the double-doors when he noticed some white guy maybe eyeing him. At the doors, an alarm sounded, and Akira clutched his belt and broke into a sprint.

Over his shoulder he saw the white guy had just burst through the glass doors, and was very clearly after Akira.

Fuck fuck fuck fuck fuck was all he could think.

Akira ducked down behind a truck, tried skipping to another row of cars while trying to figure out where the hell his car was. He crouched as he ran, deciding to suddenly change directions, hoping it would buy him some more time.

"Over here!" Akira heard someone yell, and he took off again, in yet another direction, now certainly the wrong way from where his car was parked. Forget the car, Akira thought, just get the hell out! The parking lot started to thin out, so Akira reversed once more, staying crouched between cars as he made his way back towards the store. A few rows over were some trees, and foliage — and they seemed like a decent place to hide. He hiked up his falling pants, hoping to sneak out behind a passing car.

Akira was tackled from behind — and went scraping across the asphalt.

"You like stealing purses, faggot?" said the guard gripping Akira by the back of the neck, pushing his face down into the road.

"Quit fighting," said the security guard, "I'll fucking mace you."

Akira didn't think he was fighting, but whatever he was doing he quit. The guard grabbed Akira's arm, twisted, and bent his wrist back up high behind him. Pain shot through his shoulder and elbow, and Akira thought his arm might break.

"I'm not fighting! I give!" said Akira. "You're breaking my arm!"

"You think you're funny, huh? Stealing from us?"

Akira didn't think he was funny. He wasn't sure how to answer, so he said nothing. The guard released Akira's wrist a bit, but dug a knee in Akira's back for good measure. Akira's cheek was cold against the ground, and he could feel the same chill seeping through his clothes, his stomach and thighs. When Akira finally got a decent look at him, he was scowling, dough-faced, a few years older than Akira. His hair was wispy with gelled spikes and a soul-patch on his chin. He had a thin, shiny slather of sweat, and a moist ring around his Under Armour turtleneck. He squawked into a handheld radio.

"Code red. West lot," said the guard between panting breaths. "Subject in custody."

It squawked back, something unintelligible.

"Ten-four," the guard said, then handcuffed Akira. Akira wondered if that was legal. He remembered someone saying something about having rights while being detained or whatever. It didn't much matter now that he was already cuffed. The guard yanked the three purses from Akira's pant legs, still breathing hard, as Akira froze on the ground. The guard readjusted his Oakleys, tugged his fingerless gloves down tight.

Another security guard arrived — a bigger one. He was black, older — early 40s maybe. He was tall and thick and deliberate — basically chill about everything. His age, size, and demeanor — plus a suit jacket and badge — clearly made him the boss.

The white security guard and the black guard, using a small micro-recorder, conferred about how it all happened: the white security guard recognized Akira as a subject of interest from a previous incident and notified the in-store monitors; the white security guard took up a concealed position near the first floor entrance the subject used and waited; in-store monitors used cameras to track, witness, and record the subject as he grabbed multiple purses and stuffed them down his pants while on the escalator. The subject made for the exit in a hurried manner — making no attempt at any points of sale to pay for the merchandise. A foot chase ensued. The subject was eventually detained and the merchandise was recovered. They both tried hard to sound very official.

The black guard shut off the tape, and the white security

guard then began reliving the parking lot search, and the tackling action over and over while laughing — each time more incredible than before.

"Can I get up?" Akira asked.
"Shut the fuck up," said the white security guard.
"The ground is cold," said Akira. "I'm getting frostbite."

The white security guard started towards Akira, swearing. The black security guard stopped him with a big arm.

"Jesus, man — relax," said the black security guard. The white security guard scoffed. "Twist to the side, and pull your feet up to your butt," the black security guard said to Akira. "When I pull, sit on your bottom foot, and put your other foot on the ground — okay?" Akira did, and soon he was on one knee, sitting up.
"Thank you," Akira said.
"Sit right there for a second," said the black security guard, pointing to a curb. Akira felt sitting on the curb was much better.
"Stealing purses, man — you believe that?" the white security guard said to the black one.
"Why you take them purses, man?" the black security guard said.

Akira didn't know what to say. He thought about saying he needed them for his girlfriend, or for his Mom — but he didn't think the security guards would actually care. No one cared about anything, anywhere, and so even if it was true, it wouldn't matter. Nothing ever mattered, so Akira said nothing.

A man walked by with a little girl in a yellow dress with flowers. She stared at Akira. Akira tried to smile at her, so maybe she wouldn't be afraid. The little girl smiled back. The man huffed and then dragged the little girl along.

"What's going to happen now?" Akira asked. This time it was the guards who didn't talk to him. After a bit they pulled Akira to his feet, and walked him back into the store.

As they approached the glass doors, Akira noticed he was almost as big as the white security guard. Akira told himself that, had he known that beforehand, maybe he would've fought back — even though he knew that probably wasn't true.

67

Akira was taken back in through the store, past staring shoppers, and up an escalator. Near the customer service and returns counter, the white security guard opened a door with a key card. Akira was led down a hall to a small back room, something like a broom closet that had been converted into a security office. There was a metal desk with drawers that screeched when they opened, and four small black and white monitors, controlled by a joystick, that otherwise switched to different views of the store intermittently. The little TVs were really old. There were too many chairs for the size of the room and they stuck Akira in one made of a cracking orange fake leather. Against the back wall of the room was a rack of metal shelves, with office and cleaning supplies. There was a book sitting next to an unopened ream of printer paper. Akira couldn't read the title.

"…in the loss prevention office. Second floor," the black security guard said, then hung up the phone.
"What's that book up there?" Akira asked.
"Shut the fuck up," said the white security guard.

The white guard constantly twitched his neck to one side, his shoulders forward, and was always checking and rechecking the gear on his belt — making sure everything was in its spot, that snaps were buckled, and buckles were snapped.

The black security guard asked Akira a bunch of questions — his name, age, date of birth, social security number. Akira answered. The guard filled out the information on his form. The two guards talked about what each was going to write on their incident report, then filled them out.

"What'd this guy take? A purse?" asked the black guard.
"Three purses: Gucci, D&G — whatever that is, something else."
"How much?"
"$1000, easy."
The black security guard whistled. "Big time. That's a felony, son. 3 counts. Why'd you take 'em?"
Akira looked at him. "For a girl," Akira said, "a girl I like."
"Must be some girl," the black guard said. "She worth it?"
"Probably not," said Akira.
"Be sure to tell her you got busted trying to get her something nice. Maybe she'll go for it," the black guard said. "Some chicks are crazy like that."

"Bitches," said the white security guard. "Bleed you dry, I swear."

Akira sat for a while, listening. The white guard talked about testing for the academy, how he couldn't wait to be a cop. The black guard was only half-listening, watching shoppers on the closed-circuit TV cameras.

"Why would you want to be a cop?" Akira asked the white guy.

The white guard instantly bowed up. "Well unlike you, fucko, I'm gonna do something with my life. Serve my city."

"It's better to be a flower delivery guy."

The white security guard stood. "What would you know, you piece of shit thief?"

"No, seriously. No disrespect." Akira said. "Even if you are the best cop that's ever been…if you're fair, always do right by everyone — most of the people you deal with are gonna hate you." The white guard scowled but didn't say anything. "But a flower delivery guy…hell, everyone is happy to see him."

"Yeah, well, maybe I fucking care about my God and my country! And I sure as hell didn't serve in Iraq and Afghanistan to sit and listen to a lecture from some punk-ass thief!"

"I served."

"Oh, you served? Where? At the Furr's All You Can Eat?"

"I stormed the beach at Normandy," Akira said. The black guard chuckled a little. "Me and J.D. Salinger 'saved your precious Europe...'"

White Boy stood over Akira, almost shaking. The black guard got up from the desk and stepped between them then turned to the white guard.

"Just relax," the black guard said. The white security guard started laughing — an intentionally snarky laugh.

"Fuck this punk," White Boy said. "Maybe I'll just check out the tape..."

He sat at a monitor, and rewound the video footage. He watched himself tackle Akira and handcuff him over and over — laughing every time. He was especially fond of the part when he pushed Akira's face into the ground. The white security guard asked the black one if they were going to turn over the tape.

"If they ask for it," said the black security guard, "they never do."

"Well just in case," the white guard said, and he pulled out his phone. This time as he replayed the footage he narrated like a play-by-play sportscaster while recording it all with his phone.

"…then shit-bird makes a run for it… Oh!" he yelled, right at the moment Akira was crushed into the ground. "That's gonna leave a mark, Bob!" He rewound it, showed the tackle again, rewound it, showed it in slow-motion — every time adding a "boom-shaka-lacka!" as he crushed Akira.
"Man," said the black guard, "knock that shit off."

The white guy stopped recording, then played the video back a couple times — giggling.

"I should post this shit on YouTube." He turned to Akira. "What do you think?"

Akira couldn't stand it. He wanted to smash the guy's skull in, gouge his eyes out, bite his ear off — something. Instead he sat, cuffed and beaten and boiling, saying nothing.

"Not so smart now, are you bitch?" he asked Akira.
"Hey," said the black guard. "Why don't you go scope that dude in Section H. Might be that BOLO from yesterday."

The white guard stood there, unmoving.

"Fine," the white guard said leaving.

Akira and the black security guard sat in the small room
for a while, waiting for the cops. The black security guard
told a story about a guy who got fucked up at his last
security job — some dude was accidentally run over by his
buddies in the get-away car.

"The back tire got him right up the back of his leg.
Snapped his ankle something fierce," said the black guard.
"And his buddies left him! Tore ass outta there, ran him
over, then left him." After a pause he said, "You didn't
have anyone waiting on you out there in a car somewhere?
They leave you too?"

"I don't have anyone," Akira said.

Akira looked around the shabby little room, not much
bigger than a cell, Akira thought. The black guard sat at the
bank of small TVs, using the joystick to follow the white
guard as he made his rounds. On the monitor, Akira saw
the white guard walking, arms all puffed out, saw him
start talking to a couple of young girls.

"What's that guy's problem?" Akira asked.

"Who knows?" the black guard said. "White boy takes this

shit way too personally."

On the monitor, Akira saw the white guard flicking
through his phone one-handed, chest puffed out and
posturing, re-watching the video. He held the phone up to
one of the hidden cameras in the ceiling, and pointed at
Akira on the screen, laughing. The white guard pinched
his radio, and his voice crackled through the black guard's
radio on the desk.

"So, what do you think," the radio said, "should I upload
this shit or what?" On the screen the white guard laughed
silently.
The black guard grabbed his radio and said, "You post that
shit, and they find out at corporate, you're gonna get both
our asses fired, fool."

And for a moment on screen it was obvious — the white
guard hadn't even thought of the possibility. He went back
to wandering the store.

"He's not really gonna post that, is he?"
"He damn well better not," said the black guard.

Akira asked the black security guard if he wanted to be a
cop too.

"Aw, hell no," the black guard said.

"Right? Why would anyone want to be a cop?"

"It's a job, I guess."

"A shit job." Akira said. "I'd rather work at Ginger's Burgerhaus."

"Let me guess," the black guard said, laughing. "You have a hard time with everyone, don't you?"

"They don't respect me."

"Well why would they?"

Akira didn't know what to say.

"You want some advice?" the black guard said, surprising Akira. "Don't admit anything to the cop. Just makes things worse."

"Okay," said Akira.

"And any decent girl won't need shit you can't afford, dig?"

"Dig."

Akira sat, wondering why the black guard was being so cool. It had to be some kind of trick, he thought, trying to trip him up somehow. Or maybe the cops thundered you even harder if you didn't say anything. Nothing made sense. White Boy returned from his rounds, annoyed.

"What's taking them so goddamned long?" White Boy said. The black guard just shrugged his shoulders, watching customers on the monitors. "Should I call again?"

"I doubt it'll help," the black guard said.

"I'm calling."

White Boy picked up the office phone, tucked it between a shoulder, and dialed. He asked where the officer was, that they had a subject, felony shoplifting.

"Well, I mean, how long are we talking here?" White Boy said, getting short with the dispatcher. "This is taking forever." He listened and uh-hummed before finally hanging up.

"What'd they say?" the black guard asked.

"Said they'd 'get here when they got here,'" said White Boy, "the pricks." He took out his phone, started flicking through it one-handed.

Akira smashed his head into White Boy's hand, sending the phone clattering to the concrete floor. Akira smashed the phone with his heel — two, three, four times — before White Boy even realized what had happened.

"You motherfucker!" White Boy said, running Akira into the metal shelves, and punching him a couple times before the black guard could wrap White Boy's arms, and pin him on the other side of the room.

"The hell you doin'?!" the black guard said, "He's in cuffs!"
"Fuck him!"
"Jezus...just go wait downstairs," the black guard said. White Boy didn't move. "Now!"
"Keep that motherfucker away from me..." the white security guard said pointing at Akira, who smiled back through his bloody teeth. White Boy picked up his smashed phone, turned back at the door saying, "...before I teach his ass some serious respect," then stomped out.

After a minute, the black guard said, "You okay?" Akira shook his head. "You ain't too sharp, but you got stones — I'll give you that."

The black guard took his water bottle, wet a wad of gauze from the first aid kit, and daubed Akira's lip.

He chuckled a little. "Crazy shit, man," the guard said. Akira laughed, remembering the look on White Boy's face when he first head-butted the phone.

The black guard then pulled out a new incident report form, and started filling it out — grumbling about more goddamned paperwork. Akira sat, saying nothing. When he was done, the guard gathered up his jacket, the two reports, and helped Akira up.

"Sorry about your girl, man" he said. "They drive you crazy if you let 'em."

On the way out Akira looked at the bookshelf — some kind of karate book. Akira was relieved to be led through the hidden offices and back halls of the giant store instead of the sales floor. Downstairs they both sat waiting on a curb facing the parking lot. The black guard lit a small cigar, drew on it.

"Could I have one of those?" Akira said.

The guard gave him a look and a little laugh. He unhooked Akira's cuffs, tapped one out of his pack, and handed it over with a lighter. Akira lit up — coughed.

"How long you smoked?" the guard asked.
"About thirteen seconds," Akira said, exhaling.

The guard laughed.

"It's a bad habit. You should quit."
"I'll quit after this one."
"That's what I always tell my wife."

Again the guard laughed, and they both smoked a while. A black APD car rounded the building, slowly driving the perimeter. The white guard, waiting at the far corner, hopped up and ran over to meet the car.

"Okay, show time," said the black guard, pinching the cherry off, crushing it underfoot, then slipping the cigar stub back in the pack. Akira did the same, tucked his stub behind his ear.

"Don't let me catch you here again," the black guard said and Akira nodded. He stuck out his hand. Akira shook it.

The white guard walked alongside, talking non-stop through the passenger window as the cop car slowly trawled along — eventually pulling up to where Akira and the black guard were waiting. White Boy was still yammering when the cop zipped the window up mid-sentence. The cop then sat for what seemed like a long time, while the white guard, almost bouncing with

anticipation, eyed Akira. As soon as the cop got out, the
white guard started back in:

"Like I said," the white guard said, "we need to amend the
Criminal Complaint to include destruction of my personal
property…"
"This gentleman head-butted your phone?" the cop asked.
"And stomped it," the white guard said. "Three times!"
"He used his phone to film beating me up!" Akira said.
"You filmed beating this guy up?"
"Detaining him," the white guard said, "I was detaining
him — for stealing over $1000 from us."
"He said he was gonna post it on YouTube!" Akira said.
"Sir," said the cop, "do you need medical assistance?"
"I'm alright," Akira said.

It was clear the cop was already sick of the situation. He
cuffed Akira, turned him around to look at the busted lip.
He helped Akira into the back seat of his car and turned to
the black guard.

"You the supervisor?"
"That's me," said the black security guard.

The cop closed the door and Akira couldn't hear them. He
watched as the cop and the black guard talked. White Boy

tried to interrupt, but the cop held up a hand like 'sit dog.' The black security guard handed over all the reports, pointing from Akira to White Boy to himself while relaying the story. The cop then asked White Boy a bunch of questions, while the black guard went back into the store. White Boy didn't seem to care for any of what the cop was saying, which Akira was glad to see. The cop lectured him for a minute while White Boy just shook his head 'okay.' They shook hands, and White Boy walked off. The cop got back in the car.

The cop fired the engine, and started looking at his cell phone. While he did, the black guard knocked on the cop's window. The cop rolled it down, then handed back one of the reports.

"Okay," the black guard said, and ripped it up. "He's cool with that?"
"You'll have to ask him," the cop said.

The cop dropped the car into gear, rolled his window back up, and left.

68

Akira sat in the backseat of the cop car, outside some sort
of detention facility in the middle of an empty mesa. The
cop was typing away on his various machines, putting the
finishing touches on his report. Akira thought about all the
movies he'd seen where someone was about to go to jail,
how they had to look tough, or insane so no one would
fuck with them. He hoped he looked tough and insane
enough.

"You should've done this a couple years ago," the cop said,
"it wouldn't have been a big deal."
"My mom always said I was a late bloomer," Akira said.
"She must be very proud."

The cop typed.

"Which is it? N-A-K-I or N-A-K-A?"
"N-A-K-A-M-U-R-A," said Akira.
"This says N-A-K-I..." the cop said.
"No one knows how to spell Japanese names."
"So which is it?" said the cop.
"Just put 'fat Asian kid'—that's what I am."

"So you want to tell me what happened?" said the cop.

"I think I need to talk to a lawyer," said Akira.

"A lawyer?" The cop chuckled. "What's a lawyer gonna do for you?"

Akira wasn't sure what a lawyer was going to do for him.

"Can I call someone?"

"You'll get a telephone call after you're booked," the cop said.

The cop finished his typing, then walked Akira through a backside entrance to the giant building. The cop emptied Akira's pockets, then stuck all of his stuff in a manila envelope before taking Akira to a holding cell.

"They'll process you in a while," the cop said, and left.

Akira stared around the room at the other arrested men. There was a station set up for digital photos, and another for fingerprinting, other paperwork — but everything was pretty quiet. The guards all looked angry and bored and the criminals weren't much different. Two were talking in Spanish, even laughing — but everyone was waiting to be somewhere else. One guy, the one Akira figured was the real hard case because of his tattooed neck, sat silent —

eyes shut, just waiting. Akira did the same, sure they'd all see through his bluster if he said anything.

"Hey," someone said to Akira. "That a blunt?"

Akira had forgotten all about the cigarello stub behind his ear, and somehow so had the cop. He fetched it.

"Naw," Akira said. "Just a swisher."
"Spark it," the man said.

Akira didn't know what to do. He felt sure it was some kind of test. If he gave it over, he was soft. If he didn't, these guys would probably fuck him up. He tried to stall.

"Anyone have a light?" Akira said.
A guard just outside said, "No smoking."
"Well, I mean…I'm already in jail," Akira said, "is there another jail for smoking?"

Everyone, even the hard case, laughed a little. Akira crossed the holding cell.

"It's all yours, man" Akira said, handing the stub to the guy who'd asked about it. Inside his guts wrenched and his chest was tight — but it seemed okay, like maybe no one was gonna mess with him. He sat down in a dark corner, closed his eyes, and leaned his head back against the cold, dirty paint — and didn't move until the guards called his name.

After Akira was processed he asked for his phone call. They sat him at a phone, and Akira realized he didn't know any of his friends phone numbers — they were all just icons in his contacts list to tap and dial. He asked for his cell phone and the guard ignored him.

Akira said, "Can you search my contacts then, and get me a number?"
"No."

After sitting and staring at the phone for a while, Akira gave up and dialed his father.

69

In the car, Akira's father said nothing.

Not: "I am ashamed of you, Akira."

Not: "You're a liar and I can't trust anything you say."

Not: "You have disrespected your mother and you have dishonored me."

Not: "You have poisoned our family name in the community."

Not: "You are too old to be acting like such a goddamned child."

There were no long, drawn-out pauses after each sentence.

Akira listened to the car, the tires over the tarred seams in the cracked, wet pavement. *Tha-thump, tha-thump, tha-thump* — the odd kind of rhythm of it. He was tempted to apologize, to say something, *anything*. But he could think of nothing that would satisfy his father, and it had grown so big that talking about it had become pointless.

When they got home, his father pulled into the garage, unhooked his seat belt, and simply said, "I need to think long and hard…decide if you will be allowed to remain in our home."

70

Akira stared at the ceiling in his room. He heard his father clanging around in the kitchen. Akira closed his eyes and tried to empty his mind. There was too much, and all at once — too much to sort out alone. His body was dirty and tired and ached all over. All Akira wanted to do was sleep, but no sleep would come.

He checked his phone. 37% battery, no notifications, no messages, no texts. He could still hear his father in the kitchen, fighting with some pots and pans. It went silent for a few long moments, and there was a knock at his bedroom door.

"Come in," Akira said.
"I'm going to get something to eat," Akira's father said.
"Do you want anything?"
"No," Akira said, even though he did.

His father left.

Akira logged on to Facebook. Everyone's posts were stupid, and there were no messages, no new friend requests, no alerts for him. No one had posted anything on his wall. No one poked him, or commented, or liked anything. No one posted photos in which he was tagged. No one acknowledged his human presence in any way. He posted:

just back from jail, yo. thug life.

He could see that two of his friends were online, but neither responded. Akira logged out.

He checked Twitter, Gmail. There were no Tweets or Retweets about him, only spam in his Gmail account — Canadian pharmaceuticals at massive savings, horny girls looking for a date, pills for erectile dysfunction. Akira felt that, in a way, he was already dead. Then he wondered how long it would take, if at that moment he killed himself, until anyone realized he was dead.

He logged back into Facebook — still no responses to his jail post. No "holy shit, what happened?" or "that sucks, lousy pigs - ftw!" or anything. No one said anything. No one cared. Akira posted:

don't know where y'all are. sure, you're too busy to care or whatever. I get it.

He logged back into Gmail, hoping to catch someone online. Only one of his contacts had a green dot next to their name. He clicked "Chat" and typed:

akinaki93: wuzzup, ese? just outta the clink, yo. jail.
akinaki93: shitz fucked up, man.

Akira waited for a response. The green dot next to his friend's name suddenly turned into a orange clock which seemed to read 9 o'clock.

"Motherfucker!" Akira said, and logged out of Gmail.

He scrolled through his phone, selecting contacts and calling them. He tried three people, got voicemail for all of them. He found Zoë's phone number. He selected it, and his thumb hovered over "Call." He looked up at the ceiling, eyes blurred by tears — then deleted her number.

And the more Akira thought about it, the more clear it became. He was alone. Utterly and completely alone in the world. All these so-called fucking friends of his — they had phones and computers with them at all times, they were *never* not on them, so when he tried to call or text or chat or tweet to them, they got it, oh they fucking got it alright — they just ignored him. They ignored him like he was some fucking chump-ass, whiny bitch. They weren't friends, how could they be? When he was out here, dying, and utterly alone, and they can't even be bothered to click like or return a text, a call, nothing.

They disgusted Akira, all of them — all wrapped up in their own pathetic shit as if any of it mattered at all. Who were they? What had they been through? What did they fucking know about anything? And fucking Zoë, with her Mr. Jeep Wrangler. She was the worst…entitled, preening — she didn't care. No one cared. No one gave one squirt for him, and he knew it. It made Akira physically ill. Akira felt his guts roil, and he rushed to the toilet to vomit. He retched and retched and retched, but nothing came. Just the acrid sting of pointless retching…and the deep down metallic taste of blood.

No one cares. No one. Anywhere. He could prove it, Akira thought. Yeah, I'll fucking prove it — right now.

Akira logged back into Facebook. Still no responses, no posts on his wall, no personal messages. There was nothing. Nothing. Akira posted:

dig this, bitches: killing myself if no one posts to stop me.

Akira logged into Twitter. Same old shit in his feed —
everyone on and on about their useless bullshit, no one
saying anything to him. He Tweeted:

killing myself unless I hear back. hit me up. or don't.
#AkiraSuicide #DoneFuckingCaring

There was some juice in it, the hairs on his neck stood a
little. He wondered if it would work. Maybe someone
would call the cops, try to save him. Akira sat, waiting for
his phone to ring, a text, something. Surely someone had to
say something, to respond, even if it was just to say "not
cool" or maybe even tell him not to do it. He logged into
Gmail and changed his status to "gone too soon." He
stared at his friends on chat, noticing that a couple had
little green cameras or dots next to their profile names and
were currently online. No one said anything or commented
on his posts anywhere.

He made sure the volume was up on his phone, and still
there were no notifications. He logged back into Facebook
and clicked over to a few friends' pages just to be sure that
his posts were being fed to their walls. They were — all
sitting there, glaring and ignored. Akira refreshed the page
over and over, hoping a lagging response would appear.

[Refresh.]

[Refresh.]

[Refresh.]

The same page reloaded each time, no responses. He clicked harder. And harder. A new post from someone else popped up, something about a grumpy cat and Tommy Lee Jones.

Akira clicked on Zoë's page. She'd changed her pic to a selfie — her and the blond dude, both in sunglasses, cheek to cheek, sitting in the fucking jeep as the setting sun showed pink and purple on the Sandias behind them. Akira smashed the [Escape] key on his keyboard — over and over and over.

[Escape]

[Escape]

[Escape]
[Escape]
[Escape]

The screen blitzed-out and glitched, struggling to hold the image. So Akira smashed it harder. And harder still. The screen finally went black.

He slammed the computer closed, picked up the laptop, and held it high, turned it over, and clapped it down on the concrete floor. It shattered. Akira picked up the biggest piece, and threw it against the sheetrock wall. It cut a deep, satisfying gash in the chalky gypsum before clattering back to the floor.

Next Akira grabbed his iPhone, his alarm clock, his flatscreen TV, his Xbox — anything that plugged in, anything with a low-grade, nauseating hum or buzz or crackle of white, electric noise. He smashed each in turn, one, two, three bashes or more, whatever it took. He was panting, and there were noises spilling from him — noises he was not trying to make but that came out anyway. His body thrashed, seized, bucked and a furious red heat engulfed him, starting at the back of his neck and washing over his head, flushing his face, then spreading like poison through his chest, stomach, and into his writhing limbs.

In his bathroom mirror he saw his huffing, puffing, hideous fucking face in the mirror. He punched it. The mirror spidered, showing him a thousand hideous faces. He grabbed his clippers and *buzzed buzzed buzzed* at his stupid grey hair on his fat, stupid head. He saw nicks on his palms, and a thousand tiny cuts on his thousand tiny scalps in the mirror.

Tears splintered all the points of light in the dark room, and his shirt had come halfway up his back, leaving his naked flesh cold against the floor. Sniffles and small whines pierced through the quiet. Snot ran down his lip, down his wet cheeks. Akira laid there, determined not to get back up.

On his back, he looked over at all he'd done. His father was gonna murder him. He had to get out, had to go, just get the hell away. He found his feet, grabbed his wallet, his keys, a jacket and left — he just started walking.

71

Akira walked, determined to get back to the Skyline — still sitting at the mall parking lot.

His body rocked violently with thundering jerks brought on by his silent sobs. Pain seared through him. He wanted to vomit but none would come. It wasn't crying, really. It was more of a muffled kind of deep, strangled scream — a kind of whine, choked out and held deep down inside him. The only thing that staved it off was the steps, one after the other, as he walked alone in the dark. He stuck to residential streets, avoiding any major roads. If he noticed anyone within earshot, he would clamp his insides down tight, hide his sobs until they were gone.

He found a drainage ditch, one he knew would get him close to the mall, and walked it instead. And when some goddamned jogger came up on him from behind, thankfully wearing earphones so he probably didn't hear anything, Akira took to walking in the actual ditch itself, disappearing in tunnel underpasses, and stepping over half-buried shopping carts and other trash — alone with himself. He walked. That's all he did. He didn't think, just walked. At the busier intersections above him, he'd pop up to see where he was — but otherwise he kept to his ditch.

It took a couple hours, but he made it to the Skyline. He sank into the front seat — his legs numb from walking in the cold. He turned the car on, cranked up the heater. He remembered an extra pair of gloves he had in his trunk. He punched the trunk button, and searched the back. He could only find one, next to the *La Santa Muerte* candle.

He plopped the candle in the passenger seat, dropped the car into gear, and made his way to the Interstate.

72

I-40 East was a straight shot through a deep slice between the Sandia and Manzano Mountains lining the eastern edge of town. He'd made the drive any number of times with his mother, East to the North 14 exit, through Cedar Crest, then turning off to slowly climb the backside of the mountain. For years as a child, Akira rode in the back of the car while his mother swore at everyone on the road, smoked too many cigarettes, and talked to herself — always when she was upset.

"This is no world for a woman," he remembered her saying the last time he went with her — when he was ten, maybe eleven.

She'd slow as they rounded a big corner some eight miles in — a thick granite face lining the left side of the road and occasionally dropping chunks of broken rock. To the right side, as the road finally cleared the forest was a sudden switchback to the left. She'd nose the car right up to a flat spot just next to the end of the guard rail. They'd sit on the hood, over looking the expansive horizon and the drop down the granite face to the forest hundreds of feet below.

She'd sit and smoke and Akira knew not to ask any
questions — to just wait until she said something before
speaking. Once she told him about a place called Tōjinbō,
but usually she didn't say much. He would fly his
spaceships and his legos over the chasm and wait. Despite
the deep, strange pull of the edge, he always felt the place
was serene — beautiful even. This was their place — her
place, really — another thing he didn't think his father
used to know about.

Around one bend his lights caught three deer in the road.
They sprang off before he could get a decent look.
Rounding the big corner Akira noticed that they'd installed
a brand new guard rail where they always used to park —
extending it another twenty feet. A little late for that, Akira
thought. Akira inched forward, his headlights shining on
the bright, galvanized metal, until his bumper nudged it.
They'd called it an accident — said maybe she swerved to
avoid something in the road, that she probably didn't have
enough time to brake. It was an unfortunate coincidence —
wrong place, wrong time, they said — nothing anyone ever
could've foreseen.

Akira grabbed the candle from his passenger seat, got out,
and looking back at the road, lined up what seemed like
the exact spot she'd gone over. The approaching blue

morning glowed behind the curve of the far Eastern horizon, and Akira choked on the harsh and bracing frozen air. He set the candle on the thick square block of wood newly cemented into the cliff's edge, just above the rail's rivets. Akira found three flat rocks — small, smaller, and smallest — and stacked up a tiny cairn next to the candle, then got back in the Skyline. Akira switched his only glove to his freezing hand and stared out past the candle and the cairn, out past where his headlights reached.

He felt his haggard muscles, felt the deep ache in them, how they wanted to give out. *Rest*, he thought. He knew he'd have to face his father, that there was certainly going to be hell to pay.

He'd pay it later, when he was ready — when he could stand some more.

Until then, he'd rest...*just get a little rest.*

Akira thought of palm trees, the fronds, the trunk bent in a fierce wind.

He thought of the sound of water, tumbling water, and slowly fell asleep.

EPILOGUE

Akira passed through the metal detector, and signed in with the receptionists at the front desk of the District Attorney's Office. People came in and out — attorneys and cops, people doing interviews, or moving boxes of files. It didn't seem like the TV shows. It was just an office. Akira had a seat in the lobby, opened his book, and waited to be called. He waited about ten minutes.

"Mr. Nakimura," said Akira's PPPP Officer. "Come on back."

Akira shook the woman's hand in the hall, then followed her to a small office. She pointed him to a chair, and again he sat.

"So, Akira, how are you doing?"
"Good," Akira said, pulling out a cashier's check for $50.00. He slid it over.
"Excellent," his PPPP Officer said. She jotted down some notes, entering the amount on a ledger. "Still living at home?"
"Yep."

"You ever thought of getting an apartment? A place of your own?"

"Someday. I just want to get square — get past all this."

"And work?"

"I'm still at the laundromat."

"And this is your father's laundromat, correct?"

"Yeah," Akira said. "We used to own it. Before. My dad bought it back after…with the money from my mom."

"You like working for your dad?"

"Yeah, it's okay." Akira said.

"Are you applying anywhere — schools, programs, anything?"

"We talked about registering for some classes next fall. CNM, UNM — something."

"What would you study?"

"I don't know. Film, probably."

Akira and the woman talked for a while — as they had every month since being accepted in the Pre-Prosecution Probation Program. It was — according to their shyster attorney — the best they could've hoped for. If Akira kept his nose clean, and if he paid back Dillard's for the purse he actually did steal, the case against him would be "deferred and dismissed." There'd be no conviction to sully his record, or prevent him from getting gainful employment throughout his life — his father insisted on that. The woman assured Akira he was on the right track, that as long as he stuck to his contract he was well on his way to being clear of his debt to society. She was a kind woman, attractive, and wasn't too hard or judgmental. She made Akira feel okay about having made mistakes, and even better about owning up to them. Like a man, he thought.

*   *   *   *   *

Akira wiped down the tops and fronts of all the washers and dryers with Windex and paper towels. He removed all the lint from each trap and filter, careful to check inside every machine as he did. He found a forgotten load in one of the last washers. When he first started back, Akira would ask his father what to do — but now he knew: go ahead and load it in a dryer and run it for whoever forgot the clothes.

"That way," his father explained, "the clothes were either already clean for the Lost-and-Found, or the customer would be grateful — and stay loyal to us."

Years before, when they first had the laundromat, Akira's mother insisted on sticking wet loads in plastic grocery bags, and leaving them outside to be stolen or to rot.

Akira pulled all the coin catches, and dumped them in the canvas bank bag. In the office his father would dump all the change in a fancy coin separator that was supposed to automatically roll them for deposit. The plastic hunk-of-junk hardly worked, and they often spent another half-hour checking and fixing what the hand-sorting machine had messed up. Akira was always amazed at his father's reaction to it: every single time it was one of bemused chuckles when it didn't work right, and audible delight when a coin roll came out properly.

Next Akira ran the HOKY over the old glued-down carpets, swept and Swiffer-ed the tile. He cleaned the bathroom: scrubbing the toilet, sink, mirror, and mopped the floor with bleach. Akira tossed the bathroom trash into one of the larger cans, yanked the sacks, and relined each one. Finally he rolled all the bags to the dumpster in one of the wire laundry baskets, and dumped them out back.

If he had to, he could do all the closing cashier duties too — but most nights he and his father worked the closing shift together, to save money on staff. His father handled the register, and would often pitch in and help Akira restock the vending machine with mini-boxes of detergent, fabric softener, and meadow-scented anti-static dryer sheets when he was finished putting together the deposit. Thankfully his father would also deal with any last minute customers banging on the glass after last load, or trying to sneak in and start a fresh load or bargaining for more time. His father managed to always be friendly and fair, even while rarely letting the customer in. "Only wash," his father would offer, "you can hang it to dry at home" — to which most simply decided to return the next day. It was nothing like the wars he watched his mother wage for years with customers at closing time.

"How did it go today?" Akira's father asked.
"Getting closer," Akira said. "Probably have it paid off by September."
"That's great, son. I'm proud of you."
"I'm not supposed to finish until March — but if I'm paid up early, they might cut me loose."

They talked a little more about it, but not much. Akira knew his father was interested in hearing it all, but he also knew his father tended to lecture if they got to talking about it. Both were content to leave it.

"You want a sip?" asked Akira's father, stepping from the office with a can of PBR. Akira was surprised and delighted, took the can and a big swig before he even had

time to reconsider. The beer was ice cold, and felt good —
almost stinging as it went down. "Finish it," his father said,
going back to the office and returning with another beer
for himself.

"Thanks," said Akira as he and his father supped at their
beers, nothing but the tumble of the lone drier working on
the forgotten load while they sat.

"This was your mother's favorite beer," his father said.
"She had to have the best of everything else," he said,
raising his can. "But this…this she chose over all the rest."

They each had a drink.

"Like me, I guess," Akira's father said, smiling. "She
could've done better."

His father continued: "A man in line at a liquor store once
told her — I'll never forget it — he said, 'They don't give
blue ribbons to second place beers!' She always loved
that."

His father took a long drink, looking out the window —
still sad but smiling — the warm light of sunset on his face.
They each had another sip and sat together while the

Sandias turned pink. Neither said much — they just watched the mountains go purple, and the night sky slowly crawl dark over their heads.

"Only thing left is the vending machines," Akira said. "Oh — and that new dryer belt…"

"I'm tired, son," said Akira's father, draining off the last of his beer.

"Me too," said Akira.

"It will all still be here tomorrow," Akira's father said as he got up from his chair and went to fetch another beer for the both of them.

* * * * *

They slowed to a stop at a light on the drive home. Miles Davis and the weep of his trumpet barely escaped his father's car speakers. He looked at the radio. It read "Miles Davis - Kind of Blue" then scrolled to "Blue In Green." Akira liked the song.

In front of them at the red light was a ridiculous, rusted out dually truck — the driver revving the diesel engine as it idled, spewing and stinking. The truck had two bumper stickers: one read "Try And Burn This One!" with a picture of the American flag, and the other near his exhaust pipe said, "Mind If I Smoke?" The truck impatiently lurched forward in little fits trying to make the red light change. The tailgate read, "Super Duty." *More like 'Super Doodie,'* Akira thought. From the trailer hitch dangled a pair of molded, stainless steel testicles — one ball lower than the other, a few veins etched in it for good measure. Truck nuts.

Akira wondered what the hell would make a man decide that fake truck nuts defined them as a person. *I mean jezus,* Akira thought, *does he think women will knock on his window at red lights, and beg to fuck him after seeing the fake balls on his hitch?* There had to be some kind of explanation.

"Pretty small," said Akira's father.

Akira looked at him.

"Considering the size of the truck," his father smiled.

Akira laughed a little.

"I'd be ashamed," his father said, "if mine were that tiny." "Good thing we don't have to worry," Akira said, and they both laughed.

The light changed and Super Doodie and his tiny balls tore off in a stinking plume of diesel smoke.

Thanks

To my first readers, Tina, Mema, Nana, Papa, Heavy D, Craig, cunningham, msm, Juliette, and King Lutzo — for helping me feel like I hadn't wasted years of my life. And to Pepe Arroyo, for making the border-town Spanish ring true. A special thank you to my Aunt Rita, a tireless supporter of my long-shot dream of writing since the jump, who made professional editing of the book a reality.

To Joshua Mohr — and Decant Editorial. It's important to only take artistic advice from people who "get" what you're after. Josh got me, got the book, and most importantly, got the stunted, insufferable little shit, Akira. He helped me find the book's lost opportunities, and did his level best to protect me from myself — specifically when it comes to Akira. I absolve Josh 100% of any responsibility, as I was forewarned! To Ben Tanzer, whose insight and effort gave this book every chance to succeed, and somehow made me look like a real pro in the process. And to Bill Roberts of Bottle of Smoke Press, who has supported my work through feast and famine and continues to make some of the most kick-ass editions in the American independent press — hands-down. To all the writers, artists, and creators I sought out for blurbs or even just help along the way. You know who you are. I'm honored and humbled to strive alongside you, and hope to someday repay your kindness.

And last, thanks to you — my readers. The independent press lives and breathes because readers like you decide to go out of your way, to seek out books directly from writers and small publishers. It's absolutely vital at a time when the spreadsheets of giant conglomerates basically decide what the public can stand, what they will make available and easy to find in the bookstores and libraries that remain. You're my lifeblood as a writer, and you've absolutely kept me going. If you believe in keeping books dangerous, if you believe in all the things the independent press can do that the big guns can't — tell someone, buy them a book, introduce them to this world. Hell, it shouldn't be too hard to convince them that some of the most provocative and inventive work made today ain't just gonna find itself — it has to be specifically hunted down, and word of mouth is our best hope against the increasingly tepid, cultural doldrums.

Hosho McCreesh
3 August 2018

ABOUT THE AUTHOR

Hosho McCreesh is currently living, writing, painting and working in the gypsum and caliche badlands of the American Southwest. *Chinese Gucci* is his first novel.

The best way to follow his work is by joining the *notify list* at his website: www.hoshomccreesh.com

COLOPHON

This first printing is presented in three editions:

Original Collage-Cover Hardback
An edition of 26 hand-made hardbacks with
an original collage cover by the author,
each copy signed and lettered.

Signed, Numbered Trade Paperback
An edition of 50, trade paperbacks with a
mini-collage bookmark made by the author,
each signed and numbered.

Standard Trade Paperback
[No limitation]